ALSO BY JOHN WESSEL
This Far, No Further

Pretty Ballerina

a novel

JOHN WESSEL

Simon & Schuster

SIMON & SCHUSTER
Rockefeller Center
1230 Avenue of the Americas
New York, NY 10020

10 9 8 7 6 5 4 3 2 1

Library of Congress Cataloging-in-Publication Data

Wessel, John, date.
    Pretty ballerina : a novel / John Wessel.
        p.   cm.
    I. Title.
PS3573.E8149P7   1998
813'.54—dc21   97-47758   CIP
ISBN 0-684-81464-1

acknowledgments

Thanks once again to Molly Friedrich, Bob Mecoy, Simon & Schuster, and the Aaron Priest Literary Agency for all their time and effort, generosity, and goodwill on my behalf. An author couldn't be in better hands.

Everything's for Susan

The most profound enchantment for the collector is the locking of individual items within a magic circle in which they are fixed as the final thrill, the thrill of acquisition, passes over them. . . . One has only to watch a collector handle the objects in his glass case. As he holds them in his hands, he seems to be seeing through them into their distant past. . . .

WALTER BENJAMIN, *Illuminations*

The hollow of my hand was still ivory-full of Lolita.

NABOKOV, *Lolita*

No one insures against inherent vice.

GADDIS, *The Recognitions*

one

WHAT SCARES YOU, Harding?" Cassie asks me, nervous fingers tapping the steering wheel of her burnt orange Lumina. It's the first thing she's said to me all morning. The rain is coming down in black sheets. The sky's low and tight. We're on the road in Lake County, northwest of Chicago, a Sunday in late July, the watery eye of a no-name summer storm. Even the sun looks soggy. But Cassie's glowing—her plastic raincoat's neon orange; so are her boots, her earrings, her long drugstore fingernails. Ten bright dots flicker around the steering wheel like warning lights.

"Something must make you sweat," she says, her voice rough from cigarettes, "besides this fucking weather." Her hair shimmers like ice on a Christmas tree. She's an Asian blonde, straight from the bottle. "So what is it? Nightmares? Spiders?"

"Women," I say, reaching for my seat belt as we slide through another intersection—Cassie's driving is the only thing scaring me at the moment. The roads are slick, oil and water, and Cassie's been mixing drinks—screwdrivers mostly—all morning. I don't know why she insisted on driving. I don't know why I let her. A nun in a Volvo cuts us off; Cassie lowers her window, raises her finger. Cassie doesn't feel like talking.

She was a bit more forthcoming on my answering machine last night around two A.M. I'd just returned from one of several jobs I'm currently beta testing, a Saturday night shift hauling foreign tourists around the Loop in my cousin's Yellow, padding the meter with my Chicago True-Crime Tour—Dillinger, Capone, Gacy—ending at the little-known bar where all three men liked to drink and swap stories, Gacy playing Falstaff in his clown suit, entertaining Al with his crazy antics. The German sales reps liked that story enough to add fifty bucks to the meter. They loved the authentic details I provided. Combined with the twenty the barkeep gave me for running them through his place on a slow night and the problems the Germans had with American currency, it wasn't a bad night.

I hadn't intended to enter the exciting world of travel and tourism quite so soon—I'm only forty, and was holding the idea in reserve as a sort of 401(k) plan for my retirement—but then my other jobs wouldn't be steps on anyone's ideal employment path. I started out as a private detective, back in the middle ages. Ten years ago I lost my license, my gun permit, and most of my legitimate clients to a manslaughter conviction and an eighteen-month stretch in a southern prison. Since then I've put together a patchwork quilt approach to employment—I think the MBA guys call it "flextime." My girlfriend Alison calls it unemployment.

I still work as an off-the-meter detective sometimes, taking the cases most detectives won't touch—the barely legal, the slightly impossible—referrals from lawyers or corporate security firms. So I often come home late at night to find someone waiting for me, a voice on my machine, a lone figure downstairs at the Greek restaurant that serves as my office. I get calls from everywhere. Most, I ignore.

I don't often get calls like Cassie's.

I knew who she was, of course—I'm something of a scholar of the modern cinema and so I'm familiar with Cassie's *ouvre* from the late seventies—*Biker Bitches from Hell, D-Cup Zombies, Vampire Lesbians,* or her swan song, *Humped to Death,* a Shakespearean slasher done years before Pacino and McKellen jumped on the Richard III bandwagon. And I knew she was coming to town—to sign a few autographs, drink some fake blood—for one night only, a special appearance arranged by my friend Richie Dugan.

Richie runs a cult-movie store named Video Savages. His film-school dissertation on Mexican wrestling movies—unfinished and underappreciated—is still looking for a publisher. Film scholarship is Richie's second career, after a brief fling with sports memorabilia—buying and selling, manufacturing, forging—left him with an impressive trophy case and strange friends; two arrests, no convictions. Richie loves discussing the best recipe for aging an "authentic" baseball jersey—wrap in straw, wine, and urine, bake at low heat. Richie was a finalist for the James Beard award one year, I think—for doctoring a baseball. But for the last few weeks he's talked of nothing but Cassie Rayn.

Tabloid gossip, mostly. She's been out of the limelight for years now. She hasn't made a movie since the mid-eighties—like Richie she's had two careers, neither one mainstream. And her background is a little murky. The show biz bio Richie provided doesn't list her real name, says her home's in L.A. where she lives with a boa named Snake and a rottweiler named Vincent Price, and attributes her famed exotic looks to a Hawaiian/Cherokee lineage. She retired abruptly at twenty-five, still gorgeous, after a career that started early, at sixteen, when she was second runner-up in the Miss Maui wet T-shirt competition, prepared to serve in some complicated line of succession.

Of course I knew what that contest led to—the real source of her fame, glossed over in the bio: the month she spent after that contest in southern California, the films she made as Cassie Rayn—films still legal in Europe but labeled kiddie porn here and thus highly collectible—lusted after by customs inspectors, local D.A.'s, and Richie's customers. The ethics of buying and selling bootleg tapes with an underage performer are as hotly debated on the Net as the quirk of anatomy that led to Cassie's stage name. There are only a dirty dozen, but rumors of lost treasures persist. When one does resurface it's usually with a different name, with Cassie's scenes missing, creating continuity problems only a collector would notice or care about. An anonymous post on alt.sex.movies detailing the discovery of a lost Cassie Rayn is like a film scholar unearthing missing reels from *Greed* or *The Magnificent Ambersons*. Everyone gets very excited.

Some of Richie's customers pay a lot of money for stuff like this, despite the fact that digital imaging and Hong Kong business initiative make forgery commonplace. When Richie does have a buyer for a high-end collectible I often tag along, just to hold the cash and make sure everyone stays calm. It's yet another part-time job and an easy hundred bucks, which gets you in the door at Charlie Trotter's if you don't go nuts on the wine.

My girlfriend Alison doesn't see it that way. "You're dealing with creeps and counterfeiters," she says sometimes late at night, her long body curled against mine, waking from some foreign dream. She owns a photo store and helps run a gallery in Hyde Park—performance, Paik, multimedia, not that different from Video Savages actually—and teaches kickboxing and tai chi. She holds two black belts. Very little frightens her. But everyone gets nightmares like that. "You think it won't rub off on you? What comes around, baby. It's bad karma."

"Don't go New Age on me, Alison."

"All right—it's bad *physics*. Remember that every action has an equal reaction. People push back. You could get hurt." She gets excited, too, though in a different way from Richie. It's something to see. I do my best to calm her down.

So I knew a little about Cassie. As much as you can know anyone from the tabloids or the roles she played on screen. I certainly knew her trademark voice, a lusty whisper that sounded just fine last night when I came home to a dark apartment. I played the message back twice. Still, as good as her voice sounded—she spoke to my little Panasonic like a drinking buddy—and the cheap thrill it produced, there was no ignoring the serious implication of what Cassie wanted: I would have to get out of bed on a Sunday morning.

Hello . . . Harding, is it Harding? Is that your name? This is Cassie Rayn, we've never met, and I lost the piece of paper with your address but a friend of a friend of a friend of a . . . wait, is that three or four friends—this is like blackjack, I always lose count—anyway Marcie's her name, you know her, you must remember her, you slept with her—Marcie gave me your number and God forgive me calling this late, but there's something I have to do tomorrow outside Chicago that I can't do alone, and the consensus seems to be ask Harding, he'll help, he's a nice guy—which frankly shocked the hell out of me, I didn't think nice guys lived past the age of ten . . . the thing is I'm driving down real early, so could we meet outside this dump Video Sausages around nine? And would you please not mention this to anyone? I would really love your company and of course I'll pay whatever—plus I always bring gifts—autographed posters, trading cards—the cards are real hot right now, these kids today are horny little bastards—anything but my panties, Harding, I'm sorry—the clean ones I need desperately, the dirty ones go to my fan club. . . .

"She was just here, you just missed her," Richie said this morning, when I found him in his tiny back office with a cassette he put together for Cassie's appearance—"Splish Splash," "Stormy," "Surf's Up," "Walkin' in the Rain"—the Fortunes sounded good and so did the Everly Brothers but when Neil Sedaka began laughing in the rain I lowered the volume. "She's checking in at the motel, she's coming right back. You want something to eat? A grilled cheese? I'm nuking myself a grilled cheese." I shook my head, poured unintended iced coffee from Richie's thermos, listened to the hum from Richie's microwave. I'd had maybe an hour's sleep, still had the Munich sales reps' excited discussion of Dillinger's fatal attraction for Richard Speck in my ears.

I was in a good mood, though. The weatherman predicted rain all week, but I like rain. The summer was turning out lazy, slow, and sweet. My bills were paid, my on-again, off-again relationship with Alison was definitely on, and she was coming home after three weeks in Tucson. My apartment was clean. Without tempting fate, what more could I ask for?

Video Savages was closed in preparation for Cassie's party, but someone was in the front showroom, perched uncomfortably in front of Richie's gray-market Trinitron, a short Asian man, mid-fifties. He was smoking a short brown cigarette that smelled like burning leaves, drinking a Coke Classic from a straw, watching *The Searchers* on TNT. A tan Stetson hung from the video display, as though the Duke had just stepped out for a minute.

"Guess who that is," Richie whispered.

"How would I know? Her manager?"

"No, no, he's a fan of Cassie's. Something something Quanh. He's Thai, I think. Or Cambodian. Quanh. With a silent *h*."

"Thanks, Richie."

"He was here when I opened, I had to let him in out of the rain. I hope to God he's not stalking her. But get this—he's got a copy of *Pretty Ballerina* to sell."

"I thought that was a fake."

"So did I. But this looks like the real thing. Taipei black market; dubbed from PAL to 8mm to Super VHS. I've already got a buyer lined up. And if I can get Cassie to sign it, I can triple the price. Because she's the only one who can tell if it's fake or not."

"She'll do that? I thought she didn't like talking about that part of her past."

"Well, I haven't asked her yet," Richie admitted. "She was only in here a couple of minutes. But she's on this publicity tour— maybe she's gonna make a comeback." Richie's microwave beeped impatiently. "Don't tell him I told you about it, okay? He's paranoid about getting busted." I walked into the store and watched the movie.

Mr. Quanh with the silent *h* was older than I'd first guessed, though with his small mustache and bifocals and a military shirt with upturned collar he reminded me of John Lennon on the cover of *Sgt. Pepper's*. He introduced himself, shook my hand. I didn't think he was Thai or Cambodian, but I couldn't place the accent. His English was very good; better than mine actually, though slightly formal.

"I always cry at the end," Mr. Quanh said, sniffing a bit, "when he carries Natalie Wood inside the house and then saddles up and they close the door . . ."

I nodded, handing him a Kleenex. It's a good movie, but it was a little early in the day to get misty over John Wayne. Mr. Quanh patted his eyes with the Kleenex, sat on Richie's uncomfortable chair with his legs rocking back and forth, and watched the closing titles. Richie's commemorative Natalie Wood ashtray —a small ceramic lifeboat—was nearly full of the short brown cigarettes.

Richie pulled me into his office. His desk was stacked with magazines and tabloids like the *Weekly World News*—CaveBoy was on the cover again, a wild child discovered in Tennessee—another story Dan and the networks somehow missed. This one has Pulitzer written all over it.

Pretty Ballerina was running on a small editing monitor. The woman didn't look much like Cassie. She was dressed like no dancer I've ever seen at Joffrey or Feld—white tights and a sheer bodysuit; lots of lace but not much underwear. Long white gloves, spike heels instead of toe shoes. The men were American and overaccessorized—watches, black socks, too much body hair. *American cocks so much bigger* the woman was saying over and over, trapped in the loop. Her voice was dubbed. Despite her best efforts, neither man seemed willing to prove her correct.

"What do you think?" Richie said. "Twenty years, change the hair and makeup, figure in the silicone. You've seen some of her early stuff, right?"

"How much?" I said.

"Five hundred. Two grand, if she signs it and says it's real."

"You've got that kind of money?"

"I've already got a customer, my uncle Leo Minsk, the Rhythm King—I'm really just a middleman in this. He's willing to pay three. It's nuts, I know, but that's the market. He's probably gonna resell it anyway. What's the matter? You don't think it's real?"

"I can't tell, Richie. I don't have your curator's eye for these things." I watched him pour another Diet Dr Pepper—he drinks them warm—and take a large bite out of his grilled cheese. Grease dripped down his fingers. "I'd just be careful, that's all, burning Leo with any more crap even if he is your uncle—"

"This isn't crap, Harding, it's authentic. Look at Quanh out there, *he's* authentic—"

"Yeah, just like that Woodstock tape, the one with Joan Baez and the trampoline and the donkey—"

"That tape was vetted by a sister of a cousin of a roadie who worked for Clara herself on *Rolling Thunder*—"

"See, this is where your system breaks down, Richie. Forget

the experts. Forget the vetting and the letters of authenticity. What in the world made you think there'd be a donkey and a trampoline backstage at Woodstock? I mean, why would they?"

"Orange sunshine. You're getting old, Harding."

"Besides which the woman bouncing on the trampoline looks nothing like Joan Baez—"

"She's holding a six-string, Harding. She's singing 'Joe Hill'—"

"She's at least six-two, Richie. She looks Swedish. The fucking *donkey* looks Swedish."

"And this is where *your* system breaks down, Harding. God's in the details and you have to listen to the background, the ambient. If you cross-filter and run it through noise reduction and then listen *real, real* close you can hear Hendrix playing the national anthem. But you'd have to be a professional to pick out something like that. A collector."

"Maybe you're right, because I don't hear Hendrix," I said. "I don't hear Joan Baez. All I ever hear is the fucking donkey." Sometimes I think Richie's seen too many Mexican wrestling movies. "Was Cassie alone this morning?"

"You mean was she with her boyfriend. The answer's no. Nobody. Nada. She looked good, Harding. Real good. Like a big Popsicle. She sat on my desk, in my office, her skirt came to about here. Flirted with me, looked through my mail. You've got a wild morning ahead of you. I hope you've been taking your vitamins."

"She can't be traveling alone. She must have a bodyguard or a manager or somebody with her."

"She was alone this morning. I talked to Bearmelt Bob last night—he runs VideoSleaze by Mall of America, remember?—he said Cassie was like an alley cat in heat up there, rubbing up against everybody, gonna do the whole staff. At the store, not the Mall. Though that would have made a nice promotion. You'd see more old men on those bus tours."

"So says Bearmelt Bob."

"You're forgetting how hot she was even at sixteen—like a caged animal. She fucked with such *intensity*—"

"That's called acting, Richie."

"You can't fake that," Richie said. "Are you sure you've got time to do this for me, to see Leo? I'd go, but I can't leave the store."

"I've got time."

"Because I tried resetting the date and Leo said no, it had to be today—"

"It's okay, Richie. I said it's okay. How did Mr. Quanh with the silent *h* contact you about *Pretty Ballerina*?"

"I answered a blind ad." He tossed me a page torn from a magazine, a classified circled in red.

PRETTY BALLERINA—NEWLY DISCOVERED ORIGINAL HALF MOON PRODUCTION FILMED FOR A PRIVATE AUDIENCE—ALL PARTICIPANTS CLEARLY AND EASILY IDENTIFIED—NOW FOR SALE TO DISCRIMINATING BUYER WHO KNOWS WHAT HE NEEDS . . .

"Sort of a strange ad."

"Yeah, well—who advertises straight porn in *Inches*? I'm not sure he knew what he had. And he's foreign, you know? I don't think he knows English too good." He retrieved the ad, returned it to the clutter on his desk. "I'm still worried about your schedule today, what with Cassie and all—what time is Alison's plane getting in?"

"Not till eleven, if then," I said. "She's flying Air Tucson, the rubber band might break."

"The big number twenty-nine. You get her anything besides three weeks at a baseball camp?"

"I cleaned the apartment."

"You should throw her a surprise party. Women love surprise parties." Richie dates anyone who'll take his money—employees, lap-dancers. He enjoys lecturing me on romance.

"She hates surprise parties," I said.

"Then you should have gotten her a rock, some kind of major stone. At the very least you could have given her that collectible Louisville Slugger I mentioned. Signed by every one of the nineteen forty-five Cubs, full documentation. I could probably get my hands on one by the end of the day."

"No thanks," I said. "The last time you used your woodburning kit you nearly burned the store down."

Richie shut the film off. The woman looked less and less like

Cassie Rayn the more I watched. Certainly the passion Richie talked about was missing. This Cassie spoke her lines through dry lips, badly dubbed, an Asian Fem, watery brown eyes gazing upward in supposed wonder, barely hiding the boredom—foreplay as ritual, pillow-book Kabuki. In the next room I could see Mr. Quanh lighting another brown cigarette, waiting for the second half of his TNT Silver Spurs Doubleheader, *Two Rode Together*.

"Tell me the truth, Harding. Why'd she call you?"

"She said someone gave her my name. It happens."

"You must have met her somewhere."

"I think I'd remember that, don't you? What about this morning? Didn't she say anything when she came in?"

"Nothing. Hi, hello. I think she just came in to use the john and the phone and find out when you'd get here. Where's Harding, she says. When's Harding gonna show?"

"He's here," I said. A horn beeped twice. I opened the back door, felt the warm rain coming through the screen. Richie's Mazda was parked in the handicapped spot. An orange Lumina blinked its brights. I picked up a prop briefcase designed to make me appear more professional—as though I actually know what I'm doing. Richie tossed me a final bit of romantic advice—lubricated Trojans. "Better take an umbrella, Harding," Richie said, shoving the last of his sandwich into his mouth. "It's raining like a motherfucker out there."

two

WE STOP ONCE for gas and cigarettes, then head northwest through speed traps no one lost much sleep naming—Grayslake, Fox Lake, Round Lake. Cassie chain-smokes Marlboros, fiddles with the radio dials—country, funk, alternative—nothing satisfies her. At times I think she's forgotten I'm even in the car. This is a woman who's learned to tune the world out.

She smiles faintly at the small talk I make; dodges the one or two questions I have for her, hides her eyes behind cyber sunglasses. She puts on a *TeamSexx* baseball cap. When she finally tells me our destination—her family's house on Gaines Road, near Stillwater—and our top secret agenda—moving some boxes out of a basement—I don't know quite what to say. I can't believe she grew up within a thousand miles of here, but it's too mundane a story to make up. In situations like this it's best to keep a close eye on things, and with Cassie that's not difficult. In fact it's hard not to stare. At thirty-five she's still a knockout, shorter than she looks on screen, a body slightly out of proportion. Right now her raincoat's unsnapped to her waist. A patch of red Lycra peeks through the buttons of her blouse. A stretch of deeply tanned thigh shows below a hiked-up vinyl skirt. Her dyed blond hair and candy-colored nails and lipstick are neon bright, more color than I'm used to—Alison likes black. Alison wears black in the shower.

As we drive farther west, Cassie points out landmarks from her youth, schools, churches. "My mom was real religious. My dad never went to church. But he was always driving us some-where . . . he loved to just show up, after school or at a game, and surprise us, and have some trip planned." She stops the car near a redbrick building where she says she took ballet twice a week. Cassie wanted to be a dancer.

"I was a string bean in those days," she says. "That didn't last." Neither did the dance studio; I don't see anything in the building now except dentists and insurance agents. "Once a year, at Christmas we got to do a real show in the high school gym, with live music and costumes. Not just *Nutcracker*—we did *Heidi*. We did *Thumbellina*. We did *Snow White*—"

"I think I saw your film remake of *Snow White*." We get out of the car and walk around a small river to reach a Pepsi machine outside the building. I'm out of change. Cassie treats. "I don't remember any costumes, though, and not much dancing."

"Did you know you were breaking about fifty state and fed-eral laws watching that?" she says, smiling, removing the cap, pushing her sunglasses up in her hair. It's a pretty dazzling smile.

"Actually, it was a cop who showed it to me," I say. "I think he's a judge now." It's an old-fashioned pop machine, dispensing small eight-ounce bottles. You drink them here or leave a deposit. "When did you stop dancing?"

"When I was twelve or so. When biology kicked in. But the lessons helped later . . . with those early film shoots."

"Really?"

"It's not so different. When you're dancing you have to smile and look lighter than air when actually you've got shin splints and leg cramps and bad knees. When you're Snow White you have to lie under a bunch of smelly dwarfs and act like you can't stop cumming."

"I see the similarity."

She slides her Pepsi bottle into the metal rack, returns to the car. End of discussion. Cassie doesn't feel nostalgic.

We're on the road an hour when Cassie turns the Lumina onto a shady lane the size of a bike path. Gaines Road. Another turnoff, a smaller gravel drive. She gets as far as the front yard, puts the car in park, leaves the AC and radio running full blast, stares long and hard at the empty farmhouse fifty feet away. From the way she stares you'd think the gap was fifty miles. Al Green's on the radio, preaching the gospel:

Take me to the river

"Can I ask you something?" she says. The house is rundown, hiding behind a pair of huge elms, a crooked Kentucky fence— paint is peeling from the siding and the shutters and the handmade FOR SALE sign tilting in the Johnson grass like a grave marker. The closest house is on the next ridge, and looks like an auto-parts salvage; half a dozen cars sit on the front lawn, trucks, white vans, a small bulldozer, all rusting, all sitting in the mud. There's a cabin or shed in the next valley, half-hidden by evergreens. Other than that there's nothing in sight but a few cows. I haven't been out here in years, not since Alison dragged me to a county fair looking for Arbus-like local color to photograph. We came home empty-handed. The Lizard Lady was uncooperative. I think the midgets had the day off.

"Sure."

"Do you ever get scared?"

"All the time."

"Come on—I mean really really scared—"

"I'm serious."

"And what scares you?"

"Everything. I'm a very easy scare."

"Well, that's no help," she says, laughing. Her eyes have a glow the camera doesn't show. "You have to be a little selective—"

"What makes you ask? I'd think you'd be the expert, after making *Angel with a Chainsaw, Centipede Horror, The Embalmer I, II,* and *III*—"

"Those are just movies," she says. "You get scared by movies?"

"Sure. Even the old Hammer horror flicks kept me awake. Though that might have been the actresses—they were always wearing nightgowns in those movies."

"Was there someplace in the neighborhood you were afraid to go?"

"Other than the confessional? You mean like a haunted house? Not on the South Side, no. Why?"

"When I was eight, the Wilders built that house up there on

the hill, the one with all the cars. The cabin was already there, at the edge of their property. We told them—we told their kids—we thought the cabin was haunted. Nobody, and I mean nobody, went in it. Even the Wilders. I think they were afraid to tear it down. The other neighbors laughed about it, but I never saw them go inside either. And these were farmers, sheep shearers, men who delivered stillborn calves with their bare hands." She runs her hands back through her hair like an Olympic swimmer. "That all seems so long ago now . . . the Wilders . . . almost a different lifetime."

"Haunted houses don't scare you anymore?"

"Nothing scares me anymore," she says softly. "Whether that's a good thing or not I can't tell. . . . Listen, thanks for coming, on a Sunday, and such short notice. It's probably your day off."

"Hey, I wouldn't miss it."

"You charge me whatever you'd charge for something like this."

"All right," I say. "You'll get my standard moving-boxes-from-the-basement rate."

She's chewing on the end of her sunglasses, watching the cows. They're chewing too, watching us. A huge black-and-white cat picks its way through the weeds near the pasture. "You're probably wondering how I know Marcie and what she said about you."

"I'm a little curious, yeah. Since I don't know anyone named Marcie."

"Sure you do. She used to work at a club where you were a bouncer. In Wisconsin. Tall blond, incredible body." That doesn't really narrow it down. "Come on Harding—she wore a Boy Scout uniform, used a flashlight? 'Look Ma, no hands'?"

"I knew a redhead with that act, but her name was Sookie—"

"That's her."

"She changed her name? And her hair?"

"She changed more than that. Often. She gave you a very strong recommendation."

"She did?"

"She said you were just awesome. Said I had to look you up,
you'd be just what I needed." I think the cows have stopped chewing, they don't want to miss a word of this. One of the buttons has
come undone on Cassie's blouse. Either she has amazing nipples or
she's wearing some sort of jewelry. "And don't try to deny it. I had
this independently confirmed by two other dancers, Alexa and
Lisa Ann."

"Well, I'd hate to deny it, Cassie. Really. But I can't remember
either one."

"What about Nikki and Giselle and a bootblack named Joey?
Don't tell me you didn't know that Sookie's an MP, Harding."

"She's in the army?"

"*Multiple personality.* Alexa's her Fem. Sookie's a half-cup
size larger, she gets better tips. Joey's stronger, he takes care of her.
And Marcie's the brains, sort of CEO. You must have known,
Harding." I shake my head. I only remember Sookie. The guys in
the first row loved her act. And she was a stickler for authenticity,
insisted on using the official Boy Scout model. We spent a couple
of nights together, without the mood lighting, back when Alison
and I were apart. I had no idea she was such a crowd.

I sneak a peek at my watch, trying to imagine where Alison is
right now. Probably packing. I'm not sure what I'm doing out here
in the middle of these cornfields with Cassie Rayn. And I still have
to drive to Wisconsin to see Leo. It's a very pleasant drive. "Maybe
we should get going," I say. "Before it starts raining again."

Cassie finds Tina Turner on the radio, rolling on the river,
nice and rough. She leaves her hand on the seat between us. My
briefcase's sitting on the floor between my legs; inside's a legal pad,
a pen, a package of peanut butter and cheese crackers, and Richie's
Trojans.

"I'd hate for you to miss your fans at the video store," I say.
"It's your last stop on the tour, isn't it? Besides a horror convention
outside Chicago?"

"GoreFest Ninety-eight," she says. She lights another cigarette, stares at the cows, frowning. Maybe she doesn't like animals.
Maybe she's lactose intolerant. "You don't want to do this, do
you," she says, suddenly upset, putting the car in reverse, turning

in her seat. Her mood turns on a dime. "God, I do this all the time —asking guys for favors—it's so embarrassing—it was so dumb to drive you out here—"

"We're leaving?"

"Dumb, dumb, dumb," she says, her palm against her forehead. The wheels spin in the gravel.

"Wait a minute," I say, and my hand touches her thigh. The muscle jumps. She looks at me, startled. "Maybe another time—"

"Another time?"

"Could you give me a rain check? Really, I'm flattered, but I'm in this relationship right now—it's a little hard to explain— she's a black belt and I don't like getting her mad—"

"What?"

"Maybe another time . . ."

"Oh, no, Harding, not you too," she says, a slow smile growing on her face.

"Me?"

"What did you think? Harding? That I brought you out here —that I wanted to fuck?"

"No, no, of course not." Even the cows are embarrassed for me.

"Sookie told me how you worked as a bouncer, Harding. At the club where she was dancing. And how one night there was a whole table of bikers giving her a rough time and you kicked them all out, just really kicked their butts, the whole table. And how another time when some guy wouldn't pay his bar tab you broke into his Ferrari and it was totally awesome because it had like three hundred alarms—"

"I cut a few wires," I say, feeling foolish, debating whether I should explain that the bikers were members of Golden Thunder, a Harley club for women over sixty-five. I decide to let it go. As bar fights go, it was not a pretty sight. My hand is back on my own thigh, where it belongs. "I'm sorry, Cassie."

She waves off my apology, as if I'd simply brushed her sleeve. "Marcie—Sookie said you were a private detective."

"I was, once, yeah. Not anymore. I lost my license. You have to be back by four, right?" She nods. "Then we should get going."

"We should," she says, nodding. "We definitely should. Only I seem to be having trouble getting out of the car."

More Al Green on the radio. Al says let me be the one you come running to. You can never have too much Al Green.

"The house is empty?"

She nods.

"You have family around here somewhere?"

"No, no, they've been dead a long time now," she says.

"What about your neighbors, the Wilders. There must be someone around here you'd like to see—"

"I don't think there's anybody left. Their house is empty too."

"And you said there were some boxes. . . ."

"God, I hope they're still there. The house has just been sitting here vacant, I've been traveling and putting this off for so long—"

"Why don't you let me get them? There's no point both of us getting soaked."

"You don't have to," she says, "if you don't want to."

"No, no, I want to help. Just give me the key, I insist—"

"You have to get back, I understand perfectly. I'll make other arrangements—"

"Cassie, we're not leaving until I get those boxes. Give me the key."

"I don't have one," she says.

"What?"

"A key. Didn't I mention that? The Realtors or the banks have everything. It's not exactly mine anymore. The house, I mean."

"No key?"

She shakes her head, then looks me full in the eyes. It's a good thing my hand's not still on her thigh. "Can you get me in?"

Richie will love this. "That's why you asked me along today? So I could break into your parents' house?"

"The back door's probably easiest," she says.

three

THE RAIN WON'T LET UP. I grab my windbreaker and run first to the tiny front porch, past rows of flowers dying their second death of the season—record cold and snow all winter, spring and summer floods. The porch leans slightly to the left. The shingled canopy has torn loose on one side. There's a dirty mat made of AstroTurf, a scripted *M* centered in the storm door's metal grill with a crescent, some kind of astrological sign. Or maybe just a moon. And worms everywhere, crawling on the sheltered concrete. Worms love the rain.

I wish now I'd worn older shoes. The grass is slippery as hell in the side yard. It was cut recently, not raked; my heels pick up thick clumps, heavy as sod. I slip a couple of times, nearly falling —the cows watch contentedly, glad someone's finally providing a show. There's a long back porch, partially enclosed, a stack of firewood covered with mushrooms and green moss. Clay pots sit along the ledge with matching plates, like cup and saucer.

The back door's been painted but you can still see scuff marks and scratches from the family dogs. There's just the one lock—no dead bolt, no Realtor's lockbox. Cassie gave me instructions and a motel laundry bag full of cheap tools she'd hidden beneath her seat—I think that's why she insisted on driving—but she doesn't want me breaking windows or kicking down doors. "I don't want anyone to know I was here," she says. Since I don't carry burglar tools in my wallet the best I can do is root around in the garden and backyard until I find a thin piece of aluminum planted in the flower bed, washed down from the gutter; found money. It fits nicely in the eyelash of space between the frame and the door. The latch slides back; the door pushes open. I use the same metal strip to clean my shoes and then put it back in the mud, like returning a key under a mat.

The house is empty, silent as a tomb; bare walls, surprisingly musty despite what looks like fresh paint. When I run my finger across a white pantry, the years of dust and grime come off like stale icing. The dining room's full of cobwebs; no Pip or Miss Havisham. Like most real farmhouses outside TV or coffee table books like *Country Style,* it was cheaply made. The rooms are quite small. The effect is claustrophobic.

I can see why Cassie decided to wait in the car. With the rain and the power off, the place does have a certain gloom. It's been empty too long. The kitchen appliances are long gone, though you can still see their outlines on the walls. The cabinets are here, and the countertops. The floor is light-blue linoleum, with marks from a kitchen table and chairs, Formica maybe, with chrome legs, vinyl cushions on the chairs; late Eisenhower era. There's a flashlight sitting by the kitchen sink, a bit larger than the one Sookie used. *New Life Realtors We Sell 4 U.* The Realtors must like Prince. The light flickers. It's pale but still alive.

The basement's cool and dark. There's a silent gas furnace, a gritty edge to the floor, and stone walls. Cassie gave me a brief description of the floor plan, but this area's partitioned differently than I'd pictured. I put my bag of tools down on the concrete floor and shine the flashlight across the room. There's a door to my left that's locked; the next two are open but reveal only closets. The farthest door is set in cheap wood paneling near a rusted sump pump and leads me to a series of narrow rooms, like extra bedrooms. This section is raised a few inches on untreated pine, with walls that are drywalled and covered with wallpaper. Cassie mentioned this but didn't mention the metal wardrobe sitting where I'm supposed to dig. It's bolted to the wall. I go back to get my tools.

The metal doors open when I lift slightly, like a gym locker.

The bottom isn't bolted, just fitted, and it comes up easily when I force a screwdriver between it and what's below—an old shag rug, then floorboards, not nailed very tightly. There's a light covering of dirt. Two shoe boxes sit in the crawl space, wrapped loosely in thin yellow plastic and protected by a child's warning: PLEASE DO NOT TOUCH! THIS MEANS EVERYONE ESPECIALLY *YOU* KIM! Rubber bands like dried, curled-up worms are stuck to the plastic. A black beetle crawls over my fingers. PROPERTY OF KALANI. I shove the plastic back in its shallow grave and replace the boards and the rug and close the wardrobe.

I'm walking up the stairs when I start thinking about that first door, the one that's locked. It's a bad habit of mine. I have no problem leaving the shoe boxes alone. But I'm like a cat with closed doors. Besides, the floor plan doesn't make sense. It can't be just a closet. So what is it? Another bedroom? Some kind of crawl space? I run to the car, tell Cassie I'll be a few more minutes. She nods, her eyes closed. She's switched from Marlboros to grass. Everything smells sweet and wet. The piece of aluminum is retrieved from the garden. Eventually it gets the better of the closet door, which swings open to reveal a second door much more interesting than the first.

This one's dull metal set in concrete, with a combination lock set below a steel handle. The door opens stiffly. The air inside is warm and stale. I let my flashlight wander around the room. An emergency flood's nailed in one corner with a heavy-duty battery. There are a few canned goods left. No bottled water, no radiation suits. No shotgun. It's my first bomb shelter. They weren't a high priority where I grew up, on the South Side. Even after my parents heard that we'd go in the first launch, they still worried more about the Russian tailor on South Kedzie who overcharged for alterations.

Something about the shelter triggers a memory, probably from the photo spreads in *Life* magazine I saw when I was a kid, as obsessive in their way as the ones I stared at in *Playboy*. I can't quite place it. When I take the boxes to the car and open the rear door, Cassie barely turns her head. The radio's blasting Smashing Pumpkins, so loud that raindrops dance on the sheet-metal roof like grease on a griddle, some song about rats in a cage.

One of the boxes was already sagging a bit and the rain and humidity are making it even more fragile—it's like a tapestry recovered from a pharaoh's tomb, suddenly exposed to the sun. A burst of wind catches the lid and blows it across the driveway to a small lake forming in the front yard. I step on a lily pad of wet leaves and grass to retrieve it and find a folded yellowed newspaper clipping taped inside the lid. A smiling Asian woman in a high-necked blouse sits in a rocking chair: *Lake County family sleeps on antique beds. Even the dogs drink from antique pewter bowls.*

"Just one more trip," I tell Cassie.

"Why? Is something wrong? Did you have any trouble?"

"No trouble. I just need to lock up. Then maybe we can find a restaurant. There must be a fish place around here with all these damn lakes."

"I could use a drink."

"So could I. But somebody has to drive us home."

She nods, fingers drumming the dashboard. "I guess I am home," she says, passing me the joint.

Lightning flashes; a soldier's flare. I walk back up the driveway. The clouds are swirling now, unfocused time-motion just behind the roof of the farmhouse; blue-gray clouds, celestial civil wars. The rain slashes my face. *Lake County family leaving on vacation.* The countryside comes briefly alive, thunder shaking the ground like artillery. *The entire Moon family sleeps.* The sky drops down, low and tight. The ground rushes up around me.

And that's when I realize where I am.

four

I WAS A MILLION miles away from here when it happened, doing time in the army, but the story caught my eye. When you're stuck in a Bangkok monsoon day after day, you search for any news from home, and this one hit the national wires hard for a day or two. I'd never been to Stillwater, wasn't familiar with the landscape, but still I could picture it. Later on, back home, I even talked to a cop—a uniform named Tommy Mullaney—who'd helped with the investigation, on loan from the Chicago PD. So I knew the story, bits and pieces of it anyway. And I remembered it well enough. I just didn't know it was Cassie's story.

This time when I open the front door the hinges softly protest, the storm door swings open a little slower. The house smells older now. My heart's beating a little faster. Stray footprints on the kitchen floor seem less random. Someone must have lived here since then, though . . . could it really have stayed vacant for twenty years? I can't remember if the venetian blinds were open just five minutes ago. I close them tight, and then lock the back door. Most of the people around here probably grew up sleeping with their windows open, their doors unlocked. I guess they lock them now.

The basement steps creak on cue; the wind rattles the siding. I walk through the dining room, living room, family room. My footprints disappear in the new rug; the fabric rebounds. Every noise makes an echo. *For every action there's a reaction.*

I open every closet door. Power's off but I flip every switch.
Then I walk to the rear bedroom.

This is where it happened.

Lake County family . . .

The father's name was Ellis Moon. He was from Lake County.
The mother was from Shanghai. The children were from Korea,
Cambodia, Vietnam—foster homes and youth shelters here and
overseas. Ellis had served in the navy and reenlisted twice, South
China Sea, but that was long after the war ended. It seemed ridicu-
lous to explain what went down here with delayed stress syndrome
or Agent Orange but the sheriff's department tried anyway, when
they couldn't pin it on anything—anyone—else. Besides, they
found the gun beside him and the rope and too many prints from
years of friends and family to tell exactly who was here that
day. . . .

Case closed.

Murder-suicide in Lake County farmhouse.

The bedroom's in a dark corner of the house. It's a small
room for a master bedroom, a square box really, only one window,
a tiny bathroom adjacent. They must have felt trapped in here,
rats in a cage. I try to picture the room the way it was that night,
filled with large antique furniture, oversized rage, *like a goddamn
war zone in there,* run my flashlight over clean white walls, trying
to picture the scene. *Auto-asphyxiation,* the cop Tommy Mullaney
told me later in a South Side bar, savoring both the drink and the
description. *And I don't mean a fucking Ford.*

The bed was here, against the wall. They found the mother
beneath the sheets, her arms wrapped around her stomach. One
daughter was found by the bathroom window, curled on the floor.
*She might have been trying to escape, we weren't sure. Or yell for
help. 'Cept there was nothing out there but the fucking cornfields.*
A son facedown here on an oval rug. And the dogs—farm collies,
beagles—dead outside the back door, one even tracked into the
barn and shot there. *We found the dogs first,* Tommy Mullaney
said, *then we found the suitcases.* A stack of mismatched Samson-
ites sitting neatly in the living room, ready for an early start the
next morning. Camping equipment already loaded in the station

wagon. Names sewn in all the kids' underwear, cute little dog tags around the kids' necks, in case someone wandered off.

What else? Spent shells everywhere. No weapon but the father's black .44. No unexplained prints, no sign of a forced entry, just one killer who methodically reloaded two times and missed as often as he hit, even at close range. Lots of questions, despite the rope and the kitchen chair in the middle of the bedroom and what might be old rope burns around the mother's neck. *They'd done this before, they just went a little too far this time.* Lots of questions. *Why the children,* despite finding Ellis's body in the hallway, a single shot buried in his throat, the .44 by his side. And less press than you'd expect after the initial shock, perhaps because the sexual angle was kept out of the papers, but also because the kids were adopted and well, not from around here. *They weren't really his kids, now was they.* It got filed away—murder-suicide, family tragedy—just an occasional story in the suburban editions each anniversary with a quote from a neighbor or retired deputy wondering how something like that could happen in Lake County and how the farm was still tied up in courts and the fields returning to weeds and grass and whatever happened to the daughter who survived by hiding in the basement, locked inside the shelter where police found her two days later, badly frightened but unharmed . . .

Whatever happened to her?

"You never really answered my question, Harding," Cassie says from the hallway, and I jump. Rain is dripping from her slicker. Her face has a fierce intensity; her eyes shine. The ghostly images I've conjured are chased away. The ones Cassie carries with her into the house are much stronger. "About getting frightened." She's holding a small umbrella like a sunbeaten flower. The metal snaps on her coat are now buttoned down tight.

five

I HAVEN'T BEEN HERE since it happened," she says, standing by the kitchen door, watching the rain. "Twenty years . . ." Her voice is softer here, her eyes a little crazy from the grass and the booze and maybe the one quick glance she takes of the bedroom. No wonder she drinks. It's raining through the screen door but I don't think Cassie even notices. "They were sending me to my grandparents, in Topeka. Only I missed the bus . . . I didn't really want to go. The Realtor—Sheldon—was a friend of my family and he was taking me to the bus station when they paged him and so we stopped out here. They had this crew of Mexicans to paint it and I guess they were doing okay, painting up a storm, listening to Spanish radio. And then something happened, they stopped for lunch and wouldn't move, and when we got here they were all out on the front lawn, in the rain, arguing, and Sheldon says, Wait here, darlin', and wades in, starts yelling, but he doesn't speak a word of Spanish. A minute later they're all leaving—*coño! jamas, jasmas*—Sheldon's chasing them up the driveway, trying to get his money back." She digs in her purse for her cigarettes, finds the pack but doesn't take one out. "I knew a little Spanish from school but I didn't feel much like translating. They said it was sacred ground, the bedroom. From all the blood."

"Jesus." What a thing to tell a kid. "If that was true, Cassie, half the city would be sacred. The South Side would be like Stonehenge."

She closes her eyes. "We drove to a hardware store, Sheldon and me—with Sheldon explaining how the place would definitely sell, how a certain . . . element actually liked buying a place like this. The curiosity factor. I was fourteen. My whole family was dead and he was talking to me about marketing. We bought a spray gun and Sheldon finished it himself. I helped, a little. We didn't even wash the walls. It took us four coats, in the bedroom. . . ."

"Who knows, Cassie?"

"About the paint?"

"That your name's Kalani Moon?"

"A couple people. Not many." She looks away. "I keep it hid."

"What about the rest of your family?"

"My grandparents died six months after I got to Topeka. Grandpa died one week, Grandma the next. Just from missing him. And I never knew my real family, none of us did. I was adopted, Harding. From an agency in Bangkok. You know what it's like. You were there."

"Who told you I was in Bangkok? Sookie?"

She nods. I must have been drinking. I don't remember telling Sookie much more than my pager number.

"So you're alone?"

"Pretty much." She pauses. "Lovely story, isn't it? That's why I didn't tell you everything. . . . I wasn't sure you'd come. It's not exactly a day at the beach."

She absentmindedly opens one cabinet, then another, picks at some old shelf liner stuck there like a scab.

"You must have been back before now."

"Not inside," she says. "I drove past once or twice, had a taxi bring me all the way from Midway, but I never had the nerve to come in. They couldn't sell it. I started getting nightmares. Somebody put a bunch of graffiti on it, satanic shit, totally meaningless but I didn't feel like coming in alone. Much less going downstairs. Or back there. And there's nobody around that I knew; all the other neighbors moved away."

"Are you sure? That family you mentioned, the Wilders—"

"Long gone, I guess . . . no one's living up there. It looks like a junkyard."

"And your house has been vacant all this time?" I ask her. "Twenty years? Who paid the taxes?"

"The banks, I guess. I think it was tied up in court for a while. There were a couple mortgages on it. It was never mine; it went straight to the banks. Sheldon probably got screwed." A flash of lightning fills the room. The resulting shock wave of thunder that comes barely a second later makes me jump, but Cassie's gazing at a lower cloud covering. "I don't know how they expected to sell it in this condition," she says, pointing to the kitchen ceiling. "Look at all the holidays."

"The what?"

"That's what my father called the spots he missed when he painted. You can't see them up close. From the glare. He made me stand below him on the ladder with a flashlight." I don't see them. I don't see the little girl anymore either, or her father—just Cassie Rayn in a deserted old house. I can't quite remember what the father, Ellis, even looked like. Or the others.

Lake County family all sleeping . . .

"The refrigerator was here," she says, tracing a faded line beneath the latest paint job—Norge pentimento. "See the curved top? These days they're all boxes. And we had a dishwasher over here, an old portable one, our only luxury. My mother wheeled it to the sink every night and hooked it up to the faucet . . . it would rumble and make this incredible racket and mess up the TV reception. . . ."

"Where were you the last ten years? Since you stopped making horror flicks?"

"Dancing, stripping, whatever," she says. "Under different names. I went through my earth-mother phase, in a commune, and my druggie days in North Hollywood, and the rehab . . ."

She opens the umbrella with a startling *snap* and sits it on the blue linoleum. "Fuck superstition, right?" She digs in her purse; I assume for matches. Instead she hands me an old Polaroid. "This is why we're here," she says. The boy is thin, dark featured, dressed in a white T-shirt and cutoffs, grinning at the camera. "His name's Kim."

"He's a cute kid."

"He is, isn't he?"

"Yeah." I don't know what else to say. His name was on the shoe box, but wasn't the brother named Eric or Ethan—wasn't he older than this. . . .

"Joey said Sookie said you were in the CIA."

"What?"

"That's what he said. She said." She blows her nose, wipes her eyes. "Wasn't it true?"

"No, not quite. I guess he—she meant CID, Cassie. Army police. That's how I spent my two years in Bangkok—pulling AWOL GIs out of bars. I wasn't James Bond."

"That's even better. You know how to find people."

I nod. This is not good. I'm getting a sinking feeling in my stomach. "The boy in the picture?"

"Kim," she says. "But he's not a boy, not now. The picture's misleading, but it's the only one I've got. . . . Have you ever heard the stories about boys, Asian boys, disappearing? In Kentucky, Ohio, Illinois, all through the Midwest? No? Supposedly there are lists?" I shake my head. "I want you to find him for me, Harding. I'll pay you, of course, whatever it takes . . ."

Now the cigarettes come out. With the smoke I notice other smells, the kind you can't paint over, left over from the people and pets who lived here, hot summer days.

It occurs to me that Cassie must have had to identify the bodies.

"Who is he, Cassie?"

"He's my brother," she says simply. "My little brother."

six

I DON'T REMEMBER HIM," I say, confused, "from any of the news reports—"

"That's because he was gone by then. For two years. The police said he was a runaway. But I never really believed that. He was on a bus with a bunch of other kids and a minister from our church. He got off the bus, he didn't get back on. It broke my mother's heart. She's Chinese. Family is everything. My father looked for him all over but he was just gone. Vanished. He was thirteen."

For the first time she moves away from the screen door. But she doesn't go far, just sits on the counter to the left of the sink. She still has her back to the rear bedroom. She kicks her legs nervously.

"Kids run away all the time, Cassie. Especially kids that age." Especially adopted kids, I think but don't want to say.

"That's what everyone said—it happens all the time, if he wants to come home, he'll come home, if he doesn't and he's smart . . . we might never find him. They did nothing, really. People from the church handed out flyers, put his picture on a milk bottle. He was with a bunch of other kids fixing up an old church . . . it was just downstate. He wasn't the kind of kid to run away."

"You didn't look for him before now?"

"No," she says with a sharp intake of breath. "God forgive me. My dad did but afterward . . . I thought he was dead too.

When he didn't come home. *Everyone* said he must be dead. Or crazy."

"What made you change your mind?"

She stubs out her cigarette in the sink. "Don't laugh at me."

"I won't laugh at you."

"Because I know how it sounds, that's why I can't go to the police, not with this, and if I hire someone famous in L.A. it will be all over the tabloids—I started getting these," she says, hopping down from her perch on the counter, taking a brown letter-sized envelope from her plastic purse. The purse is bright orange, too, the type only hookers and eccentric male collectors would covet. "I started getting them at my place in L.A. Then I saw them everywhere I went on tour—there was one in Denver and Minneapolis and Madison and when I went inside that store this morning I saw *another* one on what's-his-name's desk—"

"Richie?" The return address says "Administrative Office/ Record of Entitlement" with lots of small-type disclaimers. It's designed to look like it has a government check inside but of course there's just a letter from Family Dreams Travel Agency addressed to Dear Travel Lover—one of those vacation scams promising a free week in Florida or the Smoky Mountains. *We Make Your Family's Dreams Come True.*

"See where it's from?" she says, excited. "On the bottom of the page in real small print?"

" 'SunnySide Vistas—Another vacation paradise from *Lost Moon Developers . . .*' "

"It's a sign," she says. "I mean, I'm not nuts but Jesus, Harding, I get goosebumps just reading it. You see it now, don't you? You understand now?"

"The name? Just the name?"

"No, no, look here—it's postmarked Chicago except inside it says the company's downstate—at least this part is, the 'Office of Vacation Disbursement'—Pekin, Illinois, that's real close to where he disappeared. *Lost Moon,* Harding."

I nod. I wind open the kitchen window to let some air into the room. This is worse than Sookie. "Cassie, I get these all the time, everybody does. The name's just a coincidence. 'Lost Moon' —there are dozens of companies with that name. Full Moon, Rising Moon, Moonlight Productions. . . . It's just a scam. They want you to buy a time-share condo or ten acres of swampland—"

"No, no," she says, excited, standing close beside me. "See the phone number? I tried calling it but nobody answered. If it's a scam why would nobody answer?"

"Because they skipped town. Or they're going door-to-door with the gypsies, fixing people's driveways. Cassie—it's not even addressed to you."

"I know, but . . . look at this line right here—'dinner theater with Hollywood stars,' and then 'Lost Moon' . . . what are the odds on that?"

I shrug.

"I've got others," she says, pulling out identical brown envelopes, so excited half of them fall on the floor—all addressed the same but sent to different cities, all sent bulk mail. They'd be hard to trace. On the blue linoleum they're like islands in a stream.

"Did you get one?" she demands.

"Probably. I don't even open this stuff—I probably threw mine away—"

"See, that's what they'd be counting on. Only the people who'd understand would know what it meant. And not *everybody* gets them. I've asked around and most people never heard of this place. I even called a travel agent, and she said she never heard of Lost Moon or Family Dreams, it wasn't worth pursuing."

"She's right."

"Don't you see? If it doesn't exist it's even *more* significant."

I walk outside, onto the porch. Cassie stays inside. She sits on the counter again, tugging at her skirt. When I look at her through the glass, I see her leaning back beneath the cabinets, her face nearly disappearing in the shadows. All I can see are her legs kicking.

It smells like mulch back here; rotting leaves. I wipe my shoes on a brown straw mat and go back inside.

"Cassie, that's paranoia. The way you're thinking anything becomes significant."

She says nothing for a moment or two. Then she leans forward. "You think I'm nuts?"

"No, no, not nuts." I pause. She needs reassurance. I'm not

good at reassurance. I slow down, try choosing my words carefully. "I just think you've had a really, really rough time. I think you're looking for an answer or a reason when there probably isn't any."

She nods, says nothing.

"I can't imagine losing my whole family like that." It's the kind of answer she's heard a hundred times. "If something happened to him twenty years ago it would be almost impossible to figure out now. And if he's alive . . . he'd be an adult, in his mid-thirties . . ."

"Meaning you won't help me."

"You don't need my help, Cassie. Not for this. Let's say it *is* from Kim; he's decided to contact you after twenty years by sending you a free vacation. Baffling, but stranger things have happened, I guess. Why not just check it out yourself? Take the fabulous three days, two nights vacation. I don't think Kim's there, but I doubt if anything bad's gonna happen. Just don't take your checkbook. And don't sign anything without a lawyer."

"I'd rather go with you. Aren't you at all curious? What if there *is* someone out there snatching these kids. . . ."

"Let me recommend someone. I know some people in Springfield and Carbondale—"

"Sookie already recommended *you,* Harding. Don't you know how hard it was to come out here today and tell you everything? Jesus, there are guys I practically *married* I never even talked to about this stuff. And you're right, I should have done something before now. God, I lie awake nights thinking what if he's hurt or in trouble . . . what if it's him sending me a message, or the people who took him . . ."

"Cassie . . . be reasonable. It's been twenty years."

She says nothing.

"If he wanted to contact you before now . . . I mean, you haven't exactly been hiding."

"You think he's dead."

This time it's my turn to be silent.

"That's okay," she says. "I mean, I could handle that. It would be better than not knowing."

"People always say that," I tell her. "I'm not sure it's true. In any case, you can do better, Cassie, believe me. There are better detectives than me."

"Sookie says Alexa says Marcie says you're a good guy."

"Which one says that?"

"They all do. You're a nice guy. There aren't many around, especially in this business."

"Yeah, I'm a prince," I say, wondering how to get out of this. "I'm an ex-con, Cassie. I don't have a license anymore. And I'm not good at missing persons work—I'm out of the loop, cops don't like me—"

"I know."

"I did eighteen months in a state penitentiary for manslaughter—and that was from looking for a runaway—"

"I know."

"Jobs like this take a lot of legwork. They can take forever and still turn up absolutely nothing. I'd have to retrace Kim's steps, go to half a dozen towns, charge you a small fortune—and probably still come up empty. You see? It's unethical."

"That's what Sookie and Marcie said Joey said."

"She did? He did?"

"Uh-huh," she says, smiling for the second time today. "Actually, that's when your name first came up."

Good old Sookie. I have lots of questions but what's the point? I don't want this job. All I can think of is the long drive to Leo's house, and Alison's plane taking off from Tucson. How Alison's long legs never fit comfortably beneath the seats in coach. So this time I bought her a first class ticket. I see her slouched in her seat, legs on the next armrest, drinking champagne. Reading the box scores in *The Sporting News*, fending off advances from married businessmen.

Cassie comes down from her perch and blocks the door, holding Kim's picture out toward me.

There's only one way to get out of this house today. I take the picture. I take the vacation flyer from Lost Moon. And I take the only other piece of information Cassie has for me, a letter from the minister who was on the bus with Kim twenty-two years ago,

Reverend Lawrence Miner, addressed to her father, dated the same year as the killings. I don't ask her where the letter came from or why it's all she has—I don't ask her for Kim's Social Security number or adoption agency or if she knows anything about his birth parents or where his medical and dental records might be— any of the things you'd need to find him. I just shove the letter in my back pocket. Cassie's smiling. She kisses me, apologizing for the orange lipstick she rubs from my cheek.

"Too bad you've got a girlfriend," she says. "No rain checks, Harding. I would be all over you." It's the last thing on her mind —she's staring at the hallway. So much for not being afraid. Or is it more a form of respect, genuflection. . . . I give her a second, thinking she'll want to take a last look around. If it were my house, after twenty years I'd want to stay awhile, find the initials I carved in a door somewhere. But she's rooted to that spot. I realize I've asked her almost nothing about her family and the murders, and she's volunteered nothing—her words about sacred ground ring true; the subject seems taboo. If I'm not really taking the job it doesn't matter. So I make one final check and replace the flashlight and start locking the house back up again, leaving it just the way I found it. Whatever secrets it hides will stay locked up for another day.

She leaves first, waiting on the tiny porch while I lock up. I hadn't looked closely at the front door before; there are tiny scratches around the lock casing, the kind that come either from years of use or a few nervous minutes with a lock pick. Cassie's watching me now. I decide against adding to her paranoia. We retreat to Cassie's car, huddled under separate umbrellas. The one I'm using must be left over from last summer's cookouts—it smells so much like smoldering ashes I'm surprised the rain doesn't hiss bouncing off the canvas.

"Can you drive?" she says.

"I was planning on it."

I throw both umbrellas in the trunk, slam the lid down tight.

When I look up again there's a red Ford pickup sitting at the top of the drive, too far for me to see anything except shadows in the front seat. A gun rack in the back. And twin coffins bolted to the bed.

A cow's watching me too. Neither one of us has the sense to stay out of the rain.

"I've got five hundred dollars with me. Otherwise I can write a check . . . I'm a little low on funds right now."

"Keep your money for now, all right?"

"No, you have to take something. Take three hundred. For today at least."

"Wait until I find something out." But she's insistent, so I take it. It's always the way these things start. We get inside the car. I push the seat back, adjust the mirrors. It's too dark to tell but it feels like someone's watching. Like the cars and trucks in the neighbor's yard have somehow rearranged themselves. I'm getting as crazy as Cassie, who's shivering now, not from the cold. I think she's more upset out here than she was in the house.

"When do you think you'll start?" she says.

"I don't know, Cassie."

"There's a ticket in there—you could take your girlfriend on a vacation."

I nod.

"The thing is—I'm off now until Tuesday night. I'm staying with a friend until then—do you have my friend's name and number? No, of course you don't."

I do now; she takes my hand and writes it on my wrist, crossways, like a chain bracelet; Rikki or Nikki something. Somehow it's become sexy to add consonants to your name.

"I'll be back in Chicago Tuesday night for the convention, that's the last stop on the tour. Then I'm free. We could drive to Carbondale or anywhere to look for Kim."

"I'm not driving all the way to Carbondale."

I'm already thinking I could make a couple phone calls right now, before picking up Alison, then phone Cassie tonight and exit gracelessly. I already know what I'm going to find—Lost Moon will be a dead end; the Reverend Lawrence Miner will be in a home somewhere. It's too much money for so little work, but I'll find a way to deal with my guilt.

"Look, just meet me at my motel Tuesday night. Holiday Inn Libertyville. That's where the convention's at."

"Cassie—"

"I'm just hiring you to be my bodyguard, keep the weirdos off me. And there will be plenty there, believe me, since it's the last stop. . . . These shows really bring them out of the woodwork. I can pay you more when I see you Tuesday."

"Let me call you tonight, okay? At Video Savages. I've got time now to run a few things down, I'll let you know tonight about Tuesday and the convention. All right? We'll settle it then."

"You won't be there tonight?" she says, disappointed.

"No, I'm sorry. I can't."

"Then promise me you'll call."

"I'll call."

"And promise me you'll think about Kim, and what might have happened to him."

The Ford does a U-turn and disappears in the rain. Now I'm getting paranoid. "I'm thinking about it right now," I say.

seven

RICHIE'S UNCLE, Leo Minsk, is the founder and franchiser of the Leo Minsk Music Stores, self-proclaimed Rhythm King—a Harold Hill wanna-be who once ruled an empire of used violas and trumpets, sold as new to inner-city schools for a very lyrical profit. He got into the music business through acts he booked for bars and restaurants—this was in Milwaukee, circa 1958, when the city still had the Braves and Warren Spahn and Lew Burdette owned the town—and got out when he saw a future full of synthesizers and electric guitars. But Leo's from Chicago and his first love is movies, not trombones—that's why he collects film memorabilia. And that's why he built the Mindy Minsk Memorial Theater in the basement of his Wisconsin estate.

The theater's constructed in a style I would call Post-Demolition, furnished with items Leo stole or salvaged from landmark Chicago movie palaces. The refreshment stand comes from the Granada. That's where I'm waiting right now, helping myself to the house scotch Leo pours into decorative Chivas decanters. Leo's got a nice crowd today for his party, a gathering of royalty. I've been here ten minutes and already everyone's tried to sell me something; everyone's given me a card embossed with some kind of cartoon crown or scepter. The Donut King's here; so is the Transmission King, the Pool King, the King of EZ Credit, the Duke of High-Volume Discounts. I know most of them from the ads they run on late-night TV, all but the Pool King. I'm not sure if his title refers to snooker or snorkeling.

They're cartoonish figures, but they're each worth a bundle, Leo included. The huge rambling house on Lake Geneva was his wife's idea—I don't think Leo even knows how to swim—but since her death he's gradually remade it, adding a greenhouse, putting in a guardhouse where a retired fireman named Jake can work in retirement, eating ham sandwiches, waving people in. I'm waiting for Leo to finish his guided tour, which I've had myself a number of times. The theater's modeled after the Tivoli, a landmark from Leo's childhood. The rugs come from the Oriental, the drapes from the Granada, lights from the Norshore. Behind one set of drapes there's a Jacuzzi where Leo and a special guest can watch a double feature. But the real showcase is the men's room, smuggled out of the Chicago Theater piece by piece in an effort worthy of *The Great Escape*.

"The Chicago's still open," someone objects when Leo gets to his favorite part of the tour; it might be the King of Home Equity. "They never tore the Chicago down."

"You're right, it's open," Leo says. "But with a different john. The new one's all plastic, non-union. Look at mine, you'll see even the fittings are original, right down to the lime deposits." Leo has the true collector's eye for detail. He dims the lights and starts a movie—one of Cassie's drive-in monster flicks—and tells the others to enjoy themselves, he'll be right back. He's got a little business. One by one they settle back in Leo's plush red velvet seats—lifted from the Playboy Theater—and immerse themselves in *Bikini Love Slaves from Mars*. Cassie must be the Spartacus of love slaves; she's the one leading the rebellion, holding an AK-47 over her head.

Leo and I go upstairs to his bedroom, a typical widower's bedroom—always neat, the bed made first thing every morning. I think a woman comes in to clean once a month, but she never has much to do. Jake comes in from the guardhouse, and the three of them have ham sandwiches and play cards. Over the double bed there's a framed poster of a naked swimmer from some restored Busby Berkeley film. "She had dancer's tits," Leo says, admiring the picture as he swings the frame away from the wall. "No surgery. You wanted tits like that you had to work for 'em." There's a gas fireplace and a white mantel with a row of awards—an

Oscar, two Golden Globes, other trophies from various trade groups; none with Leo's name, of course. Leo has a dozen more in storage; he likes to rotate them, like a kid playing with toy soldiers. They might be real, I don't know. I don't think he bought them from Richie. He's got a collection of ceremonial knives and a Japanese sword I think he bought on late-night TV, maybe from the Sword King.

Leo forgets what he's doing for a moment, then turns the combination before I can politely look away. Not that I'd need the numbers—the safe's so Mickey Mouse anyone could pull it from the plaster, but I guess it makes Leo feel better. That's all most home alarm systems do anyway. "You must have had some morning. Cassie Rayn, in the flesh. Tell me something. Is she still just as beautiful as she was in *Pacific Rimmed*?"

"She looked good."

"What did she smell like?"

"She smelled okay, Leo. I didn't get real close."

"Richie said you rode in a car with her."

"A big car, Leo. With wide seats." Through the bedroom window I can see an old swimming pool, built maybe by the Romans—no shiny blue fiberglass, just gray stone, pebbly concrete, covered now with moss and ivy. It looks more like a pond. Leo should stock it with trout.

"Richie said it was you that got her to vet the movie—you must have been closer than that. He gave you all the credit. He doesn't usually do that."

I shrug, waiting for my money.

Leo's smiling, waiting for an answer. He's looking very dapper today, as always; summer sport coat, tan loafers, a bit of cologne, every hair in place. It takes me a minute to realize what the question is.

"You didn't fuck her?" he says finally.

"I didn't fuck her, Leo."

"That's something you'll regret when you're my age, when you're a grandfather. Try having sex after joint replacement." He takes an envelope from the safe, spins the combination, replaces the poster. "Richie said two and a half, right?"

"I think he said three, Leo."

"Three? You're sure?"

"Pretty sure, yeah. You want to call him?"

"No, no, I trust you."

"He's your nephew, Leo."

"That's why I trust you better. Did you watch the tape?"

"If you're asking me whether it's fake or not I couldn't tell you. That's your department."

"I was wondering if Richie made a copy. I told him not to, he never listens."

"I have no idea." I'm anxious to get going but Leo's in no hurry. He's still holding the money. "I'm just a courier, Leo."

"You don't think it's real?"

"I didn't watch it."

"Of course it's real. I wouldn't be paying you three grand for a fake, would I?"

"There's a certain logic there, I guess."

"And I've got your word, right?"

"I didn't see her sign the paper, Leo. I was waiting outside in the car. I'm not a notary."

"But you spent the whole day with her. She must like you. And that's good enough for me," he says, paying me the three thousand in very crisp hundreds. The top bill, though, feels a little moist, as if splashed by the water in the poster. "And I'm sure it's going to be good enough for Marty, the Pool King."

"You're turning it around already?"

Leo nods. "For six and a half. Don't tell Richie, it'll break his heart." I wish he hadn't told me; my percentage is from Richie's take, not Leo's. "And don't let on I told you, either. I'm sworn to secrecy. Marty thinks the vice cops will raid his swimming pool company. You want some coffee? I can make some instant, it's no trouble."

I shake my head.

"How about some flowers for Alison? I've got a white rose out there I have to cut or it's just gonna die—"

"She doesn't like cut flowers."

"She's picky."

"Yeah, she's picky."

"Did Richie tell you how he got this thing, this *Pretty Ballerina*?"

"No."

"He didn't say who he bought it from?"

"I told you, Leo, I'm just the middleman."

"Every time I hear that word in a commercial somebody's eliminating the middleman. What happens to all the fucking middlemen?"

On the way downstairs Leo tries once again to interest me in an Eldorado—Leo used to collect cars—that he says appreciates every time I open my mouth to breathe. I tell him no. I close my mouth. He shakes the keys in my face—"Take it for a test drive, Harding. There's a slight oil problem, easily fixed." I tell him no. Cars to me are transportation, and trouble. There is always an engine in need of a simple tune-up or an oil problem, easily fixed.

We return to the Mindy Minsk Theater. Cassie's on the screen in a ripped bikini, holding off a prehistoric monster with a Thompson machine gun. For some reason she's speaking in Italian. The monster's spitting fire. He isn't dubbed.

"Marty, I want you to meet someone," Leo says, and the Pool King stands. He's about Leo's age—early sixties—but heavier, with a thick head of hair. He's wearing a red blazer that might have fit him in college. Like a lot of men he shakes hands as if it's a contest. It's not a game I've ever felt like playing.

"An old friend," Leo says. It's not clear which of us he means.

"Harding," he says. "Where have I heard that name?"

"I don't know. Possibly you saw my *Time* magazine cover."

"Harding brought the Cassie Rayn I was telling you about," Leo says, and Marty smiles. It's more like a squint, as though he's looking into the sun. I wish Leo wouldn't bring me into these deals.

"You're the one spent the weekend with her?" Marty says.

"Just a couple hours."

"Leo said you spent the whole weekend with her, she's an old friend. You must have had a ball."

"She's very nice."

"Did you get wet?" he said. "I bet you got wet."

"He didn't get wet," Leo says, sitting down in a recliner. "Mr. Devlin's a major collector, Harding. Cassie Rayn, A to Z. A real expert."

"What a loss," Marty says, shaking his head; this comes straight from the heart. "What a loss to the adult-film industry when Cassie Rayn retired."

"I didn't know you were in the industry," I say.

"King of the Loops," Leo says, "thirty years ago, the peep shows on Wells and State, every one of them came from Marty Devlin Enterprises."

"You wore two crowns," I say. "That's an awesome responsibility."

"That was my pre-pool days," Devlin says. "We took Swedish health films, sliced 'em into seven-minute loops. Times change. The sex business changes. One thing doesn't change—people are always gonna want to jump in a pool. Aboveground, belowground, whatever." It's cool in the basement but Devlin's sweating; I think he's the kind of guy who starts sweating the minute he steps from the shower. "Any chance this little tour of Cassie's means she's coming out of retirement?"

"Doing porn again? I doubt it."

"So why's she doing it? Going on the road?"

"I don't know. Money, probably."

"You two are old friends?"

I shake my head.

"A talent like she has, that's God given," Devlin says. "It's like playing the violin. Quitting's almost sacrilegious. It's an insult to God."

"She checked with the Vatican, Marty," I say. "The pope signed off on it."

"These days, what with all the diseases, I don't know how they get girls willing to do it," Leo says, moving his loafers back and forth on the footrest. He sees me watching. "Bursitis. If I stand too long in one place the blood stops moving. I get leg cramps something awful."

"Now I remember," Devlin says. "Harding, the ex-con. You work a lot of security jobs, don't you? We met ten years ago or so, when I was starting up my business and auditioning security firms—"

"You've got a good memory."

"No, I just remember your boss, Donnie Wilson, giving his spiel while this guy sat in the corner—one of his 'trained operatives,' Donnie said, except when I checked you out I found you'd done eighteen months in jail. We gave the contract to somebody else. How's Donnie doing these days?"

"He's prospering."

"You still work for him?"

"I see him occasionally, yeah. Leo, I have to get going—"

"You can't stay?" Devlin says. "I'd love to hear about Cassie."

"Details, Harding," Leo says. "We want details. Was she wearing stockings? Panties? How did she sit?"

"Maybe another time," I say. Leo doesn't want details, he wants me to help seal the deal with Devlin, be part of his sales pitch. And Devlin's questions about Donnie Wilson and my past have irritated me, though I've done my best not to show it. Otherwise he'll want details on that too.

"Let me give you my card," Devlin says. "I would love to give you a good price on a swimming pool." The Pool King's card has a crown with tiny arms and legs diving off a board. He gives me a rubber refrigerator magnet too, with the same picture and the slogan of the Devlin Pool Co. *Swim for Life.* "These are new. We're running a special right now on our AquaWonder 2000. Full fiberglass lining, state-of-the-art construction."

"Thanks but I live on north Broadway. My landlord doesn't even like waterbeds."

"You did some time in Kentucky, right?" Devlin says. "That's horse country."

"I've heard that."

"I tried selling the governor on swimming pools in the prisons down there. Good therapy, keep everybody a hell of a lot cleaner."

"You should have hired Harding as a consultant," Leo says.

"I don't guess they had a pool in that hole you did your stretch in, did they?" Devlin says.

"The johns backed up into the showers once or twice a week —that the sort of thing you mean?"

Devlin chuckles. "You don't just work for Donnie, right? You work freelance?"

"Why?"

"I might have something for you," he says.

As I'm leaving, Leo's beginning the second part of his tour, explaining how the Tivoli came to be such an important icon for him—how it was there at age eighteen that he took his second cousin Mindy Minsk from dance rehearsal to a Saturday double feature and fucked her in the Tivoli's balcony. It was the last time outside of his marriage that Leo didn't have to pay for sex.

"I guess I'm sentimental," Leo says.

eight

REVEREND LAWRENCE MINER lives in Waukegan, land of enchantment. This is blue-collar Lake County, where the maids and gardeners who run the mansions in Lake Forest and Winnetka rent apartments or buy cheap tract housing and sit at night dreaming of ways to slit their employers' throats. All the streets are named Elm or Oak or Maple but the trees died long ago. It's my favorite part of Lake County, the only part of the North Shore that looks and sounds and smells like Chicago. I returned a Mazda with a steering problem to a dealer near here once, and was given a choice by Del, the service manager—full price during business hours; half price at night, on Del's time, with Del's tools. Since the car was under warranty, the offer didn't make much sense until I heard the rest of the package—let Del do the job at night, pay Del in cash, and I'd get to keep my tape player. And get my car back. It drifted to the left for another year or so before I traded it in.

I got Miner's address by calling Stillwater Methodist, the church on Cassie's twenty-year-old letter, and finding an overeager youth minister who's never heard of Miner or the Moons but has access to the church records and, like me, has several hours to kill before Sunday night services. I've prepared half a dozen phony excuses for needing the information but none are necessary. I think he trusts me. It catches me a little off guard; it's not something I'm used to. All he asks is that I bring my wife and family to church sometime soon.

"We have a lovely candlelight service tonight," he says, but since I'll be picking up Alison I explain that I'll indeed be worshiping tonight, though at a different altar. This is fine with him. "We all serve the Lord in different ways," he says.

The letter that Miner sent to Cassie's father is full of minutiae from a finance committee meeting; both men were on the church board. After three paragraphs bemoaning a decision to use mission funds from the outreach program for a new air conditioner, Miner abruptly changes the subject.

> . . . not much use pursuing this, Ellis, I think there's nothing to do but accept that if he wishes to come back he will, and trust that God watches over him from the same sky as you and I. . . . Right now I am frankly more concerned with you—perhaps counseling or a different doctor might help lift your spirits— certainly your obsession with finding him has taken its toll on you and your family, and your suspicions have alienated you from your friends and neighbors . . . the Wilders and the Lees, everyone at SunnySide . . . and now I hear you're making another trip. . . . What possible good can this do? Your seventh trip?

This doesn't tell me much, other than Miner was concerned about Ellis's health. You could read more into it, about Ellis's state of mind, but it's still a giant leap from this to psycho killer. He made seven trips looking for Kim. It doesn't sound much like someone who would kill the rest of his family.

The youth minister wasn't familiar with SunnySide, confirmed what I knew about the Wilders, that they used to be Cassie's neighbors but didn't have a current address. He did know of the Dr. Arthur Lees, though; they still lived nearby, in Lake Forest. Lee was still on the church board. I stopped there before seeing Miner but found the house—a huge colonial on a shady street— dark and quiet. The whole street was quiet, North Shore quiet. People pay a lot of money for quiet like that. I'm as impressed as I get over real estate.

Waukegan's just a short drive from Lake Forest but much noisier. Neighborhoods change rapidly. The sonic booms you hear as you cross the city line are property values dropping at the speed of sound. Reverend Miner's address turns out to be an old courtyard apartment building, yellow brick with air conditioners humming like seven-year locusts. I don't see Miner's name on a mailbox, so I walk around back where a driveway curves to the basement garage and find a middle-aged man sitting on a footstool, repairing screens. He's dressed in work clothes. There's a ceramic coffee mug on the cement floor, near a large oil stain. When I ask about Miner, I'm told the woman moved out last month, good riddance, thank you very much.

"I was looking for Mr. Miner, used to be with the church?"

"That would be Selma's brother."

"That's right."

He puts down the screen, reaches for his coffee. The mug says DO UNTO OTHERS—THEN RUN LIKE HELL. "Is it good news or bad?"

"I just want to talk to him."

"You a lawyer?"

"No."

"Doctor?"

"No."

"You're nobody?"

"There you go. That's me."

"Well, he ain't here. He moved out, nearly a year ago—after he'd been here five years at least, staying with his sister—I kept thinking he'd move out, but his sister's got the extra room and I guess he needed somewheres to stay. When they let him out. You know."

"Yeah."

I wait a second but he's too interested in the screens to help me any further.

"That was something," I finally say. "When they let him out."

"Whadja mean."

"I just remember something, in the papers—"

He looks up at me, scowls. "You believe what you read in the papers?"

"Not always, no." His attention is already back down on the

screen. This could take all day. "You didn't think any of what they said about him was true?"

"They never proved he hurt nobody. That's the bottom line."

"Right."

"He just went a little nuts is all. Not that I condone that sort of thing."

"Absolutely not."

"His sister's the one they shoulda locked up."

"Selma?"

He nods. "What a fruitcake. Always thinks somebody's watching her. Every time I see her I want to tell her she's got a piece of food or something on her face because she's got this little mole over her lip with these two little hairs—"

"Where's Reverend Miner living now?"

"He's two blocks over on Cypress. I don't know the number but it's the house with the flag. They're supposed to take it down when it rains, but Miner never takes it down. He's got it nailed up there. He should take it down when it rains."

"You knew him pretty well?"

"Both of them. She more than him—she was here a lot longer. This is their screen I'm fixing. She threw one of her flatirons right through it. Miss Miner collects flatirons. Hundreds of 'em. One of the movers collapsed on the front lawn, he's wearing a truss now, I think. The apartment's vacant—you know anybody needs a place?"

I shake my head.

"I get a bonus anytime I find a new tenant for the owner—pretty good deal, huh?"

"Yeah."

"Can you imagine collecting flatirons?"

"People collect all sorts of junk. None of it makes any sense to me. Which way is Cypress, east?"

He nods. "You tell the reverend that Selma left some stuff in the basement. Hey, if you're going over there now maybe you could take it with you."

"Sure, as long as it's not more flatirons."

"No, no, just some junk mail they don't forward. I'd do it

myself except I've got all these screens. This is a real bad year for mosquitoes. That's what I wished I'd studied in school. If I'd gone to school. Bugs, I mean. Insects. Then I could see the screens like they see 'em. Take a different approach. Outside looking in."

"How do you fix a screen exactly?"

"To do it right? That's quite a bit of work, an art like weaving a rug or caning a chair. Take the Amish, for example. The Amish have a way with screens."

"And you?"

"I'm Unitarian. I just dump glue all over it—like this—kind of mash it together, hope it sticks. That's my method."

"That's how I generally fix things," I agree. "Where's Selma living now?"

"In Florida somewhere, probably waxing them two hairs—"

I take the junk mail with me to the truck and glance through it while driving the two blocks to Cypress. Reverend Miner's house is a two-flat sitting with a dozen others in disrepair. I have no trouble finding a parking spot. There's a vertical mailbox, the kind that holds maybe one gas bill, hanging from a nail beside the door. Miner's name is on a strip of tape sliding off the box. The first floor gets the enclosed front porch. Miner gets the view of downtown Waukegan.

The front door's unlocked, then there's a long stairwell. I knock and hear someone trying to be quiet. I knock again, and the door opens an inch or so. It's five o'clock, but Miner's in his bathrobe. I don't think I woke him: I think the bathrobe's pretty much full-time. I'm hoping he's got something on underneath. Defrocked clergy make me nervous.

"I'm not Miner," he says right away, as though that would suffice—oh, all right, sorry to bother you. He's older than I pictured. The whole house smells like cooking gas.

"Come on, Reverend, open the door. Where's that evangelical spirit? I just want to ask you about someone."

"You're not from the city?"

I shake my head.

"If that's a summons you can forget it because Miner isn't here."

"It's not a summons," I say patiently.

"You're not from my sister's lawyer? Miner's lawyer? I mean Miner's *sister's* lawyer?"

"Easy now, you're gonna hurt yourself." I put the mail on the floor behind me, take the picture of Kim from my wallet and hold it to the inch of space that Miner's giving me. He's looking at my wallet more than the picture. "Remember?"

"No."

"If I give you ten bucks will you open the door?"

"Twenty," he says. With the bathrobe he looks like an ad for NyQuil. "The door's hard to open sometimes."

"Fifteen," I say, giving him the money, "and I'll stay out here. What about it? You remember him?"

"I said no." But something in his face says he remembers him very well.

"His name's Kim Moon. You gave him a bus ride twenty-two years ago."

"Twenty-two years?" he says with a laugh that turns into a hacking cough. He wipes his mouth on his sleeve. "Are you crazy? I have enough trouble remembering what I did yesterday."

"Here's the thing, Miner—I'm betting yesterday wasn't all that eventful. But this you should remember. The kid disappeared. Now, I know you were on the bus. Just answer my questions and I won't tell your sister where you're living."

"You talked to my sister?"

"I heard all about it—the fight with the flatiron, everything."

"Did she say I hit her with the flatiron? Did she tell you that?"

"Just look at the picture, Reverend. And calm down."

He pauses, looks at the mail on the floor. He doesn't look at the picture. A dog starts barking from a back room. Miner keeps the chain on the door and leaves to yell at the dog, who comes bounding toward me. It's a pit bull with a face like a smashed tin can. I don't see a leash or a collar. I don't like pit bulls. They tend to attach themselves to the legs of small children.

"Sit!" Miner says, with an authority in his voice I didn't know he had. The dog sits. I feel like finding a chair myself.

"That the only picture you have?" he says after a minute.

"Afraid so."

"Nothing from church, with the other kids? So I'd remember better?"

"No."

He pauses a second. "Did he turn up or something?"

"Good, you remember."

"I didn't say that. How'd you find me anyway? I'm not in the phone book."

"It wasn't real hard. Come on, Miner. Someone's looking for this kid."

This is not good news to Miner.

"You got a cigarette?" he says, both hands in his bathrobe pockets. I shake my head. I get out the letter he wrote Ellis, though it occurs to me the man who wrote that letter has disappeared almost as completely as Kim. "You have to understand, I haven't thought about this in years, that's all. I'm not a member of the parish anymore—"

"I gathered that. What was it, Reverend—a crisis of faith or just a few too many cups of sacramental wine."

"I needed a rest," he says. "Who sent you, anyway? The hospital?"

"No."

He looks toward the picture. "Who's looking for the boy?"

"I am. I'm looking for him. Just tell me what happened and I'll be out of your life."

"Nothing happened." He's staring at me with each sentence, as if he's waiting for something. Probably a drink. "He ran away. That's why I finally just left, it was too much, worrying about kids like that, chasing after boys, always running away . . . not just him. His sister, too."

"Kalani?"

"The little slut," Miner says. "Give me the rest of the money. I've got soup boiling."

"I've got a letter here that you wrote to Kim's father—"

"What?"

"Take a look at the letter."

He holds it against the door. His lips move slightly as he reads.

"Where'd you get this?"

"From a friend of the family."

"There was no more family," he says, staring at me now, " 'cept one. Tell me who sent you."

"What did you mean here about the Wilders and the Lees—"

"I don't remember. I didn't know anything then, I know even less now. I just want to be left alone."

"Just one more question."

"I told all this to the cops years ago. You're not a cop?"

"No. Did Kim have a friend, someone he might have confided in?"

"How in the world would I know that?"

"Who was he sitting with on the bus?"

"Are you kidding? Twenty-two years ago? Now I'm warning you—move your foot out of the door or I'll dump hot soup on it. I'm not a man of the church anymore. This is my house, my property. Besides, anyone'll tell you—I'm crazy as a loon—there's no telling what I'll do. And this soup is hot—"

"Take my card," I say, finding one in my wallet for someone named Jack Wallace, Insurance Appraiser, writing in my real phone number on it. "Call me if your mood improves. Oh and here's your mail. You should check your box more often."

"Insurance?" he says, fingering the card. "Is there some kind of money involved in this?"

"Just the fifteen."

"There must be money to make you come out here, after all this time."

"Call me if your memory improves, Miner. We can discuss it."

He thinks about this while I hand him his mail. Most of it's ads and coupons and department store closeouts but one postcard intrigues me enough to let it fall to the floor where I can get a better look at it. I must have missed the message side earlier.

Don't forget to clean out your attics and basements for the annual SunnySide DayCare garage sale.

What catches my eye is the logo of a crescent moon in the

corner—it's just a coincidence but it reminds me of the one on Cassie's storm door. All moons look pretty much alike, right?

Drop your items off at any of SunnySide's four convenient locations.

I ask Miner three or four more questions while he looks through the mail. He seems a bit more nervous than when we began. I think his fingers are shaking just a bit. Maybe it's the lighting in the hall. Maybe it's my imagination.

He leaves me alone at the door. I try talking with him some more but his temperature goes up a few degrees. So does the flame on the gas stove. I ask him how he could let such a young kid just vanish like that. How could he live with himself, a man of God, letting one of his flock wander off. Suddenly, the interview's over. I go back downstairs to get a towel. The soup's chicken rice.

nine

WHOEVER SHE WAS, she's a lousy kisser," Alison says, rubbing my face with a wet Kleenex. Apparently I've been walking around with orange lipstick on my cheek. "She missed your mouth by a good two inches. And I hate her perfume. You smell like chicken soup."

"It was a gratitude kiss from a client. Potential client. She thinks I'm helping her with something."

"You're not?"

I shake my head.

"This money you put in my purse isn't from her?"

"Most of it's Richie's, not Cassie's."

"She wears frosted orange lipstick?"

"She's in show business. Was."

"Is there a reason she wrote this on your wrist?"

"Body art, Alison. She suggested piercing a different appendage but I said no, fading Bic blue is as far as I go." We're in a holding pattern at O'Hare, just outside the Skycap Lounge, jammed in a crowd of frequent fliers. Alison's plane was one of the last to land, before most of O'Hare shut down from a combination of rain and night fog. She's sitting on her luggage, drinking very expensive Gatorade, wearing a black baseball jersey and extremely red, extremely short shorts—she's looking very leggy, very bronze from the Arizona sun, her long black hair hanging past her shoulders. Each time I cross the terminal to use the phone a different guy tries picking her up. I wish she'd at least let one of them pay for the Gatorade.

"I thought we were going home and celebrating my birthday," she says. "It's been three weeks."

"I know. I bought new sheets. Silk."

"You did?"

"And I cleaned the apartment."

"Oh God—"

"I dusted, too."

"Harding, you can't tease me like this—"

"Have another Gatorade," I say.

"Why are we waiting?"

"Richie paged me an hour ago. His line's still busy."

"Call him from the truck."

"I hate cell phones. It won't be long, I promise."

"Is this another one of his deals? You should quit helping him," she says. "Find something better."

"Uh huh." To distract her from this line of thinking I give her a postcard that came yesterday, from her father, Stan. It's a picture of albino fish.

" 'Here I am at Mammoth Cave.' Another tour. He spends too much time around old people."

"He's sixty-two, he's retired. You want him picking up young girls in bars?"

The airport's hot; too many people. The United terminal looks like a big greenhouse. Alison takes off her cap, pulls her hair back, wipes her brow on her sleeve. Her earrings are new, I think; sterling silver—I have trouble remembering earrings unless they need to come off in certain situations. "He says the lake is forty-eight degrees year round. Absolutely pure, like a spring. Can you imagine diving into water like that?"

"They don't let you swim in Mammoth Cave, Alison. It's not a resort. And they've got vampire bats in those caves. Didn't you ever see *Nightwing*? Or *Lifeforce*?"

"This will surprise you, Harding, but people often take vacations without being randomly slaughtered by vampire bats."

"Not in my world. Incidentally, that's what the tour guide always says, Alison. With a reassuring chuckle. Right before the bats suck out his eyeballs. You need a refill?"

"Please." I get her another Gatorade from the bar and then

walk across the terminal, carrying my briefcase so I look business-like. Without a briefcase in an airport you're just a tourist. There are four banks of phones nearby; the lines are slightly shorter than those at the rest rooms. The johns and bars are as jammed as the runways are empty; flights canceled, airports closed; too much rain, fog, flooding. Alison was lucky; she flew in from Tucson, where rain's an Indian myth. It's beginning to look like the Midwest will fall into the sea before California.

The number I've been dialing is Video Savages' office line. Alison's right—I could have called Richie from the truck. But since it's not his home number it probably has to do with Cassie, and I'd rather clear this up right now. The fewer interruptions later, the better. This time Richie finally answers. He sounds like he's been doing some defensive drinking.

"What's wrong, Richie?"

"She never showed, that's what's wrong. I've got a store full of very horny people and no Cassie. What the hell happened with you two?"

"Nothing happened," I say, trying to remember the last few things she said. "Have you tried her motel room?"

"Of course I have. She checked out hours ago. Apparently she never even checked in, not really. Never touched her room."

"That makes no sense. Her car's gone?"

"Of course her car's gone, Harding—*she's* gone—"

"What about the agency that booked her?"

"It's Sunday night, Harding. Nobody's there. Nobody's anywhere. Except here—*everybody's* here."

"Calm down, Richie. Just apologize, give away some of those old used rentals and some popcorn—"

"I don't think you understand. There's about a hundred people here, half of them horror freaks, half of them porn freaks; some of them in PVC and leather could go either way. And some of these guys are real old, Harding, they've been waiting all day in the heat and humidity—I'm just waiting for someone to throw a clot and drop dead and sue me. I'm not insured for this. You're the only one who knows CPR."

"Didn't you talk to her when we got back?"

"She came in, signed the movie, and left, said she had to change her clothes, take a shower."

"She didn't look at the movie either?"

"No—who cares about the fucking movie?"

"I thought you did. That's why I had to drive all the way to Leo's."

"I care about my money. You've got my money?"

"Yeah."

"Thank God. At least I cleared a profit on that part of her trip."

"So did Leo."

"He's selling it? How much?"

"You don't want to know. I wasn't going to mention it."

"Three and a half?"

"Five." I don't have the heart to tell him the truth.

"Fuck," he says. "Five. Who pays that much for a Cassie Rayn?"

"Some guy named Devlin. The Pool King."

"Who?"

"I don't get it, Richie. Cassie seemed fine on the drive back. A little stoned but generally happier than on the way out."

"Well, something happened. You're the detective, you find her. Listen, I gotta go; the crowd's growing restless. I thought I had them boxed in behind the laser discs but they're forming some sort of human catapult—I might have to sleep here tonight."

"Welcome to show business, Richie."

The person behind me wants the phone. I could leave now, I guess—if Cassie's gone maybe so is my obligation. I wish now I hadn't taken her money. I feed another quarter in and dial the number for Lost Moon. *Call now for a message that may change your life!* Cassie said no one answered but I get a recording.

The speaker's a young boy.

Thanks for calling the Lost Moon hot line! To help you learn more about us we've prepared a video that's sure to answer all your questions, including rare historic pictures of the area. It's not yet available but will be soon—watch your local papers! Remember—Lost Moon is for families!

At this point the guy behind me coughs impatiently—I tell

him that my mother's just had a stroke, it's a family emergency, so back off. This doesn't impress him. "My mother had three strokes," he says. "I never once tied up the phones." I try finding SunnySide DayCare but strike out. I call a couple travel agencies but they're all closed until Monday morning. I plan to be in bed then, with the woman now watching me from across the terminal. She's starting to wonder what I'm doing over here, what Richie has to say that could be so interesting. I guess I could follow up on Ellis's letter, look harder for the neighbors, the Wilders, find out enough to convince Cassie if she does contact me that her brother's long gone; there is no Lost Moon; there is no serial kidnapper of Asian boys—

"I sense a troubled spirit," a woman says, suddenly beside me. She's dressed Elvira-black with long leather boots and appropriate cleavage. "The Flying Psychic relieves all fears. She knows the wind. She knows the sky. She can see rain, dense fog, she has your regional and national forecasts." What she sees is my pile of change. The Flying Psychic has a Slavic accent that comes and goes and long nails that would flatten a tire. "Give me your hand," she says, taking it before I can object. "Don't you wish to know if your plane will land safely? For only one dollar?"

The other guys want a look, too—not at my hand, at the Flying Psychic. It's not a bad scam. For the second time today I find myself doing my best not to stare at a woman's breasts.

"I see many interesting things," she says. "Many lines. They go here, they go there. What do they say? What do they tell us? Warnings from the Gatekeeper, the Keymaster, the sun, the moon —oh no, look at that one—"

"I don't have a dollar."

"The Flying Psychic sees one seventeen in change."

"All right. But if you were really psychic you'd know how much you annoy people."

The coins disappear somewhere in the sleeve of her dress. She drops my hand like a rock. "You're okay," she says.

"That's it?"

"That's it."

"What about the warning from the Gatekeeper?"

"Twenty-eight bucks for a lost ticket," she says. The accent falls away, too. "The Flying Psychic does not recommend short-term parking." As she walks away someone beside me says *What a piece of ass* and another man laughs and says *Read* my *mind, darling* and we all watch the way her rear end moves in the tight black dress.

While someone lifts my briefcase.

There's nothing in it, but I hate to be taken so easily. They're going to be pissed when they open it. A job like this usually takes three—probably one of the guys behind me, the woman dressed for Halloween, a third man who right now has the briefcase—it's an awful lot of work for what I'm carrying. If they're any good the woman's changed clothes and they're heading for their car and the Gatekeeper. I hope they lose their tickets. About all they can do with my briefcase is eat peanut butter crackers and take notes while having safe sex.

I go downstairs to find a bathroom, trying to avoid more con artists—packs of Moonies and Hare Krishnas in search of the way —I tell them yes, the john's right over here—and then walk past the baggage carousels to the up escalator. Everywhere I go I see black briefcases. When I step off I see someone getting off a parallel escalator who reminds me of Richie's customer, Mr. Quanh. Or rather I see a cowboy hat, floating through the crowd near customer service.

Because of the floods and canceled flights there are circles of people huddled anxiously beneath the monitors, waiting for the numbers to change—it looks like the stock exchange on Black Tuesday. The cowboy hat disappears behind one of these. I let a flood of people pass around me, waiting, but the next time I see the hat it's on the floor near a maintenance room, minus its owner. I wander over and pick it up and dust it off, creasing the brim, feeling a little like Glenn Ford. The next thing I feel is a small gun against my ribs.

"An old trick of Hopalong Cassidy's," Quanh says.

"And very effective it is, too." Alison was right. I should have phoned from the truck.

"Let's go in here," he says, motioning to the maintenance room. He has one hand on my elbow. I'm holding the hat.

ten

THE ROOM'S SMALL, filled with sweepers, brooms, a lunch table. It smells like fast food. Only one of the lights works. Quanh motions me to the wall, kicks my legs back and pats me down like he knows what he's doing. He's old but still fairly strong. Sometimes the old guys give you the most grief.

"If you're working a briefcase scam," I say, "you should tell your people they're supposed to *switch* briefcases. Now I don't have a briefcase."

He keeps checking for a gun; around my legs, under my arms. It tickles a little. I think he's surprised to find I'm not armed. It's a common reaction.

"What, then?" I say. "If you're upset about Cassie not showing, I can't help you."

He kicks my legs out farther, removes my wallet. "Harding," he says. His breath is full of the brown cigarettes. "Why are you here tonight? Are you following me?"

"I'm not following anybody." He has the small gun tight against my side. It might be a derringer—outside of *Wild Wild West* reruns I've never actually seen one. The Stetson's on a card table beside me. "Are you crazy, pulling a gun in an airport?"

"You're not following me."

"I saw your hat, that's all. I thought you lost your fucking hat. I was being a good Samaritan."

"Who are you with?"

72

"Nobody. Put the fucking gun away."

"You're meeting someone?"

"No." Let's leave Alison out of this.

"You just come to the airport for no reason?"

"Yeah. I'm funny that way."

He kicks one leg out farther. My head smacks the concrete wall. I turn slightly; his expression hasn't changed. Mine has, just a bit.

"If you do that again," I say quietly, "you'd better be willing to use the gun." He looks at my driver's license, turns my pockets inside out. I'm hoping it's too dark in here for him to read wrist writing.

"You were at the store this morning because you work for Richard?"

"No."

"Why, then?"

"I was returning my rental copy of *The Green Berets*." It's taken me this long to place the Vietnamese accent, buried beneath his formal English. "Someone's going to come through that door very soon, Mr. Quanh, and when they see you have a gun you'll be in a good deal of trouble. This isn't Tan Son Nhat."

"Were you in the war?" he says, more polite than interested. Other than the head smack and pulling a gun on me he's conducting a very polite interrogation.

I shake my head.

" 'Jack Wallace, Insurance,' 'Robert Lamb, Attorney at Law,' 'J. R. Andrews, V.P. Banking.' In my country, you see," he says, trying to make sense of my business cards, "everyone was in the war." He gives up; files them carefully back in my wallet. "What is it you do exactly, Mr. Harding?"

"I sell aluminum siding. The ASA's holding their annual meeting over at the Hilton."

"ASA?"

"Aluminum Siding Association. What is it you do exactly, Mr. Quanh?"

"This is quite a coincidence. I too am a salesman."

"No kidding."

"Why don't you tell me who you're working for?"

"Right now I'm kind of in between jobs."

There are voices in the corridor but no one tries the door.

"Let's talk about the movie you transported today," he says. "How did you get involved in this?"

"You've lost me."

"Who purchased this movie?"

"I really should get back to the association."

"You spent some time today with a Martin Devlin, did you not?"

"No."

"You're working perhaps for Mr. Devlin?"

I shake my head.

"You're an associate of Mason's?"

"I don't know who that is."

"You don't know Mason, or Mr. Devlin?"

"Are they members of the siding association? Look, why don't you come with me—I could sponsor you for membership."

He gives me back my wallet. He hasn't moved the gun. "Would I be very successful at this, do you think? Selling aluminum siding?"

"You'd do all right."

"Just all right?"

"Based on what I've seen tonight I'd say your sales technique's a little rough. I'd work the inscrutable angle harder, maybe lose the gun. The ASA frowns on the use of handguns, at least on the first sales call."

He smiles. It's not much of a smile. His teeth are the color of straw.

"I know Cassandra contacted you—"

"Now how would you know that."

"And I know you're a private detective, at least by reputation. You were escorting Cassandra today. So you must know why she canceled her appearance. What I can't determine is whether you're helping her or not."

"And that's what you're trying to do? Help her?"

"Most definitely."

"Didn't you see her when she came in the store?"

"Just briefly. From a distance. You must know where she went."

"Sorry. I can't help you."

There are more voices now. Quanh walks toward the door, keeping the gun pointed at me. He's wearing the Stetson again.

"A word of advice—"

"Oh good."

"I'm afraid you don't know what you're getting into."

"Really? Did you just figure that out?"

Someone tries the door, says "damn" when he finds it locked. I hear the lovely sound of jangling keys.

"You would do well to watch your back," he says. "There are a number of parties involved besides Devlin or Mason—"

"I told you, I don't know anyone with that name."

"You will," he says softly.

That's all he has time for—two men in neat blue suits come through the door—not cops, just janitors. I can be damn lethal with a push broom when I want to, but he's gone in a second. The crowd fills in around him. The hat's gone, too. Very inscrutable.

When I get back to the Skycap Lounge there's a crowd of guys around Alison. She has a chair now. And some flowers. And a pen —at first I think she's signing the bar tab but then one of the guys rolls up his Polo shirt so she can write on his chest. I don't see the cowboy hat anywhere.

"Thanks, guys," Alison says. She stands, stretches, unfolds blue sunglasses and slides them over her ears. "Gotta run. Big photo shoot in the morning with Herb Ritts."

"God, Tawnni, thank you—"

"Don't forget to send me a picture, Tawnni, please—"

I pick up Tawnni's suitcase. "What's going on?"

"They think I'm some Playboy bimbo flying incognito—not bad for somebody pushing thirty, huh? I think it's the tan. I've never really had one before. You don't tan in Hyde Park, you go straight from white skin to second-grade melanoma."

"It's the flight delays. Those guys have been here so long they're starting to hallucinate. You're like a mirage."

I keep expecting to see Quanh. I don't know how you can

hide a hat like that. Except the place is so crowded the whole terminal's like a Moroccan bazaar. And with the rain everyone's got hats. And briefcases.

I could go hunting for him but I'm not sure what I'd do if I found him. And I'm determined not to let any of this spoil my night with Alison. It will wait until morning.

"Something the matter?" Alison says.

"No."

"I'm over here," she says.

"Sorry. I thought I saw someone I knew—"

"I can go home with Doug if you have other plans."

"Who's Doug?"

"The one in the Armani T-shirt."

"The short one?"

"Don't be a size queen, Harding. Besides, don't complain, Doug paid our bar tab. And he sketched in a very special evening if I could get away from my handlers—dinner and dancing and some drug he came up with at Abbott that the FDA might see around two thousand ten, increases the libido to the third or fourth power. We were just about to cruise home in Doug's new Porsche and double-check his math."

"You haven't seen the roads. It's still raining. What you need tonight is a boat, not a Porsche."

"Dougie doesn't have a boat. Just the Porsche."

"You asked?"

"I did, yeah," she says, smiling.

"That's my girl."

"I missed you, baby," she says, draping an arm around me. "So much."

"Then we'd better get going," I say. "Unless they bought you a golf cart. It's a day's walk to the car."

eleven

THE EDENS and Kennedy Expressways are dotted with shiny lakes. I drop Alison near the back door to my building, wait until she climbs the stairs and lets herself in the kitchen door. "Ten minutes," she yells. My next-door neighbor, Mrs. Loomis, sticks her head out her bathroom window and waves hello, shaking a yellow dust rag like a flag at Indy. I leave the truck in the alley and then walk up Broadway to what passes for my front door, the entrance to Athena Gyros. I shake the water from my slicker like a cocker spaniel. Inside it's warm and muggy. My landlord, Minas, hands me today's mail and then points to a back table filled with salad, bread, the day's special.

"Watch your back," Minas whispers.

"Why?"

"Looks like Turk," he says. A man in a badly fitting black suit glances up, continues eating. I don't recognize either one, the special or the man.

"You're Harding," he says.

I tell him I am.

"Your buddy puts too much garlic in his octopus."

"I didn't know that was possible."

"And he keeps watching me. Like I'm gonna steal the silverware."

"He's a good host, that's all. He's being attentive. You should leave a nice tip."

"He could set himself on fire with the saganaki, he won't get more than ten percent. Don't sit down," he says. "You're not talking to me."

"I'm not?"

"Across the street," he says, pointing with his fork. "Frozen foods. Aisle ten." He's very sure of himself. I'm about to ignore him when he touches my arm lightly with his fork, holding his jacket open just long enough for me to see a shoulder holster. Wonderful. "Aisle ten," he says.

"Look, I've been waiting all day to see my girlfriend—"

"She'll wait. This won't. Believe me."

"And what's this about exactly?"

"Frozen foods," he says, again showing me the gun. What the hell, I think. I can always use more fish sticks.

He coughs, sneezes, blows his nose in his napkin.

"I need some of them tiny time pills," he says, wiping his nose. "Summer colds are the worst." I expect him to follow me, but he doesn't make a move, other than a fresh assault on his dinner.

"You're not coming?"

"I get dessert," he says. "It comes with the meal."

Treasure Island's parking lot is worse than the expressways, full of abandoned shopping carts, some still turning in slow circles like windup toys. The store's crowded despite the rain. Marvin Gaye's in the background: "Trouble Man." A woman in produce gives me a slice of kiwi, the wonder fruit. I fill a basket with a few essentials: milk, eggs, the *Weekly World News*. It's another special edition featuring CaveBoy, now spotted hanging from a power line in Kentucky. Maybe Alison's father can join the search team.

There's no one I recognize in frozen foods. But then I walk to paper products and see Leonard Toth.

Leonard used to be a suburban cop, though he never got past detective first grade—other opportunities came his way. He does collection work now, for bookies mostly. It's surprising how squeamish bookies can be about violence. Leonard's not squeamish. His specialty is hardware—C-clamps, vises. He pinches knees, he pinches toes. And he's very tight with a dollar. His first jail time was from a bank job; Leonard was the driver. Everything went fine until his buddies ran outside and couldn't find the car— it was across the street at the car wash. There was a Wednesday special on hot wax. Leonard had a coupon.

I worked with Leonard years ago, just after prison when I needed money and was less particular than now about the jobs I took. I ran surveillance for him on a podiatrist who liked to bet on the Cubs. Leonard bought the note. He settled with the doc late at night, while I watched the door. It was over fast. I think he offered him a professional rate.

I haven't seen him in years, thought he moved away years ago, to the West Coast.

Right now he's squatting in aisle seven, checking the unit pricing on paper towels.

"The goon in the restaurant said you wanted to see me."

"That goon's my brother Luther," he says, irritated. "Don't sneak up on me like that. And show a little respect, will you? We just came from St. Mary's Cemetery. We had to put Aunt Martha in the ground."

"I hope she was dead." He's not exactly dressed for a funeral —an oversized Hawaiian shirt, white pants, canvas loafers.

"Listen, you're the college guy, what makes these fucking towels cost so much? The little houses with picket fences and cats and dogs they paint all over the borders here?"

He makes it sound like one of the decorative arts.

"Just buy the generic, Leonard. Your wife must love you, doing the grocery shopping now between jobs, breaking people's knees."

"My wife hates me, she walked out three weeks ago. And her lawyer thought today would be a good time to serve the papers, right at the grave site—I think he thought that might be safer, I wouldn't pop him right in front of my relatives."

"Well, he doesn't know you very well, does he?" I seem to recall Leonard actually leaned on the priest performing his son's first communion, leaned on him *during* the ceremony. This was for unpaid bingo tributes. Leonard is a "Render Unto Caesar" strict constructionist.

" 'Gross mental cruelty'—what the hell is that, I ask him. He gives me a list half a page long. It turns out I shake the table when I cut my round steak. I breathe funny when I watch TV. My aftershave's too flowery."

"No kidding. Let me get you a sympathy card, Leonard. Aisle five."

"So I'm gonna be a bachelor again," he says, pushing his cart slowly forward, "after nineteen years of marriage. Like you. You never married what's-her-name, Wonder Woman, did you?"

"Alison. No. We can double-date." The idea of Leonard Toth reentering the singles scene is a little frightening. *DWM. Thrifty, sweet-smelling. Enjoys maiming, torturing, and killing. Seeks female with similar interests.* Leonard's pushing his cart nearly as slowly as he's moving this conversation. "It's getting late, Leonard. I've had a long day. Alison's waiting for me."

"She's got her own business now, I hear."

"The photo store? She's had that a couple years now."

"I'm just thinking—I've got half a roll of vacation 110 in my car I should get developed—"

"She'd love to have your business. If they're candid shots of the Toth family maybe they'll show up at the gallery. Can we maybe move this toward the express lane, Leonard?"

"Sure, sure," he says, leaning over the plastic clicker he's got taped to the cart. He does smell a little flowery but it might be the scented Puffs. "I was hoping you could help me out a little, that's all."

We're at the end of the aisle, staring at prepackaged chickens.

"I've got maybe twenty bucks on me, Leonard."

Leonard examines the selection of roasters. "I was thinking more along the lines of information."

"About what?"

"Your other girlfriend. The one you spent the day with."

"Cassie?" I say, not hiding my surprise very well. "That was you watching us today, in the red pickup?"

He shakes his head. "This is a third-party report, like a rumor." He rings a buzzer and a butcher comes out and explains to Leonard that they don't sell day-old chicken, they don't mark down the meat. He's lost a customer.

"I thought you lived in L.A., Leonard. How long have you been back?"

"Not long."

"How long have you been following me?"

He shakes his head. "You know, I thought this was gonna be such a simple job—I'm back in the city anyways for the funeral, why not pick up the extra money—then who shows up today right in the goddamn middle of the fucking pasture—"

"What's the job?"

"I need to talk with Cassie. I was wondering what she told you today, about her plans. And where she is tonight." He selects a mixture called Chicken Surprise; no breasts, wings, thighs, or legs. I think that leaves Leonard with the beak.

"That's it?" I say.

He pauses. "For now."

"I don't know where she is. I'm starting to wish I'd never heard of her."

He starts up the next aisle. Snacks/Party Supplies.

"Somebody else interested?" he says casually, looking at microwave popcorn.

"Short VC, cowboy hat instead of black pajamas. Is he yours?"

"No," he says, frowning. He opts for generic low-fat butter, with Genuine Artificial Butter-Flavored Crystals. He saves a quarter over the Paul Newman. "But I can guess who he is. . . . Did she hire you for something, Harding? Find something maybe, safeguard something . . . those shoe boxes, for example."

"What shoe boxes?"

"Come on, Harding," he says, smiling. "I've got you on tape carrying them out of the house."

"Just shoes, Italian pumps. Cassie's lending me a pair for the prom. What's inside the shoe boxes that's so important?"

"You really didn't look?" he says, laughing. "I guess I'm not surprised. For such a smart guy you've always made lots of dumb moves. Why should you look? Some broad talks you into breaking into Hell House, the place probably still smells like blood, you come out with a shoe box she hid twenty years ago—why look? And she's so sweet, am I right? You see the papers today?"

"Not yet."

"Interesting story in the *Sun-Times*," he says. "Ten-year-old kid in Cabrini Green kills his two brothers when they won't go get him some candy. This kid wanted his Snickers so bad he empties a .32, reloads, and keeps shooting."

"So?"

"Sometimes kids develop early, Harding."

"What are you saying, Leonard?"

"Only this, and for your own sake—if she's trying to hire you I would first talk to someone who knows the case. One of the Lake County cops, for example. A guy named Reese used to work up there, he wasn't a total asshole. Now, this is not something I generally recommend to people, that they talk to cops. Especially county cops. It goes against my nature just to say the words. But I think you should read the case file. The papers left a few things out. And there's a few things Cassie might have left out today, if she was crying on your sleeve, trying to get your help. Though if you're not working for her, then what's the difference? Right? It's this funeral making me all sentimental—I'm out there with my brother Luther at St. Mary's, standing in the rain putting Martha under the wisteria, and I just decided out of the blue, let's give Harding a call. Get him out of the line of fire. 'Cause if you don't have friends what have you got?"

At this point—as a gesture of friendship—Leonard decides to show me his gun, a small Davis automatic tucked inside his pants. There are people everywhere, but this is Leonard's special genius. No one the least bit sane would think of opening fire in a place so public.

Which leaves Leonard.

"How much does she owe?"

"You don't need to know what she owes or doesn't owe. You just need to listen to me. Because you know the rules—if I have business with Cassie and she comes to you—then I have business with you."

I nod. It's a basic Mob syllogism, Goon 101. Leonard makes a quick turn, heads down the next aisle, which is full of soft drinks and bottled water. "You're saying there was money in those boxes?"

"Nobody said that. Did I say that?"

"Then what do you want with the boxes?"

He starts to say something, then stops, an act of self-restraint unusual for Leonard.

"You know too much already," he says finally. He finds a bottle of water on sale, imported from a spring in West Virginia. "You know what I forgot? I forgot the fucking lime."

"I don't like being threatened, Leonard."

He laughs. "Harding, you've known me a long time. Would I be threatening you in a public place, right here by the Perrier? No, I would not. We'd be over in the butcher shop, customers would be buying overpriced salami sliced from your ears, on special— and it would serve those old broads right the way they crowd in there. Pushing and shoving. And do they take a number? No, they do not."

He takes out his grocery list and checks something off: *ground chuck, Tuna Helper, lean on Harding.*

"You get back to me on this," he says. "Maybe next time we can meet at a Jewel. This place is too pricey. None of my coupons match."

"What's the time frame, Leonard? Days? Weeks? Hours?"

He shrugs. "It's all the same thing, isn't it?" More philosophy. "Do us both a favor. When she gets in touch with you, give me a call. And step back. That's all you have to do. Otherwise . . ."

"Is this the threat?"

"No, no. But there's a nice spot out there, I noticed, by Aunt Martha. Oh, you'd like it, Harding, it's real pretty, lots of trees. Just like the pictures on these fucking towels. Give my best to your girlfriend. Maybe I'll drop by her store one of these days."

He turns his cart around and heads down the next aisle. I watch him go. I pay for my groceries. There's not much of a line.

Outside the store I walk toward Broadway and see the same Ford pickup I saw earlier today, out of place among the Grand Cherokees and Explorers everyone around here drives. I must have been blind not to have noticed it before. I wonder who's paying Leonard. And what it is I've walked into.

There's a pay phone on the corner. I've got a cell phone, but I don't like using it, I leave it in my truck. I've got a phone in my apartment, but I don't feel like involving Alison in this. I call Richie, get his machine, leave a properly frantic message. Leo isn't home either. I can't think what else to do. Of course, I'd like to talk to Cassie. What I have on my wrist is a first name—it looks more like Nikki now, the ink beginning to blur and bleed—and a phone number with an unfamiliar area code. I let it ring a long time but there's no answer. I dial information for the area code and discover I'm calling Altoona, Illinois. The number's not listed. Who keeps an unlisted number in Altoona, Illinois?

The traffic lights on Broadway are still scrambled from the afternoon storms, flashing yellow. Beneath the rain the air is turning close and hot. I make one more call, trying the person who usually bails me out of this kind of firestorm, a corporate security CEO named Donnie Wilson. I do a lot of work for Donnie; we go way back. But he's out West somewhere. "White-water rafting," says the lady at his answering service. "A management survival course. No phones." As though Donnie would need a course on survival. Drop him in the jungle, he'd come out with the natives signed to contracts for burglar alarms and invisible fences.

He won't be back till Wednesday. So I'm on my own. The day hasn't turned out quite as I'd planned. It's after midnight now. Across the street the restaurant looks like shelter from the storm, lit like a cozy taverna. I don't see Luther, he must have finished his dessert. On the third floor I can see Alison crossing the living room to pull the drapes. Her bags sit unpacked in the middle of the room. She turns her back, pulls her shirt over her head. The light goes out. The bedroom light goes on. I cross the street against traffic. The rain's a constant drizzle, mist from a distant waterfall.

twelve

WE HAVE A LATE DINNER, catered from Athena Gyros on chipped Fiesta ware. We drink too much Greek wine. We break in the new sheets. My first thought is to postpone any discussion of Cassie Rayn and Mr. Quanh and Leonard Toth until morning. It doesn't seem particularly romantic.

The evening's turned very humid. Alison and I are in bed, sweating from the heat and serious aerobic exercise. I have a window fan that succeeds in moving dust bunnies around the floor. The radio's on low, a pirate station that was heavy metal when we began but has since turned to polka. Occasionally we get a breeze, along with street noise, filtered through the softly whirling blades. I'm drinking Wild Turkey from a grape-jelly glass.

"You do look a little like her," I say, my fingers in her hair. "Tawnni." She's lying on her stomach reading *Gothick Abs & Delts* magazine.

"Really."

"Your hair's like hers. A little. It's black."

"That's it?"

"And the eyebrows—the eyebrows are a definite match."

"That's the best you can do? It's gonna be a long night, baby. You'd better do a whole lot better."

I switch the radio to something designed to relax her, death metal.

She shows me a new tattoo I'd somehow missed in the earlier

innings, a shortstop fielding grounders. "Ernie Banks," she says. It looks like my grandfather weeding gardenias. Since she has Ron Santo on her ankle I'm afraid she has plans for the entire '69 Cubs. "I had the best time at camp," she says, kissing me. "You were a doll to send me."

"Did you ever actually see Ernie Banks?"

"Oh yeah—didn't I tell you?" she says, turning on her back. "Wednesday afternoon during batting practice—this kid from some Pony League downstate was showing off, throwing nothing but junk, and I was nervous and pulling everything—and Ernie Banks walked by and said 'Nice swing, kid.' God, I almost came. Do you think you could work it into your repertoire?"

"I guess. Here I thought the catcher's mask and spikes would be enough for you."

I'm just drifting off when a very worried looking Mrs. Loomis knocks on the front door. Her hair's in curlers. She's wearing a robe with quilted squares that look stronger than the space shuttle's heat tiles. I'm in my underwear, hiding behind the door. My jeans are where Alison threw them, somewhere in the apartment, I think. Sometimes I wish Alison could be a little neater. Not often.

"Someone's outside my window," she says.

"On the fire escape?"

"My bedroom window."

"You're on the third floor, Mrs. Loomis. He'd have to be a hummingbird."

"I'm afraid to open it and see—would you come? Please?"

"I'm not dressed, Mrs. Loomis. And it's very late. Why don't you call nine one one—"

"There it is again," she says, turning back toward her apartment. "That noise. Hear it?" I shake my head. "Please, just check for me or I won't go back to sleep. This reminds me of when I was a little girl . . ."

She drags me across the hall and into her apartment, gives me a terry cloth robe I assume belonged to the late Mr. Loomis and leads me to her bedroom. The drapes are closed. "When I was a little girl," she says, "I was sure someone was outside my window and so I lay awake all night just waiting. I was too frightened even to call my parents."

"That's happened to all of us, Mrs. Loomis. I used to think someone would attach a wire to my bed and electrocute me."

"Yes, but—just before sunrise I decided to see and so I pushed the drapes open a bit and peeked out the venetian blinds and sure enough someone *was* out there, right there, staring back. I jumped ten feet." We stand, waiting. "There were just two big eyes." Then it comes, a noise like someone throwing pebbles against the screen. "This could be a prowler."

"There's no fire escape out there, Mrs. Loomis. If I see two eyes I might jump too."

I open the drapes and the blinds, unlock the window, pull the screen into the room, and see someone in the shadows. He's walking away, to the other side of the building. I think it's Marty Devlin, the Pool King, but I can't see much. A car starts up directly below me.

"Wait," I yell, but he doesn't stop.

"You know him?" Mrs. Loomis says. "It's all right?"

"I know him. It's all right. I'm sorry, Mrs. Loomis. Go back to sleep." On my way past the bed I stumble on something sharp.

"Watch out," she says, "for the flour sifter."

I nod, rubbing my ankle. I nearly killed myself on a common household item. "Any reason it's by your bed?"

"It keeps ghosts away. Put a flour sifter by your bed; when the ghost comes it counts all the holes and leaves when morning comes."

"What about the next night? What ghost is gonna fall for that two nights in a row?"

"Dump pepper around your bed. That works too. And turning your pockets inside out takes a ghost's breath away."

"I'll remember that. Can I give you the robe tomorrow?"

"Two in the morning, throwing rocks against my window. Keep the robe. It looks better on you than it did on Mr. Loomis."

Alison's sound asleep, doesn't even stir when I close the bedroom door. Her head's buried under the covers. I go through my apartment to the kitchen door and undo both sets of locks and throw the chain and then walk down the back stairs. The night air is still uncomfortably warm, the rain more like drifting fog.

The car that was beneath my window sits halfway down the

alley. There's a man and a woman in the front seat. A lot of drug deals go down around here; it's an odd place to park unless you're doing business. And they're not in a typical dealer's car—it's a small Rabbit. I watch for a moment. Then the woman's head disappears beneath the steering wheel and the man's head tilts back and I realize they're not interested in drugs or me.

There are hustlers on the street, hoping for one last trick. Minas has closed the restaurant, but he's inside cleaning, tearing the broiler apart. A cabby sitting on Broadway puts on his lights and pulls into the alley, winds down his window. Brook Benton's on his radio, describing a rainy night in Georgia. He asks if I'm the one that called. I say no. "Do you have a name for the fare?" I say, and he shakes his head. He's looking at my legs. I keep forgetting I'm just wearing the robe and some underwear. It's a very comfortable robe.

Now Devlin comes back, staring stiff-necked at the windows. He's wearing the same red blazer, smoking a cigarette. He looks a little like Jackie Gleason around the time of *Sting II,* which was not a good time for Jackie. He's got another handful of pebbles.

"Marty?" I'm annoyed at being disturbed in the middle of the night. Especially this night.

"Harding, Jesus, finally, I've been around this building half a dozen times." The blazer's unbuttoned—underneath there's a pair of beltless slacks and a silk or shiny rayon shirt, both much too tight. Some of Devlin hangs out below the shirt, some tries to get out from the spaces between the buttons. It's like the second re-make of *The Blob.* "Why don't you put your name on the buzzer for crissakes—"

"It keeps out the paparazzi. What are you doing here?"

"I need to talk. Can we talk?"

"Sure we can talk. I have something approximating office hours, generally during the daytime—"

"This won't wait," he says. "You wanna go back upstairs, change your clothes?"

"No, it's late, Marty. We're not gonna talk that long."

I want to sit on my back steps but he pulls me over behind the restaurant, out of the light. Maybe he doesn't think I look good in the robe.

"This has been a crazy night—I've had alarms go off at my home, at my business. This fucking weather."

"We've had a lot of weather," I agree, waiting. I wonder if Mrs. Loomis is having better luck getting back to sleep.

"I've got a job for you. If you're for hire. Are you for hire?"

"I'm not a cab, Marty."

He pauses, shifts his weight from one foot to the other. "I wasn't a hundred percent you even did this kind of thing. Leo said you might." He stubs out his cigarette. "If not . . . I can look elsewhere."

"What's the job."

"There's someone I want you to talk to. A guy that's bothering me."

"Like what, he's following you home from school?"

"It's complicated. . . . Let me show you something first," he says, handing me a very familiar envelope. "Damnedest thing . . . I've been getting these fucking things twice a day—at work, at home."

Lost Moon Developments

As far as I can tell it's the same as Cassie's, but I don't read the fine print. What catches my eye is a short paragraph about Lost Moon's *wonderful family recreational facilities . . . including Olympic-sized swimming pools.*

"So what," I say, giving it back.

"So there's no such place."

"It's junk mail."

"That's what I thought, yeah," he says. "Believe me, I don't usually spook this easy. But there's this guy, he says his name's Quanh. He pays me a visit, out of the blue. No hello, who are you —'I think you're disgusting,' he says. This while my secretary's still in the office. 'I think you should be locked up for what you're doing.' 'What the hell are you talking about,' I say. 'You bought the tape, didn't you?' he says. '*Pretty Ballerina*? You answered the ad, bought the tape.' 'So what,' I say. 'I'm a collector, I like Cassie Rayn.' "

"It sounds like Mr. Quanh is a little nuts. Did you call the police?"

"No," Devlin says. "He's a nut all right but a nut with a gun.

I sat. I listened. Finally he went away. 'I'm watching you,' he says. 'Some night you'll wake up and I'll be there and I'll cut your heart out.' "

"Jesus."

"He has quite an attitude, let me tell you. And this tape he mentioned, the one Leo sold me—*Pretty Ballerina*—it's a piece of shit. It's fake. I don't even want the fucking thing. I sure as hell don't want some crazy Jap cutting my heart out because of it."

"But he's not after you just because of some tape—"

"I don't know why he's after me."

"He just selected you out of the blue—"

"All I know is he's nuts, Harding, and my talking to him or even getting a restraining order isn't going to work. If you'd seen him you'd know what I mean."

This doesn't sound like the Quanh I ran into at the airport—calm, deliberate.

"You still haven't said why you want to hire me."

He hesitates. "Before I give up the rest I have to know if you'll take the job."

"Good night, Marty."

"No, wait—it's just very confidential. I'll pay—"

"How much?"

"Two thousand, half up front."

"That's an awful lot for just talking to somebody."

"I want the guy talked to so he doesn't come back. Ever. Understand?"

"I think so. But I don't do that sort of thing. And if I did, it would cost you a lot more than the two."

"So you're not interested?"

"Is this Quanh you're talking about?"

"I didn't say who it was. It shouldn't matter."

"Believe me, it would matter." I pause, not for long. "I think I'll pass, Marty."

He nods. He hasn't done much of a job selling this to me. I'm not sure what he really wants. And I'm surprised he thinks I do this sort of thing routinely. Except he knows I did time, and he knows what for . . .

"Is all this gonna remain confidential?" he says.

"For that we'd need to establish a professional relationship. Money would have to change hands."

"Jesus, how can you live with yourself," he says, putting two fifties on the porch steps. The alley light makes them look fake. I take them anyway.

"Is this something from your past?" I say. "From when you were cutting porn loops?"

He shakes his head. "That was nickel-and-dime," he says.

"You said someone broke into your place?"

"Yeah, nothing's gone right today. They took some cleaning supplies, pool cleaning, maybe they're going into business." He extends his hand. I take it. "Like I said, if you're not interested that's okay, I can go elsewhere. Let me know. You have a good night." He's awfully understanding about being turned down. It's a very abrupt exit, stage left, but then his entrance was equally surprising. He takes another look at my legs and then walks out toward Broadway. And away we go.

On my way back to the stairs, I take another glance at the couple in the car. She's straddling him now, her shoulders gently rocking. She has frizzy hooker's hair. Her halter top is pulled down to her lower back. The car engine's on, either for the air or the radio. They're not going far, halfway round the world, about as far as you can go in a car that size. You can't hear the radio, just the beat from the bass, like an amplified heartbeat in reggae time.

I stop in the kitchen and find a new bottle of Wild Turkey hiding under the sink. The only clean glass is covered with Power Rangers or Rugrats—the dye's so faded there isn't much action left in the figures. I can't remember where I got the glass. I drink two shots, pour a third, but leave it in the glass.

I take the bottle to the couch and sit for a minute, trying to make some sense out of the day. For some reason the bourbon tastes better straight from the bottle. I have a feeling it's a short step from this to drinking Thunderbird out of paper bags. Let's see: Cassie Rayn, Marty Devlin, Mr. Quanh, Reverend Miner, the Flying Psychic . . . lots of new friends today. And a few names— the Wilders, the Lees, Kim Moon—deserving of more attention.

And a few questions. What does Leonard Toth really want with Cassie? Why didn't Cassie tell me more about what I might be getting into? Didn't she know? I should try calling her again.

I decide it will wait till morning.

I check the locks on both doors and turn off all the lights. With any luck Alison's asleep.

She's waiting for me in the bedroom. She turns on the radio.

Let it rain

She doesn't like the robe. "This better be good," she says, undoing the knot. Maybe my luck is changing. She doesn't wait for the explanation.

thirteen

A LITTLE LATER something wakes me and I struggle, coming to the surface. The room's dark and hot, Alison has one hand on my chest, another over my mouth. At first I think I'm snoring more than usual. There's the sound of traffic, and an odd bump coming from the living room. It must be almost dawn.

"Someone's out there," Alison whispers.

"What?"

"In the front room."

All my clothes are still on the living room floor. I lost track of the robe when I came back to bed.

Let's see: my gun is where?

I can't hear footsteps, but a familiar board creaks a familiar warning. Something's heading our way. There's no time to do much except scramble—push Alison off the bed and then high jump the sheets. I make it behind the door just as it swings open. Two arms and a gun enter, rising to a military stance. When I reach for the gun a shadow grabs my arm. For a shadow he fights back rather well. I shove him against the chest of drawers, fighting for the gun, yelling at Alison to stay low. He's covered with sweat, like a junkie in detox. I wish now I'd slept in pajamas.

Two shots rip into my pillow.

"Son-of-a-bitch," the shooter says when we hit the floor, mostly because I'm on top. The gun goes off twice on the way down; shots rip into my headboard and pillow. The goose gives up his feathers a second time. The designer sheets now look like less of a bargain.

He's younger than me, strong and wiry, and his clothes and sweaty skin smell like body odor and grass. I don't know the voice. Something cracks in one of our arms. Alison says "shit" and scrambles past us, heading for the living room and her clothes.

"Easy now," I say, sitting on his chest, one hand on his throat. "Take it slow." The gun's a clumsy revolver, heavy and slick with oil. There's a bit of oil in his hair as well, slicked back fifties style. I think the gun's been cleaned more often.

"You broke my fucking arm," he says, struggling, with an accent I can't place. I don't have the slightest idea who he is. The only light is from the street, what the fan lets in the window. "You wanna get your dick out of my face?"

"Sorry. It's nothing personal, believe me."

"The phone's dead," Alison says from the next room, pulling on her shorts. "Should I use the one downstairs?"

"Not yet." His wallet's in the right rear pocket of very baggy jeans. I toss it over my shoulder to Alison, who catches it like an infield pop-up. "There's a small flashlight by the stereo."

"Right."

A beam of light crosses the floor, lands on an unfamiliar face. He's mid-twenties, a little manic, maybe from drugs. He doesn't look scared.

"You're sitting on Professor Josef Grabowski of Spertus College."

"Like hell."

"Or maybe not. Let's see what else we have here. We have a nice calendar, we have major credit cards, gym memberships—three or four different names—we have a woman's picture, she's cute, maybe thirty—"

"I like older women," the kid says, his teeth gleaming somehow in the dark. If he were standing Alison would probably knock him down. The accent's Spanish, but it seems to shift around, like a radio that can't stay on the station. The grass smell is everywhere. It's not just his clothes; his skin and hair smell like he's been marinated in the stuff.

"Come on, Professor, we're getting up." He grunts; he's not happy with this either. "And don't move too fast. I'm not good with revolvers. The damn thing could go off right in your mouth."

"I gave up already," he says. "What's your problem, man?"

"You. You're my problem. Where'd you get the wallet?"

"From the trash, down the street." His accent comes and goes, like the Flying Psychic's. Maybe I'm being attacked by a troupe of bad actors. "Don't call the cops. I didn't do nothing."

"You tried to kill us."

"Hey, I must have the wrong place, you know? Look, man— I'm on probation. Let me go, you'll never see me again. I never did nothing like this before in my life, I swear."

"Right. That's how you got on probation. The cops are going to love talking to you."

"Just lemme go . . ."

"How'd you get in anyways?"

"Picked the lock," he says, the first thing that makes me uneasy—I've never known a junkie who could pick a lock. The need is too strong for that.

"Let me go, I'll be out of here so fucking fast—"

"Where'd you learn to pick locks?"

"I'm going for the police," Alison says, and there's a strange grunting noise.

Then the light goes off behind me.

"Alison?" I say. There's no answer. The kid laughs, an annoying high-pitched giggle. I back off him quickly, like a rodeo cowboy with a skittish bull, fumbling for the wall switch. Nothing happens. None of the switches work. I hear other voices in the kitchen. My stomach growls. I could use a snack myself.

There are footsteps moving toward me. I can't see Alison.

Then everything lights up, though not in a way I'd planned. The back of my head slams forward into the door frame. I don't lose consciousness, but somehow now I'm on the floor, a hand yanking my hair back, a shoe placed squarely in my back. The same smell of grass is now overhead.

When he kicks me my mouth meets the floor. At least the rug's clean.

"Now you're the cocksucker," he says. But I realize I'm still holding the gun, cradled beneath my stomach. I wish now I'd checked the chamber.

"Give us the gun," someone says. I think it's a girl's voice. It might be the Flying Psychic. It's too dark to tell how many there are. Flashlights light up like matches, dart across the floor. I feel like I'm in Jeffrey MacDonald's alibi. The shoe presses more insistently. It's joined by the tip of another revolver, against my neck. "Take his gun, Mason."

"Why don't you just give him our fucking address?" Mason says. I recognize the voice from the airport. *What a piece of ass.* I wish now I'd turned around to get a better look at his face. And asked Quanh more about him. "I told you not to use no names. And I can't believe you kept those fucking IDs, you are so small-time—"

"*Put the fucking gun on the floor.*"

"Alison? Where are you?"

"Shut up."

"Here," she says, somewhere behind me. I can hear her struggling with one of them.

"Fuck," he says. "You fucking bitch—"

"Put the gun in front of you, man. Do it now."

"Not until I know she's all right."

"*I don't see it, I don't see it back here—*"

"Hey man, you're in no position to be telling us what to do, you know?" He cocks the gun. "Give me the fucking gun."

"*—damn shit could be fucking anywhere—*"

"Alison?"

"Crazy bitch," someone says.

"I'm all right, Harding," she says. "*Let go.*"

"You see?"

"Don't give up your gun, Harding—"

"Lady, will you shut the fuck up—"

"Put her down, Zane—"

"No, wait," I say, not liking the sounds I'm hearing. The second one, Mason, suddenly has a very mean edge to his voice. It's not an accent that he's faking. Alison can usually take care of herself, but I have no idea how many there are back there, or what they're carrying. "Here's the gun. Leave her alone. Take what you want. There's money in my wallet. I can show you—"

"Slowly, man. . . ."

"*Will you just put him away? Zane?*"

My head hits the floor harder than before. The gun becomes less important. When someone grabs my arm I let it slip from my fingers.

"Is she tied?"

"Yeah. But they saw my face, man. Why don't we take her?"

"We're not taking anybody."

"This is fucked up, man. Hiding in that closet, *what kept you, man, what kept you—*"

"There's a couple thousand here, let's just go—"

"*Look around, look everywhere. I'm not leaving without it. Jesus, what a fucked-up night—I'm working with fucking amateurs—this is just like when we were kids—*"

"There's people downstairs, they had to hear the shots—"

"Is he out?"

"I think so. Yeah."

"Better make sure. And check the woman again."

"You check her. That bitch kicked me in the fucking stomach. I'm gonna lose it."

"If you're gonna lose it, lose it here. Not in the car. We got a long drive ahead of us."

"We gotta go."

"*Put this fucking cocksucker out.*"

"*No! I've had enough for one night—we'll be three hundred miles from here, so let's just go. Goddammit, who's gonna fucking know—*"

"Nighty-night," someone says.

I flinch, expecting a shot. Instead the gun comes down on the back of my head. I try pushing off the floor but my arms are rubber.

A siren comes up Broadway, an ambulance, not a squad car— I've ridden in enough of both to know the difference—but they're spooked enough to think it's the cops and so they leave, though not before someone kicks me in the ribs and someone else yanks my head back and whispers in my ear—with breath smelling of

Wild Turkey—to keep my mouth shut or they'll be back, they know where I live. *You'll get what the other guy got.* The siren grows louder. Then I black out.

When I come to there's a pounding in my head like someone knocking on the door. It takes me several minutes to realize it *is* someone at the door. I call for Alison. No one answers. The power's still off, the early morning light too hazy to show me much. Or maybe it's my eyes—I'm so dizzy when I stand that I grab at the headboard for support. My ribs ache when I breathe. I feel worse now than I did when they were kicking me. The back of my head's sore. There's a cut inside my mouth. Alison's purse is on the floor, minus Richie's three thousand. I don't see Alison.

Where is she? Did they take her?

What scares you, Harding?

I'm still undressed but getting my softball bat seems more important right now than getting my clothes. I head toward the door—bat cocked back, grain out, left arm parallel to the floor, perfect form.

But the thumping begins again, this time behind me, along with the sound of splintering wood. Before I can reach the closet door Alison has both her feet through it. She's kicked the slats halfway across the room.

I peek through the hole. I can't contain my smile.

"Hell of a birthday, huh?" I say, relieved.

She's covered with sweat, but she's okay. Her mouth's taped, her arms tied with rags. I pull the tape off slowly. The rags have knots that would surprise a sailor. "God, I hate surprise parties," she says, leaning against me. I notice the name and number Cassie scribbled on my arm are gone now, lost in the night's feverish sweat.

We hold each other for a few moments. I'm too dizzy to close my eyes. My head hurts so much I barely hear Minas come in the front door. He looks at Alison, her legs still stuck through the door like Puritan stocks, her hands tied together with rags. He looks at me, sitting beside her in my shorts, blood on my hands and face.

"Turks did this, I bet," he says.

fourteen

THE LINCOLN PARK ZOO can be pretty even on a rainy day, but it's not a favorite spot of mine. You don't have to be an animal rights nut to see that the tigers pacing in their tight boxes don't have much room. Of course, the condo high-rises across the street aren't much bigger but then the people in those boxes are paying for the expensive view of the lagoon and the lake and the pacing tigers.

It's just past nine-thirty. I'm watching a cop named Tommy Mullaney navigate through a crowd of school kids with a cardboard tray filled with hot dogs, potato chips, and Cokes.

"You got enough food here, Tommy?"

"I missed breakfast," he says.

Tommy's like me, a South Sider exiled to the North. I know quite a few cops, scattered through the city, guys that grew up in my neighborhood or played high school ball against me—it's a South Side Old Boys' network, Skull & Crossbones via Back of the Yards. Tommy's father is an Area 5 commander, he's got one uncle in construction, another running a local Teamsters shop. Tommy's bounced from precinct to precinct, even worked in the suburbs. What he's doing still in uniform is beyond me. He has to be the only connected Irish cop still walking a beat.

"Look at this fucking rain," Tommy says.

"Don't worry, Tommy, the water's beading on your hot dogs."

I guide Tommy indoors to the ape house. It's nice and empty

today. We walk along the rising walkway that encircles the animals.

"I love this place," says Tommy, looking around. "You remember my uncle Sandy? He poured the foundation. Sixteen-bit steel, solid concrete."

"It seems very sturdy," I say, jumping once or twice on the ramp.

"Of course it's sturdy, asshole," Tommy says. "What's important is the shape. It's round."

"Nothing gets past you, Tommy. Your uncle Sandy built the Guggenheim of ape houses. Who'd he bury in the foundation?"

"Nobody you know. You want this information I got for you or not?"

"I do, yeah."

"Then get me another Coke. And tell the girl not so much syrup." He takes a bill out of his favorite hiding spot, the pinned cuff of his trousers, then remembers I'm paying. "And get something for yourself, willya? I hate eating alone. Or did your girlfriend pack you a lunch." He means the Star Wars lunch box I'm carrying around. "You should have filed a report, Harding. You don't know who those three were last night. They might have killed you. And they might come back."

Which is exactly what Alison told me early this morning, sitting on the floor of my apartment, performing minor surgery on the back of my head. But I reminded her that I'm an ex-con with a manslaughter conviction and a possession charge that was thrown out but that never seems to quite disappear. Cops sometimes jump to conclusions, make connections where none exist. They take the shortest route. Which in this case leads to me. I don't like giving them a reason to rummage around in my apartment, or my past.

I prefer to do that myself.

We were lucky, I told her. My landlord, Minas, is very understanding about major structural damage—"You don't need that door," he said, dragging it away, giving the room an open California Closet effect. I've got a headache that will go away. And Alison wasn't hurt. They tied her up, told her to be quiet. Fat chance. She ended up in the closet after a nasty free-form groin kick. "But not a clean shot, Harding, or he'd be gelded, talking like Tweety Bird." The apartment's a mess. So much for vacuuming and dusting. I should have taken pictures.

"You're lucky you don't need stitches," she said, looking at a small cut above my eye. "Minas says he has a cousin at Mount Sinai who could look at you for nothing."

"If you mean his cousin Dimitri, he's a cook, Alison. He'd stick me with a meat thermometer."

"I still think you should have called the police. They broke into your house. They had a gun."

"We had a gun, for a few minutes anyway. My apartment's been broken into five or six other times. You know that."

"Not with me there," she said. "It's not something I want to get used to."

I told her I'd install a security system first thing tomorrow. I didn't mention that technically no one broke in; that no system could protect an idiot who leaves his back door open while strolling through the alley in his bathrobe. I didn't mention that this morning I'd found the 4Runner broken into, tossed much like the apartment. I still hadn't mentioned Quanh or Leonard Toth or my nighttime talk with Marty Devlin, which hindered my explanation somewhat.

But as usual she was several steps ahead of me.

"Excuse my worrying," she said. "See, the break-in was bad enough, but if you tell me don't worry, I won't worry. The creep hiding in your winter clothes, listening to us make animal noises —that bothers me, but I figure with years of therapy I'll get over it. Okay. No problem." She puts something on the cut that stings. When she sees me flinch, she applies some more. "But where I draw the line is this—when the man I'm sleeping with would rather spend hours running around an airport and then *grocery shopping* instead of going straight to bed with me—that's when I get upset. That's when I start to worry." She puts a small Band-Aid on the cut, nods at her work.

"I take it Minas told you where I was last night?"

"When you didn't show. At first I thought you were picking up last-minute aphrodisiacs. Candles. Condoms."

"You're on the pill."

"It's been three weeks, you might have forgotten."

"Why didn't you ask me about this last night?"

"It didn't seem very romantic," she said. "And I thought I'd give you a shot at bringing it up yourself. I was pretty proud of myself, I don't usually have that much restraint." I think she's more upset with me than with the guys who tied her up. "Who was he, Harding?"

"The guy in the grocery was Leonard Toth. He's a collector, Alison. Past debts."

She studies me. "I thought you were free and clear."

"It's not me he's interested in. It's someone else."

"Orange lipstick?"

I nodded. "Her real name's Kalani Moon. At least that's one of her names, her adopted name. She has sort of a history."

"I love history. Enlighten me."

So I told her about Cassie's family and the murders and Kim and Lost Moon. I told her about Quanh and my trip to downtown Waukegan to see Reverend Miner and enough about Leonard Toth so she knows to stay clear of him. I told her about Richie and Leo and Marty Devlin and *Pretty Ballerina*. I can't tell her what it all means because I don't have the faintest idea.

"What can I do?" she said, no-nonsense. Her anger was gone. She faces things head-on, likes direct, simple problem solving. Most of the shit I get involved in has a lot of gray areas.

"You don't have to get involved," I said. "I can handle it by myself."

"Excuse me again, but isn't that what the tour guide says right before they rip out his eyeballs?"

So I told her I had one lead on our uninvited guests, that I was asking a cop I knew, Tommy Mullaney, to check it out. She shouldn't worry, I had no intention of letting them get away. After all, they've got my briefcase. They've got Richie's three thousand. They've got my percentage of Richie's three thousand.

"But they weren't after money," she said. "And they weren't junkies, they didn't touch our medicine chest."

"I know."

"We have two names, right? Mason and Zane?"

"Yeah. And the VC, Quanh, used Mason's name last night at the airport."

"The guy who sold the tape? What makes this tape so valuable?"

"I'm not sure. I didn't watch it."

"You didn't open the shoe boxes, you didn't look at the tape. Aren't private detectives supposed to be curious, nosy—"

"You may have hit upon the reason I have trouble succeeding in this business."

"Laziness?"

"Apathy. Ennui."

"I don't think it's that existential, Harding. A little more sleep, a little less Wild Turkey. Do you think our guests came from Toth?"

"Maybe, though it's out of character. He likes doing those things himself. Letting them rough us up would deprive him of all the pleasure." What I'm wondering about is Quanh's part in this. And whether Marty Devlin walked me over to the restaurant steps not to get me out of the light but to get me away from my back door. If so, he got his two fifties back. There's something slimy about Devlin, like the algae-covered fiberglass in one of his pools. "Plus the makeup was all wrong. Toth never hires women. And he hates drugs. You smelled the grass on that one guy's clothes."

"At least he had clothes. I felt like Patty Hearst in that closet."

"I'll put in a security system, first thing tomorrow. Like the one I did for your place. Lots of bells and whistles. We'll sleep like babes in a manger. Or that woman in the mattress commercial. Safe, secure, rain on the roof. Till the clouds roll by. Okay?"

She nodded. She wasn't happy.

My own mood dropped somewhat when I followed up again on the name in Cassie's letter, Dr. Arthur Lee. I pictured a phone ringing quietly in that large colonial house. A woman who identified herself as Mrs. Lee answered the phone.

"Is this some kind of joke?" she said when I began my insurance sales pitch. She wasn't laughing.

"We offer a number of professional health care plans tailored to your husband's needs—"

"Will you vultures just leave us alone?" she said, in a pleading tone I found unsettling. Even as she hung up I was picturing the drive north to Lake Forest. It's a very scenic drive.

At the zoo the hard rain from last night has softened but not disappeared. Luckily the refreshment stand at the zoo's shaped like a giant pith helmet. I stand just under the brim, out of the rain, and wait for my food. I hand the cashier a twenty. She looks even grumpier than Alison. I'd hate to see her after being locked in a closet.

"Nine-forty, out of twenty, you got nothing smaller?"

"Afraid not. And can I have a dollar's change?"

"I'm already out of fives. I'll have to give you the rest in singles. You're taking all my singles."

"Sorry." She sighs, the sigh of a cashier without any singles. "We may as well close. You wiped me out. Anybody else in line needs change, see this guy, he's got all the singles." This is my new goal in life, to make people miserable. I seem to have a natural gift for it.

When I get back from the refreshment stand Tommy's herding a group of kids from Francis Parker around the cages. He backs me away from the railing and motions to the smaller kids to move up front. Even on his day off he's directing traffic.

"No bars, Harding. Just glass."

"You think they notice?"

"Sure. They're smart, like dolphins. Big monkey brains."

A little kid stomps his foot. I think he's about to kick Tommy in the shins. "They're not monkeys," he says, squinting up at Tommy. "They're orangutans."

"Well, they sure smell like monkeys," Tommy says. "See? They've got little red monkey butts."

"What a role model you are, Tommy," I say.

"Listen, it's my day off, Harding. I should be over there at the seals, yelling at my own kid." He leads me to a spot near the exit, as though the eight-year-olds might be wired. "You asked about the Moon case. Christ, I haven't thought about that in years. I can't get you a file, it's closed."

"Just tell me what you remember."

"I remember the blood," he says, unpacking his Coke. A teacher points at the universal NO FOOD OR DRINK sign—a pouting cheetah on a doctor's scale—and Tommy pulls out his badge, as though it gave him unlimited Coke privileges. "It was like a battlefield. I was one of the first ones there."

"I know. How soon did they close it?"

"Officially a week or so. But it was closed the minute we got there. It was a strange family for that area, that time. They didn't really fit in. And Ellis had a drug charge—two of them—both dropped, but you know what that means."

"Yeah," I said, thinking of my own dropped charge. "Did you know Ellis or his wife?"

"Naw. Everybody knew the kids; from church, from school. That was the worst part. The daughter that came out of it was in a state of shock. Couldn't say a word. How she survived is beyond me."

"Kalani."

"That's the one."

"She was in the basement, hiding."

"That's what she said," Tommy agrees. "God knows she was dehydrated enough, sealed in that tomb. Some parts of her story didn't quite match. What the hell, you're fourteen, you see your whole family killed, it's gonna throw your recall off a little. Though I'm telling you, she looked like no fourteen-year-old I've ever seen."

"She saw them killed? She wasn't in the basement?"

"That was her story. There were a couple discrepancies—"

"You found her?"

"I was there, yeah. I didn't open the door."

"So what was her story?"

"She was downstairs, in her room, and she heard gunshots, and screaming, and I guess somebody yelled for her to hide. The door hadn't been used in years, it jammed when she closed it."

"How'd you know she was in there?"

"We didn't, we were just opening everything. She was damn lucky."

"Who yelled for her to hide?"

"She wasn't sure. A female voice, maybe her mother."

"Do you know whatever became of her?"

"Naw," he says. "I transferred to McHenry County right after that. Then I finally got into Area Two down here. They might know up there in Lake. But I don't think it's high priority. It's closed. Hell, it was never really even open. What's all this about, Harding?"

"I'm not sure yet."

"Because these are strange fucking questions for a Monday morning."

"What about the other kid, the one that ran away?"

Tommy shrugs. "That was before my time, so I didn't know much about it. Nobody on the homicide case thought it was real important."

"Did they look for him, really look?"

"Of course. You know how hard it is to catch a runaway, especially one that's smart—if it doesn't happen right away you're probably out of luck. Unless he wants to come home."

"What about a kidnapping?"

"There was no evidence of that. The middle of the day, a church outing—no one saw nothing suspicious. The minister vouched for that."

"Reverend Miner."

"That's him."

"What did he say exactly?"

"That the boy got off the bus. That's all they knew. 'And it was as though the hand of God just swept him away'—"

"You've got a good memory, Tommy."

"It's the case, the family. The bodies. You don't forget a case like that."

"Something happened to him later on, the minister, he got sick, left the church—I was wondering why."

"How the hell would I know. Maybe he had a crisis of faith. Or too much booze."

"I never met a priest in my life who'd let either one take his collar."

"Yeah, well. Miner's Methodist. Maybe the rules are different."

"I heard he had a few problems."

"We all got problems. I got problems."

"No one considered the boy or the girl suspects?"

"Hell no. There was one suspect: Ellis. They were fucking kids. What angle are you working on this, Harding? Are you holding something? Because if you're holding something you should give it to me. Especially if it's something that would make me look good." I shake my head. "The kid ran away, the father went psycho. That's it. You should worry about shit a little closer to home, like what are you gonna do about those three broke into your place?"

"Actually, Tommy, I thought maybe you could help me out with that."

I open my lunch box and use a handkerchief to show Tommy the glass I've got wrapped in a paper lunch bag.

"Don't tell me," he says. "You're collecting kids' milk glasses now."

"It's gonna have my prints on it, Tommy. And some Wild Turkey tracks. But one of the three picked it up after I did. He finished the drink. And they weren't wearing gloves. Could you run it for me as a John Doe?"

"I don't like doing that, Harding. First of all, I'm not a detective. Secondly, I don't like processing hard evidence. There's paperwork, all kinds of shit—"

"It's all I've got, Tommy."

"You should have phoned it in. If it's important enough to run this then you should have phoned it in."

"I know." I'm still holding the glass. Finally he says okay, taking the lunch box with as much enthusiasm as I took Kim's picture from Cassie. "If it turns up some kind of serial killer I get the collar."

"I don't want his collar. I want his ass."

"I can't do this until later," he says. "When a guy I know comes on."

"That's okay."

"And I can't rush it or people get nosy."

"That's fine, Tommy. Did you find out anything about Toth?"

"Another name from the past. You're a fucking gravedigger here, Harding. He lives in L.A. now. Locally, he's kept his nose clean. Or else he's doing a better job of hiding the bodies. There was a hit last year on a North Side dealer. It went down as gang related but Homicide's not so sure. They would love to make him as the shooter."

"He's doing hits? I thought it was just muscle and juice."

"Hey, a fella's gotta improve himself. These aren't his prints I'm gonna be finding, are they?"

"No."

"Harding, if you know something about this guy Toth—"

"I know, I should give it to you."

"He's a psycho, Harding. So's his brother Luther—he's a real piece of work. I busted him once for turning an old woman's knees into soft soap. He pulls scary shit. The whole family's section-eight, but Leonard's the worst."

"He was a cop once."

"Yeah well. The two aren't mutually exclusive. I've got a nice picture for you. Did you know he was Special Forces, when you were in Bangkok playing policeman?"

I never knew Toth was in the army, much less stationed in Southeast Asia. It's a large area, but the coincidence is still unsettling. So is the picture of Toth that Tommy's holding—full camouflage, a necklace of human ears, and a very shiny gleam in his eyes. He looks nuts all right.

"He looks young," I say.

Tommy laughs. "That was taken in seventy-four. He did three tours and then reenlisted again after the war." He hands me the photo. "You probably looked young then too, Harding. I mean, I'll give you the benefit of the doubt."

"I was young and stupid," I say. "Not quite that nuts."

"I never could see that, stringing ears around your neck. Is that like carrying a rabbit's foot or something?"

"Like warding off death? I don't know . . . people collect all kinds of crazy shit, Tommy."

I fold the picture, which is printed on cheap fax paper, and put it in my wallet. "Does Narcotics have anything else on him?"

"Nothing they'd share with me. What's this all about, Harding? You on some kind of case?"

"No. I'm trying my best to avoid that." We walk outside, past a concrete amphitheater probably built by Tommy's uncle. You could bury a small town in there, not much different from a mausoleum, I guess.

"I'll get back to you if I turn something up," he says.

"One other thing. Who would I talk to downtown about a story I heard, kind of an urban legend about Asian kids disappearing, going back years and years—"

"You got some specific kid? You don't mean the Moon kid, do you?"

"I was wondering if there were others."

"Of course there's others. All kinds. A thousand a day running away. Where are you going with this, Harding?"

"I'm not sure."

"You got a client?"

"No. Well, maybe. You remember Cassie Rayn?"

"Sure, the actress. The one who fucked her way out of junior high."

"I spent the day with her yesterday."

"No kidding. I'm in the wrong profession," he says. "She's not connected to any of this shit you're asking me, is she?"

"No, no."

"Urban legends about disappearing kids—where do you get this shit, Harding?"

The kids are running wildly around the stage. "It's a long story, Tommy. Forget I asked. Look, I gotta go."

"You can't stick around? They've got a nice monkey show later. Cute as hell, riding bicycles, wearing little tuxes."

"I need to check a few things out. Thanks for your help, Tommy."

"Sure," he says, watching the stage. "They're cute little fuckers, aren't they?" I can't tell if he means the kids or the monkeys.

fifteen

RICHIE'S RED MAZDA is in its usual space at Video Savages, near the back door. The same leaves that were plastered beneath its wipers yesterday are there now. It's a sports car, which means it's uncomfortable, noisy, and overpriced. The door to the back room's propped open. And the music's the same as yesterday, Cassie's tribute tape. *Uh-uh, oh no, don't let the rain come down.*

"Don't move anything," Richie calls to me from his office. "We're preserving the crime scene for dramatic effect." It looks like my apartment. The furniture's overturned. Richie's sitting on a three-legged chair that's about to crash forward, like in a Caravaggio painting.

"When did this happen?"

"Last night, I guess. After two sometime. It was like this when I opened."

Since I had trouble of my own last night—trouble which seemed to begin with my visit here—I'm less than sympathetic. But Richie shuts up when he thinks he's in trouble. If you scare him you lose him. So I go slow. He already has the store robbery to worry about. Wait till he finds out about his money.

One of the employees is fiddling with the Julia Strain display figure from *Naked Vengeance* or *Vengeful Nudity*. Cardboard lust. He has chocolate on his mouth. Richie sends him to straighten Action/Adventure. "And don't put Van Damme under *D* again," he says, shaking his head at me. "Carl. The new guy." There's an endless succession of new guys.

"What did the police say?"

"The police? The police expressed remorse over the phone. Apparently a grade-two storm passed through here last night, whatever that is. Half the city had wind damage. Nobody's got power. This didn't seem to impress them."

"Nobody got hurt?"

"Nobody was here." He comes outside his office, sidestepping a pile of junk that was yesterday, I believe, a new point-of-purchase candy display for the front register. There are still a few Baby Ruths and Butterfingers squished on the floor that Carl missed. "It's hard to tell what they were after. The registers were empty. And the safe's okay. The receiving room's fucked up. A lot of the new releases are missing."

"They're always missing. What about back there, in the office?"

"I don't know. What could they take? Some pencils?"

"You didn't have anything valuable, something you were holding or about to sell—"

"Not outside the safe," he says. "You know me better than that." He notices my little bandage for the first time, taps his own head with a pencil. "What happened to you? Some kind of wind shear?"

"We had some visitors, too, Richie, in the middle of the night. We bumped heads." This gets his attention. He actually reaches for his wallet.

"Don't tell me," he says.

"Sorry, Richie. Maybe I should have stopped at a bank."

"All of it?"

"Yeah."

"I don't believe it . . . were your cops more helpful than mine?"

"I didn't report it."

"You didn't report it," he says, nodding. "Wonderful."

"Did the cops have a theory at least?"

"Disgruntled customers, junkies, random chance. . . . Of

course that was before I knew you'd been hit too. A pattern begins to emerge. Why didn't you report it, Harding?"

"Take it easy, Richie. There wasn't much point."

"Take it easy? I was counting on that money. There's a deductible on the insurance I have to pay. When you add that to my losses from Cassie—"

"You never heard from her?"

He shakes his head. Carl the new guy is back, waiting for new instructions. Richie sends him to Family Drama. In this store Family Drama is *Basket Case*. Carl ambles off, talking to himself. He's still an improvement on the last new guy Elliott, who complained of wet feet on dry summer days, propped his shoes on a cold radiator, then spent the day with his feet wrapped in paper towels and rubber bands. Elliott was here almost a year, remained a New Guy to the end.

"Richie, do you remember a guy named Leonard Toth."

"I don't think so—"

"Collected for Mickey Davis, half a dozen other bookies, started out a cop, did some occasional body work—"

"The name doesn't ring a bell."

"Are you sure? Think real hard."

"I'm thinking, I'm thinking. Did I owe him money? Did I sell him something? 'Cause I don't know the name."

I think he's telling me the truth. Richie's a pretty good liar but he's not pathological about it. You have to give him a half-decent excuse.

"Tell me more about your buddy Quanh, Richie. Everything. And the truth this time."

"I told you the truth. There's nothing to lie about. He sold me a fucking tape. It happens all the time."

"How did you set up the deal?"

"Standard stuff, nothing unusual. . . . Why?"

"He came after me last night in the airport."

"Quanh? Are you kidding?"

"What did he talk about yesterday morning? Or when you answered the ad and set up the sale—"

"Nothing unusual. He came after you? There's something I'm

missing here. He's just a short guy crazy about Cassie—I had fifty others here last night just like him, maybe a little taller."

"Did he know you were selling the tape to Leo?"

"I doubt it. How would he know?"

"What did you really think about the tape? Was it genuine?"

"You mean did it come from Hong Kong? I'd say it's more likely it came from Gary. But she signed it, right? So there must be something genuine about it."

"She never even looked at it."

"And Leo?"

"Leo took my word on it. I took yours. You took hers."

"You think that's why the place got tossed? *Pretty Ballerina*?"

"I don't know."

"Because I've sold half a dozen other things the last month just as bogus. And *Pretty Ballerina*'s only a big deal to a handful of collectors. And the county D.A. Who cares?"

"Who got burned?"

"Leo's customer Devlin, I guess."

"See, this other guy came after me last night, too, the bill collector I mentioned, Leonard Toth. About an hour after Quanh shoved me into a closet. This was a couple hours before my night visitors broke in and shoved Alison into a closet."

"Geez, you might have told me this, Harding. Before my place got taken apart. I would've been more careful if I'd known you got your lights punched out."

"Not all my lights. Just one. The rest of my lights are fine. Have you talked to Leo?"

"Not this morning. The phones were out for a while."

"They work now?" He nods. I go into the receiving room. The phone's over the copy machine, still here. So is the fax. Otherwise, Richie's right; the place is a mess. I turn down the amplifier—the Cowsills are in the park with the rain and you and me—

"Toth?" Leo says, sounding grumpy. I think I woke him up. "Leonard Toth? The name means nothing to me."

"Your place is okay, Leo? Nobody broke in?"

"I'm fine, Harding. I just can't get any sleep. The damn phone keeps ringing—"

"You're a popular guy, Leo."

"No, nobody's there. Just silence, then a dial tone."

"When did this start?"

"Middle of the night sometime."

"Is Jake outside today?"

"He's here. I'm all right, Harding. It's probably just kids."

"I don't think so." I tell him about the break-ins. He doesn't seem surprised. "The neighborhoods both of you live in. I keep telling Richie, move to the suburbs. They don't like horror movies in the suburbs?"

"Tell me about your customer Marty Devlin."

"He's an old friend. Why?"

"Did you sell him the tape?"

"Of course I sold him the tape."

"Can you give me Devlin's address?"

"He's in the book, I don't have it here—"

"Get it, will you, Leo?"

"No, I mean—all I have's a phone number and I think it's his business or pager—he travels a lot. He's never home."

"Would you read it to me, Leo?"

"It's a long-distance call."

"That's all right."

"You'll have a surcharge."

"Fine." Jesus—Leo's getting as cheap as Leonard Toth.

He reads me the number. It's long distance, but just to the northern suburbs. It might cost me forty cents.

"And his home?"

"It's in the book."

"What book? The northern burbs have fifteen different books."

"No, no, he lives in the city. Not that far from you, though I couldn't tell you the street."

"How did you connect with Devlin anyway?"

"Like I said, I've known him a long time. He was a general contractor and we did some business together—"

"What kind of business?"

"Real estate. Nothing, Harding, just residential—"

"So you see him a lot?"

"Actually, no, I hadn't seen him in a long time. He called a couple weeks ago saying he saw some ad in a local rag, he asked me about it, could I find out if it was genuine. He knows I'm in the trade. I told him sure. Then I called Richie, asked him the identical question."

"So Richie answered the ad for you and bought the tape. Why would Devlin do that? He could have bought it directly from Quanh and saved a lot of money."

"I guess he wanted our expertise."

"He probably still wants it. I don't think he ever got it. Nobody even looked at the fucking thing."

"I haven't heard any complaints from Devlin," Leo says.

"He's not waking you up, throwing rocks at your windows?"

"What are you talking about?"

I tell him only that Devlin paid me a visit, he wants to return the tape.

"You tell him forget it."

"Haven't you heard from him at all?"

Leo says no. I remind him to keep his doors locked, ask him to call me if he hears from Devlin or if anyone asks him about Cassie. He has one last question for me.

"You're sure you didn't fuck her?" he says.

"I'm sure, Leo." He yawns and says good-bye.

Richie stands at the door of the receiving room. He's yawning too, but I think it's a fake yawn.

"You should buy me lunch," he says. "At Blue Mesa. Since you lost my three thousand the least you can do is buy me some blackened shrimp fajitas."

"You didn't tell me everything, Richie. You didn't tell me you were the bottom in this deal."

"What's the difference how the fucking deal was set up?"

"Both our places got tossed, that's the difference, and Leo's getting strange phone calls. I have Vietnamese cowboys and L.A. hitmen on my back. What else aren't you telling me here? Are you sure Quanh sold you the tape? You didn't buy it in Gary or Merrillville and throw Quanh into the equation to make the deal look more 'authentic'?"

"That would have been way too much trouble, Harding. I bet

none of this has anything to do with the tape. We've both been robbed before. It could be coincidence."

"Now you sound like me reassuring Alison." The floor of the receiving room hasn't been cleaned up yet; there are newspapers, Styrofoam peanuts, pieces of cardboard and tape and brown cigarette butts from Quanh's ashtray. I bend down to pick up a blue matchbook with ARGYLE STREET MERCHANTS ASSN. on the cover. "Did you have something in the mail that Cassie was looking at? One of those phony vacation deals?"

"Maybe, I don't know. She was only in here two seconds." I've pushed him too hard; he's clamming up. I don't have any money to bribe him with. I sure don't feel like taking him to lunch. A little flattery can be substantially cheaper than the luncheon menu at Blue Mesa.

"Richie, I need you to do me a favor," I say.

"What kind of favor."

"You've got lots of contacts."

"So?"

"You know guys in the business I could never get close to." I give him the flyer that Cassie gave me. "Would you check this out, see where it came from?"

"Why don't you do it yourself," he says, examining it. "There's a number right here."

"The number's a recording. Just see if you can find out who printed the thing. You've got friends who handle paper, right? Ask some of them."

He thinks a minute, then shrugs. "Yeah, okay," he says.

"I'll pay you, Richie. Whatever you discover." His mood improves. I dial Devlin's number and get a salesman at Devlin Pools who tells me his boss is out of town—could he be of some assistance, could he possibly get me an outstanding price on a pool? No? When will Mr. Devlin be back? Probably tomorrow. Where is he? Working, always working. His home number? He's in the book, isn't he?

"Look at it this way," Richie says. "Nobody got hurt. It could have been worse, a lot worse. We were actually pretty lucky. You too, Harding."

"Yeah? Why don't I feel that way?"

• • •

Argyle Street near Devon is the center of Vietnamese culture in Chicago. A lot of expatriates settled here, opening grocery stores or restaurants. There are gift shops and clothing shops. All belong to the Merchants Association. Nobody remembers Quanh or sells white cowboy hats. I get a few strange looks, but I'm used to that. I wish I had a picture of Quanh or the hat. Finally I stop for some rice noodle soup at Pho Hung. I ask at the counter about the cowboy, but get blank looks. I get that a lot too. The man next to me looks like he's four hundred years old, full of wisdom. He's reading the *Weekly World News* story about CaveBoy. I ask him about Quanh. He puts down his newspaper, shakes his head.

I use a pay phone by a painting of water puppets in Vietnam, manipulated by unseen hands below the surface. Alison answers on the first ring.

"One bit of news," she says. "SunnySide DayCare, the name on that flyer? You can't find it anywhere because the name changed to KidKare, Inc., ten years ago." She gives me an address in Evanston. "It gets better. I called the state licensing office. The director of KidKare is named Evans. But the Director Emeritus is Dr. Arthur Lee."

"I talked to his wife, she was upset about something."

"I talked to the maid. Maids always know. There's nothing in the papers. But Lee's dead. She thought I was calling from the funeral home."

"Do we know what happened to him?"

"An accident," she says. "In the water."

I reach Tommy at a pancake house; now he's eating breakfast. He puts me on hold to call his station and then calls me back. I can just see him doing this at the front counter of the restaurant, tying up two lines, getting toothpicks from the little metal dispenser. Tommy doesn't use pay phones.

"It was a boating accident, Harding," he says. "Typical rich guy's checkout, powerboat with a lot of fog and an unlighted dock."

"They're sure it's an accident?"

"They must be, they consider it real routine. And you know those North Shore cops, they don't have much to do. Some doctor crashes his boat, they get out the vests. They'd kill for a good homicide."

You'll get what the other guy got.

"What kind of pancakes are we having, Tommy?"

"Some kind of wheat germ, they weigh a ton. I hope I don't have to chase any bad guys today."

When I'm paying for my food an elderly woman comes from the kitchen and pulls me aside, wiping her hands on her apron.

"He was here," she says.

"Really? The man I'm looking for?" She nods. "When?"

"Sunday night, very late. Right before we close."

"Did you talk to him?"

She shakes her head. She sees the picture of Kim in my wallet as I pay. "Your child?"

"No—someone I'm looking for."

"Very handsome boy."

"Did anyone talk to him?"

"Several customers."

"Do you remember who they were?"

"No. But he was like you, going to each person, asking each the same question. No one would help him."

"Why not?"

She hesitates. One of the customers turns his head to look.

"He was *cong sung*," she says.

"How do you know?"

"That's something you just know."

"What did he ask them?"

"He was like you," she says. "He showed them a photograph."

"Yes?"

"That is all I know."

"Did you see the photo?"

"No."

"Why was he like me?"

"He was looking for a boy."

sixteen

I FEEL LIKE GOING HOME and getting some sleep, but I'm not far from the address Alison gave me for KidKare, on Montebello. It's a city street made to look suburban, mostly residential but with a Burger King on one end and a long low brick building with swing sets and a fenced-in yard on the other. There are just a handful of kids here now. It's nap time. The mats are out on the floor.

I tiptoe past the sleeping kids to the office where two women sit watching TV. It looks like an all-new *Maury* on pet makeovers. I knock on the glass door before opening it.

"Can we help you?" asks the younger one. Her companion eyes me suspiciously. Her right hand's holding a cigarette. I think her left's going for the stun gun. Both women are wearing navy blue jumpers with KIDKARE FUN KOUNSELORS on them.

"I just wanted some information."

"My name's Kathy, this is Sylvia—"

"Harding," I say.

"Did you have a child you wanted to enroll with us, Mr. Harding?" she says. "Because our open enrollment times are generally the first of the month."

"No, I just wanted some information. About the trips you sponsor? With Stillwater Methodist?"

Kathy looks at Sylvia, Sylvia looks at Kathy. "You must be mistaken," Kathy says uncertainly. "At least I've never heard of any trips like that—"

"Me neither."

"And Sylvia would know, she's been here much longer than I."

"Let me ask you something else while I'm here." I take out Kim's picture just to get my foot in the door. "I'm looking for someone. His name's Kim Moon."

Sylvia shrugs. "Not one of ours," she says.

"Do you keep records of the children enrolled here—"

"No," Sylvia says.

"Why do you ask?" Kathy says.

"Because he'd be older now," I say, "much older."

"How much older?"

"Mid-thirties. Thirty-three, I guess."

"Since we don't accept children past the age of twelve," Sylvia says, "he might have a problem fitting in."

"He disappeared a long time ago."

"Was he one of our kids?" Kathy says.

"We don't lose kids," Sylvia says with a frown. She seems a little grumpy. Maybe I interrupted her nap time.

"What makes you think we would know anything?"

"He disappeared on a trip that was cosponsored by a Methodist church in Stillwater, and SunnySide DayCare. I've been told that's KidKare's old name—"

"You should phone the office," Sylvia tells me. I think Sylvia's the glass-half-empty type. She'd like me out of the room. She'd like me in Outer Mongolia. "I never heard of any trips."

"I never heard of that name."

"Well, this would be a long time ago—"

"And I don't know of any connection to a Methodist church."

"Bottom line—we don't know your kid," Sylvia says. "And frankly, mister, even if we did we wouldn't tell you."

"Thanks a lot."

"No, she's right," Kathy says. "It's for the children's sake." They're both a little defensive, but that could be any of a million things.

"What about getting information on the man who led the trips, a minister named Miner."

I explain everything that's public record. "I'm just running down every lead I can. You understand. For the boy's sake."

"You said he's thirty-something," Sylvia says. "I doubt he needs you holding his hand."

"You should talk to this Reverend Miner," chirps her friend.

"I did."

"You should phone the office."

"I thought this was the office."

"Sylvia means the main office. They're in North Chicago. But I hate sending you all the way up there on a wild-goose chase. Not that I'll get much help this time of day. Everybody's out for lunch." She picks up the phone, speed dials, and talks for a few minutes to someone in a low voice. She gets transferred once or twice, put on hold—I only hear one word that rises above a whisper— "Really?"

Sylvia eyes me with boredom, takes another Doral Light from the pack.

"I have a cousin named Sylvia," I tell her. "Second cousin actually. She teaches third grade."

"Lucky you," Sylvia says.

"She's on leave right now, in Betty Ford. Hooked on phonics."

Sylvia yawns. I don't think it's a fake yawn.

"I spoke with someone in administration," Kathy says. "This isn't the biggest company. We don't keep records past eight years. But this woman remembers Reverend Miner. He took the children on field trips, part of the church's day school in the summer. Their children and ours. That was before he left the church."

"So he drove them to places, for picnics or something?"

"I guess. That's all she remembers. I'm sorry." She hesitates. "I shouldn't tell you this but she mentioned something else. Maybe you should talk to his church—"

"What did she say?"

"Just that there was talk, when the trips stopped, and I guess our association with the church was broken off—"

"What kind of talk?"

"About his conduct. With the students. Not the young children."

"Teenagers?"

She nods.

"Boys or girls?"

It doesn't embarrass her. "Boys," she says.

Sylvia frowns. "Kathy, what if he's a lawyer?"

"I'm not."

"It's just gossip," Kathy says. "But maybe someone at his church remembers—"

"They won't tell you anything," Sylvia says. "They might get sued."

"Could you give me that woman's name?"

"I don't think I should."

"Is that when the name was changed? When the trips were discontinued?"

Kathy doesn't know.

"Maybe I'll come back for your auction."

"Auction? What auction?"

"You're not having a garage sale and charity auction next week?"

"No. I wish we were."

"You should phone the office," Sylvia says. "We used to have garage sales. All the time. But someone bought a mixer with some bad wiring and they got lit up like a Christmas tree. We got sued."

"Sylvia knows all this a lot better than I," Kathy explains. "She's been here a lot longer."

"I thought she looked more experienced," I say. "Is there a pamphlet or brochure or something describing SunnySide—I mean KidKare?"

"Just this," she says, getting me a booklet from a filing cabinet. I skip the color pictures and turn to the list of officers and board members on the back, scan the names quickly. There's no mention of Stillwater Methodist Church.

But the founder and Director Emeritus is indeed Dr. Arthur Lee. The name's not in very large print. I mention his accident and get blank looks from both women.

"I'm sorry about your boy," Kathy says. "What was his name?"

"Kim."

"I hope you find him. I really do."

"Yeah, let us know," Sylvia says. "Or we won't get any sleep."

seventeen

I TAKE THE TOLLWAY north to Lake Forest, a North Shore suburb where the true test of status is which side of Sheridan Road you live on. Old money's to the east, near the lake. The Lees are new money, they live a block west, on Astor. The house would be impressive anywhere else but here it looks routine. Even so I would have to start the bidding at a million five. Money, money— the two most important words in real estate, so sayeth Century 21 and Tommy James and the Shondells.

I ring the front door, get a butler who looks like he doesn't have much to do, and talk my way into the front parlor. It's a comfortable room, informal, with a nice leather lounge chair the butler keeps me a good three feet away from. He's wearing a black suit similar to a tux—he looks like an ex-fighter doing color commentary on HBO. I don't see the maid. A radio's playing soft jazz, probably WNUA. There's a fireplace made of green marble and several pictures on the mantel, none with children. Dr. Lee looks sixty-five, his wife early forties. She might be a trophy wife. People collect all kinds of stuff.

A woman comes to the doorway but doesn't sit down. She's the woman in the pictures, very thin with short brown hair parted like a boy's. It's the kind of simple haircut that can cost you a hundred bucks and most of an afternoon on Oak Street. She's not wearing black. Her eyes look tired.

"Can I help you?" she says.

"Mrs. Lee?" She nods. "My name's Harding. I'm sorry to bother you—"

"What is it."

"I just wanted to ask you a few questions."

"You told Edward you were a friend of my husband's?"

"That's not really true. I'm sorry, but I didn't know what else to say. I'm trying to find out what happened to someone and I wondered if you could help me—I believe you or your husband may have known his family. Their name was Moon, they lived in Stillwater."

"I'm afraid I don't understand—"

"You used to live in Stillwater, didn't you? You belonged to Stillwater Methodist?"

"No," she says, shaking her head. Her arms and legs are tan —lightly tan, North Shore tan, not from the beach, from playing tennis at the club. She's not wearing stockings. "That is, we lived in Stillwater for a year or so. We didn't attend that church . . . if you wanted a donation we already give to Lake Forest Methodist—"

"Your husband was the founder of SunnySide DayCare? What they call KidKare now?"

She nods, looks around for the butler. I think she's about to kick me out but that's not what's on her mind. Instead she asks me if I'd like a drink.

"No, I'm fine."

"I'm fine too," she says, "but I'm having a drink."

"Sure, whatever you're having," I say.

"I'm having a Manhattan."

"That's fine." I haven't had a Manhattan in years. I rarely have any kind of mixed drink; it's too much like cooking.

"I hope you're not trying to sell me something, Mr. Harding," she says when Edward brings the drinks. She sits down now, on a settee; she's giving the leather chair a wide berth too.

"No."

"Because I've had a flock of calls and inquiries since my husband's accident, people trying to sell me something or collect something. Apparently my husband moved in wider circles than I realized." Edward brings me my drink, along with three napkins and a coaster. "The things you find out at funerals."

"I didn't realize your husband had died. I'm very sorry."

She raises her hand a little, like a pope giving a blessing.

"I won't keep you long, I promise. I'm looking for someone," I say, "and trying to get information about the church and the youth trips they sponsored. This goes back twenty years."

She nods. She doesn't seem surprised. I don't think it's her first Manhattan of the day.

"The family was named Moon."

"I remember them, of course," she says. "From the papers."

"You weren't friends?"

"No."

"But you lived nearby?"

"We weren't friends," she says.

"Do you remember Kim?"

She nods. "A little," she says. I hand her the picture. She stares at it, finishes her drink, sets the glass on the coffee table with wobbly fingers. She doesn't use a coaster. "Poor boy. He never turned up?"

"No. Did you know anyone named Wilder, or Miner?"

"The Wilders lived close to the Moons. We lived a mile away but that was close in those days. Reverend Miner? The last name sounds familiar—"

"Reverend Miner, Lawrence Miner?"

"Maybe, I'm not sure . . ."

Edward appears again. "Don't forget your dinner meeting," he says and she nods. I don't think there's a dinner meeting. I don't think Edward likes me.

"Let me give you a number," I say, giving her a card with my real name and number. "Just in case you remember something." Edward hasn't left. He must have been a boxer—he keeps watching my hands, the way a cat watches your feet. "I'm very sorry about your husband's death. If you don't mind—could you tell me how it happened?"

"He was on his boat. I'm afraid he had too much to drink."

I nod.

She sips her drink.

"He was alone?"

"That's what they tell me."

"Meaning?"

"Meaning . . . why am I telling you this, Mr. Harding?"

"I was just wondering. . . . Did he often do that, take the boat out by himself in the evening?"

"At his age, you mean? Sometimes. He said it helped him unwind. But he wasn't usually alone. He had other friends, Mr. Harding. And lately he's been under a lot of stress. Would you like another drink?"

"I shouldn't, no. I have to go."

"That's a pity."

"The police were sure it was an accident?"

"What an odd question."

"You said he was under a lot of stress . . . was this from his work?"

"Arthur was retired," she says. "It was something else."

"Was anyone else here recently asking some of these questions?"

She says no.

"A Vietnamese man, very polite, named Quanh—"

"No one's asked me about those days in some time, Mr. Harding. I'd forgotten all about them." I doubt this. Edward reacts to Quanh's name as if the corner bell had rung.

"Would it be prying too much to ask what exactly was bothering your husband?"

"Yes," she says. "I think it would."

I nod. If I'd brought a hat this would be the time for Edward to hand it to me. "If you see the man I mentioned or if you remember anything please call the number on the card. I'd appreciate it, the Moon family would appreciate it—"

"Don't you think it's a little late to be doing this? Looking for him?"

"I don't know."

"This other man—is he dangerous? If I see him should I call the police?"

"No, he's just asking questions, like me."

She reads my card. "Are you dangerous, Mr. Harding?"

"No, I'm a pussycat."

She pauses, tapping the card against her fingers. "Have you talked to some of the other neighbors?"

"No, she . . . I was told most of them have moved."

"If I ask you something will you tell me the truth."

"If I can."

"Are you working for Kalani Moon?"

"What?" I say, surprised.

"You must be . . . who else would care after all this time? Who else is left?"

I don't answer.

She drains her drink.

"Watch your step, Mr. Harding," she says.

"Oh?"

"With Kalani. If she's anything like she was then . . ."

"What was she like?"

"Predatory."

"Really."

"She had boyfriends—the Wilders could tell you more about that. Always a different boyfriend—"

"That's not so unusual."

"If that were it, yes . . . Edward? Would you get me another drink, please?" Edward clears the glasses.

"I'm fine," I tell him.

"I don't remember asking," Edward says.

"So it was something more than boyfriends?" I ask Mrs. Lee.

"Fathers," she says, "the boys' fathers. And the year we lived there she was going through the Wilders one by one, each brother. You should ask their neighbors."

"Like I said, everyone's moved away. Or died."

"Are you quite sure you wouldn't like another drink?"

"I'm sure."

"Don't pay any attention to Edward. He's grieving. Edward dear, quit being so glum. Get Mr. Harding another drink—"

"No, I can't, really. Did you know the parents, Ellis and his wife?"

"Just by sight. They were hard to miss."

"Because he was black? And she was Asian?"

"Not just that. She had these marks on her throat that she went to great pains to hide, wearing silk scarves and turtlenecks in the middle of summer . . . it was sad, really."

"You saw these marks? When?"

"Why? I don't remember exactly. They were always there. I only know because of a swimming party we went to once, at the Wilders'—"

"Did you tell the police this when the Moons were killed?"

"I never spoke with the police."

"No one interviewed you?"

"They talked with my husband."

Edward clears his throat again. He probably needs a Sucrets.

"The Wilders were much closer to the Moons," she says. "I don't think Beth and Tom are still alive. But the boys must be around."

"Do you remember their names?"

"Of course. Mason and Zane." It's a good thing I don't have a drink. I'd have spilled it. Edward would not be happy.

"I want to thank you, Mrs. Lee—"

"Helen," she says, shaking my hand. "If you see Kalani Moon you can give her a message for me—"

"Yes?"

"Tell her to forget it. He's dead."

"Her brother?"

"My husband."

Edward follows me to my car, stands in the rain as I back out, and watches me until I'm on the road. I drive a mile south and then double back, stopping at the Lees' mailbox. But Edward knows my tricks, he's waiting for me. I manage to palm a familiar brown envelope from the mailbox before he gets to my car. He's wet, more from the walk than the rain.

"Just leaving," I say, handing him the rest of the mail.

"You mentioned the Chink," Edward says. "Something something Quack."

"Quanh. He was here?"

"Maybe." I take out my wallet. Let's see—I'm in Lake Forest, but Edward is more like North Chicago. Tipping etiquette can be such a problem.

"He was here last week," Edward says, pocketing a twenty. "Asking for Mrs. Lee. I didn't let him in. I don't like Chinks."

"That's it?"

"Not quite. I don't like you either." He takes the mail and returns to the house. I open the brown envelope, addressed to Dr. Lee. His vacation offer from Lost Moon is slightly different from Cassie's. I have to hold it closer to read the fine print. I need glasses.

Safe Reliable Day Care Provided

. . . rest assured your children will be in the loving professional hands of Dr. Arthur Lee. . . .

Edward's disappeared. But I see a face at the front window, watching until I back out onto the road.

eighteen

I DRIVE EAST to Waukegan, past the apartment building where Miner lived with his sister. The screens look good. Then
I drive the two blocks to Cypress and park on the street. It's only
twelve-thirty but the sky's dark enough to suggest sunset. There
are no lights on in the second-floor windows. I knock on Miner's
door, and ring his bell, but no one answers. I check his mailbox
and find today's junk mail—another sweepstakes offer. It looks
like Cassie's, though something's different . . . it takes me a minute
to spot it. The wording is the same on this one, it's the picture
that's different. Instead of a second picture of the proposed developments, there's a shot of a boy sitting alone on the beach.

I go around back, to a small fenced-in yard with a BEWARE
OF DOG sign and plenty of evidence on the grass of the dog's
presence. But I don't see the dog, and when I open the chained
gate I don't hear any barking coming from the house. It's an empty,
afternoon silence, not particularly ominous. I climb the back steps
and knock as loudly as I can but Miner never shows. A woman's
watching me from a kitchen window next door. I think she's
frowning or scowling but it could just be a crinkle in the solar film
taped to the window. I wait until she leaves and then I let myself
in by breaking a small pane of glass in the back door.

The rooms are dark. I leave them that way. Miner's bowl is
still in the sink, full of milky water and cold soup. The saucepan's
still on the stove. Everything in the apartment feels half-finished.

The bedroom's furnished with grocery-store boxes full of Miner's clothes. I run my finger over the wallpaper and find greasy dirt.

One end of the bedroom's been made into a sort of office, with a cheap desk and a pile of books. There's a stack of typing paper and a small piece of correction tape but no typewriter. The apartment's not large enough to hide anything. I check both closets, then I notice a thin cord hanging in the shadows of the back hallway, and when I pull it down I find very steep stairs leading to a very dark, very hot attic. When I get to the top another cord brushes my face, turning on a single overhead bulb.

Someone's been through here recently. A white T-shirt on the floor has a shoe's imprint, with crumbs of mud that despite the heat are still barely moist inside, like a cake half-done. There are bags and bags of clothes and old toys and halfway to the wall the floor becomes just beams and insulation. I look until I'm coughing from the dust and then I find it, locked in its case. It's like the locked door in Cassie's basement—I carry the heavy case down the narrow steps, nearly breaking my neck, and get a knife from the kitchen to force it open.

There's a piece of paper in the cartridge and a handful of letters sitting on top, some with envelopes, some just carbons—most are from ministers and must be important for Miner to keep them like this, but the first one that means anything to me is dated three years ago and was forwarded several times, from Stillwater Methodist to his sister's house, eventually finding him at Longview Hospital. The letterhead says TWIN LAKES METHODIST CHURCH.

> Dear Reverend Miner:
>   My name is Simon Gates. We haven't met, but I've found something that I believe to be yours. A boy from our church found this while exploring the caves near our town . . . as you can see it's suffered from the elements and time, but I was still able to make out the names on the dedication page—Lawrence Miner & Kim Moon—and though the second name was unfamiliar yours rang a bell with an older member of our church board, who remembered your trips here, assisting in the building of our chapel and the way the children sometimes played near the caves. Were this any other book, I probably wouldn't have

bothered, but as it seems to be someone's personal Bible I felt compelled to retrieve it from its premature burial and send it to you. I'm hoping you can return it to Kim or its rightful owner.

A letter's in the carriage, too, the paper curled back at the top. Half-finished. I turn on an old pharmacy lamp. The first thing I notice is the date—six months ago today. The second thing I notice is the letter's intended recipient:

Dear Cassandra:
    This will seem like the voice of a ghost and perhaps it is— God knows I feel half-dead sometimes, nearly separated from the pain and pleasure of this world—nearly but not altogether, not yet, and so I feel I must write to you and ask your help, as indeed I wish to help you. I believe we can help each other.
    Let me be blunt. I know you are the child I knew as Kalani Moon. I know you remember me and the part I played in your life. There isn't a night I don't go to bed with the image of your family's faces staring at me from the darkness. My own life has not been easy but I will explain that in a minute—what I've been doing all these years to seek repentance and arrive at this point, where I could write you this letter.
    First, again I must be blunt. We both know your brother was killed. I fear there were others. Are others. Your father believed it too—that's what drove him to look and look again, not for Kim but for the man who took him—drove him so he mistrusted everyone around him—
    Now something new has developed. I have been getting strange pieces of mail—contests, sweepstakes, sent from some- one . . . I'm wondering if you know anything about them. . . . They are so artfully done I wonder if they're not from the devil himself . . .

The letter stops there. The last few lines are hard to read—the typing slowly becomes more erratic, with misspellings, crossed-out words, as if mimicking a breakdown. I read it again, then put it back in the machine and line it up. Even if Miner were here I doubt he could preach anything as powerful as those last mistakes.
    The mood's broken by my pager, sounding twice as loud in the bare apartment, and I use Miner's kitchen phone to call a

Gretchen. The name, as Leo would say, means nothing to me. But Gretchen says a Detective Reese would appreciate my dropping by the Lake County Police Department, at my earliest convenience. I say I can be right there. She says, Well, that would be fine. Everyone's so polite in Lake County.

I haul the typewriter case back up to the attic. This time I notice something I missed before, in all the dust—a shoe box, the same kind I found at the Moons'. Inside are what look like missionary items and a number of form letters, not addressed, which from their text seem to have been sent to the Red Cross, or adoption agencies.

If I were looking for a child

I leave the shoe box. Downstairs, I look in Miner's refrigerator for something cold to drink, without success. Then I go into a small bathroom and run cold water over my wrists and try to wash my face and hands and maybe get some of the day's dirt off me. When I reach for the towel and the light so I can see to take a piss, Miner's decorating scheme for his powder room becomes clearer—vacation flyers from Lost Moon, many of them different, though with a similar theme—each has a different picture with a different family, a different black-haired boy sitting on a different beach with a bucket and sandcastle, taped floor to ceiling so neatly they might be wallpaper.

nineteen

Y OU KNOW you're in the suburbs when you go to the cops and they smile and shake your hand and offer you hors d'oeuvres. The mood at police headquarters is festive. I ask for Reese, expecting a pass to the back, but instead a desk sergeant hands me a plate of cookies and directs me next door to the coroner's office, where they're having an open house for the new morgue. A woman there with a corsage gives me a brochure and more cookies and tells me a tour has just begun, would I care to join in? I fall in with a group of senior citizens who listen intently as a technician demonstrates how the new autopsy carts lock to the wall. As he talks, a short guy beside me introduces himself and tucks a red comb in my pocket—WALT MASTERS REALTORS—WE SELL WAUKEGAN.

"Wonderful facility," he says, and I nod. "With the old one they had to park the vans outside, carry the bodies across the backyard. It got messy in winter."

"I bet."

"Now they just drive 'em right in." He points to the refrigerator room. Like everything today, it's perfectly clean, shiny brushed metal like a polished bedpan. I've never seen such a holiday atmosphere at the morgue. "It holds seventy-five," Walt says.

"Why? Are they expecting an invasion from Green Bay?"

"Lots of coroner's cases," Walt says. "It's not just for homicides. We had more suicides than homicides last year."

"You know a lot about the morgue, Walt."

He hands me a different red comb: MASTERS & SONS FUNERAL HOME—WE TAKE CARE OF WAUKEGAN.

I decide to skip the slide show. I find Detective Reese guarding a lazy Susan full of dip and raw vegetables. He's dressed in street clothes, with just an ID badge to show he's a cop. "Harding, right?" he says, handing me a carrot. "Let's go next door." He leads me to an office in the rear of the station. Everyone jokes with him. They ignore me. The station's new, like the morgue, and filled with furniture that looks like it came from the Mart, and young white cops that look like they were ordered from a catalog.

The walls are covered with memos and outdated CPD and FBI bulletins on one side, a large travel poster for Bermuda on another. It leaves the Ten Most Wanted in perpetual anticipation, watching as a bronze-skinned woman in a white bikini walks toward them from the ocean. Since the air conditioning's broken it feels a little like Bermuda in here. The morgue was much cooler.

"You want some coffee?" he says. "I need some coffee, I've got this damn celery stuck in my teeth." He gets us two cups of black coffee from a table outside the door. I've never seen a Krups machine in a precinct house before.

"There's cream and sugar out there."

"I'm fine."

He nods. He looks like my high school health teacher—barely six feet, buzz cut, steel-rimmed glasses, powerful arms. His face and skin are white and stiff looking, like a bleached hardwood floor. He sips his coffee, goes behind his walnut veneer desk, opens the center drawer and takes out a business card. He turns it back and forth as though seeing a hologram, chuckles, and holds up the card I gave Miner last night. "How's the insurance appraisal game these days, Mr. Wallace?"

"I can explain that."

"Oh, I'm sure you can," he says. "What were you doing, bothering old Reverend Miner on a Sunday?"

"Just asking him a few questions."

"What sort of questions?"

"Nothing too tough. Did he complain or something? Because

I thought I was very nice to him. I even gave him fifteen bucks. And I brought his mail over from his old address—"

"You're not licensed, are you, Harding," he says. "You've got a record. And you don't live around here. So I've got no reason to be nice to you. Let's cut the bullshit. What's your interest in Reverend Miner? And does it possibly have something to do with Cassie Rayn? Or Kalani Moon?"

"You know about her?"

"Of course we know about her. We're not complete idiots up here. We'd like to know a little more. Like what she was doing with you out there at the Moon place."

"Was it on the AP wire or something? Everybody knows I went out there. It's a closed case, right? I don't understand why you care."

He sighs. "This case still makes people crazy around here, Harding. I mean, we've got some younger guys now, good kids, real good training, could make it in the CPD no problem. But in those days it was just a few county sheriffs. They weren't used to shit that brutal. Kalani disappeared and Kim never turned up and so it's down as Ellis going psycho. Period."

"But you're not so sure?"

"I would like to talk to Kalani, that's all."

"She hasn't exactly been hiding the last twenty years."

"She's been in L.A., overseas. . . . Look, I didn't work the case, I inherited the fallout. I wasn't there when they found the bodies. So I really don't know anything. I just have a hard time swallowing the scenario they created. I don't see a father doing that to his wife and kids."

"Were there any other suspects?"

He shakes his head. "It's just a feeling. A cop's instinct. But I knew Ellis from when his boy disappeared, and I know he was convinced somebody took the boy—somebody who knew him pretty well, who'd be able to get him off that bus. I know he was looking for Kim right up till the killings. Why would a father who cared that much about one child do all that to the others?"

"Didn't anyone else have the same doubts?"

"They kicked it around for a while. But they couldn't find anything."

"I thought they closed it right away."

"Who told you that?"

"A cop I know. Tommy Mullaney."

"Mullaney? You a friend of his?"

"Yeah."

"No shit. Well, Tommy's memory must be deserting him in middle age. He knows it wasn't closed. Hell, he's one of the ones who finally closed it. He found the girl downstairs in the shelter, got the story from her—she was the only thing close to a witness."

"He was the one who found her? Who opened the vault?"

"Yeah."

"He never told me that. Did you ever really look for Kim?"

"That's all you're getting out of me unless you tell me what Cassie wanted with you."

I pause. It can't hurt to tell him what I know. I don't know anything.

"This won't exactly break the case wide open. She wanted a couple of shoe boxes she'd hidden in the basement."

"Shoe boxes? Hidden where?"

"Under some floorboards in the basement."

"Bullshit. We went through every inch of that dump. You're telling me we missed something as big as a shoe box? How long was it there?"

"Nobody dated it for freshness."

"What was inside?"

"I didn't look close. Family pictures and diaries. I didn't know they were important."

"She took them with her?"

I nod.

"How'd she get in the house? With a Realtor's key?"

"No, she didn't have a key. I helped her with that. At first I thought that was the only reason she'd called me."

"And then?"

"Then she showed me a picture of Kim. Told me how he disappeared, how she never really searched for him the way she wanted. She wanted somebody to take another look. That's it."

"She hired you to look for Kim."

"Something like that."

"All those years—the other tenants that lived there since—
and nobody but you could find the shoe boxes."

"She said the place was empty."

"For twenty years? It's had three different owners since Ellis.
Plus one who never moved in."

"Maybe she didn't know that."

"Of course she knows that. Even our friend Reverend Miner
rented it for a year when he got out of the nuthouse."

"Miner lived out there?"

"Six months or so, never really moved in."

"It sounds like you keep an eye on the place."

"I drive by," he says, "from time to time."

"What's so important about the shoe boxes?"

"Just curiosity, Harding. You weren't a little curious yourself?"

"I restrained myself."

"And Cassie gave you Miner's name?"

I nod.

"And you asked Miner about Kim disappearing and stirred
up lots of painful memories about the trip and the kids. . . . I guess
it plays."

"What does?"

"You haven't heard?" He shoves a folded Lake County *Sun*
across his desk, turned to a small story in "Neighborhood News."
All that made it news was the weather angle.

WAUKEGAN MAN DROWNS ON JOGGING PATH

The body of Lawrence Miner, a former Methodist minister, was
discovered Sunday evening near a Lake County reservoir that
recently overflowed its banks. . . . Police have not yet ruled on
cause of death but there was no sign of foul play . . . only inches
of water on the path where Miner lay . . .

"They found him facedown on cinders and blacktop," he
says, stirring his coffee. "Six inches of water, half a bottle of pills
in his stomach. The pills are some kind of sedative, the lab work's
two weeks away, but right now they're calling it suicide."

"How do you drown on a jogging path?"

"You run real slow, I guess. He was seventy-two, Harding. Besides, you can drown in a bathtub, you know that. His lungs were full of water. Be glad they closed it so quick." He hands me my insurance card. "If they thought it was a homicide they'd want to discuss this with you in much greater detail."

"Which they don't."

"Which as of now they do not," Reese agrees. "Where's Cassie now, Harding?"

"I don't know. I wish I had a dime for every time somebody asks me that."

"Who else wants to know?"

"Just fans of hers." I pause. I'm wondering what happened to Miner's dog. The place didn't really look like it had even been searched. "Actually it's growing into quite an interesting crowd."

"How about a trade?" Reese says. "You tell me what Cassie really wanted out there, and where she is, and who's looking for her—"

"Are you sure that's all you want?"

"—and I'll let you look at the case file. Briefly."

I don't even hesitate. "Done," I say.

"You first."

I give him Quanh's name, and Toth's. I tell him most of what Cassie told me. He's not happy that that's all I know. I run into this feeling quite often.

"You've seen this Quanh, talked with him?"

"I've run into him once or twice. Do you know who he is?"

"I've heard things, that's all."

"You don't seem surprised about Toth."

"Toth doesn't worry me. He's small-time. He's not connected."

"But Quanh is?"

He shrugs. "The ground rules on looking at the file are you take nothing with you. You can't make copies, you can't write anything down. You get two minutes and that's it. Okay?"

"Okay." The file may be closed, but he's got it in his office already. It's not very thick for a triple homicide. I look briefly at the crime scene photos. They're as bad as any I've seen. I skip the household inventories and all the other detail work that cops do hoping for a break and go to the interviews. I'm looking for something regarding Kim's disappearance but there's nothing here. I do find Mrs. Moon's cause of death, listed as multiple gunshot wounds. There's nothing to indicate the auto-asphyxiation Tommy mentioned. The full coroner's report isn't here.

"I thought the mother had weird marks on her neck, like from kinky sex."

"Never heard that."

"Tommy Mullaney said he found them—"

"Mullaney again."

"Where's the full coroner's report?"

"Isn't it there?" he says, frowning. "This is what happens when we let outsiders look through the files. There wasn't anything unusual in there. They were shot to death. You have to remember, in those days the M.E. out here was like a circuit preacher. He didn't have a lot of time, and he didn't get real subtle."

Reese's looking at his watch. I pull out the checklist of interviews. The names that I recognize are Lee, Miner, Devlin, Wilder.

"That's it," he says, taking it away.

"There's a name on the interview list—Marty Devlin—can you at least tell me why he was interviewed?"

He glances at the list, checks the name. "That was just part of the process, talking with everybody who'd been around the house. Repairmen, plumbers, whatever."

"What was Devlin doing there? He builds pools."

"He was a general contractor then. He was doing work on the house being built on the next hill. And I guess he came over to the Moons and gave them a bid on some foundation work. That's all."

"You sound like you've been reading up on this yourself."

"I looked through it," he says. "There was talk—nothing substantial. About Devlin. Just rumors, I can't remember what. It never made it into the report."

"And the other name here—Wilder? They were neighbors, right?"

"Yeah."

"Do you happen to know what happened to them?"

"The parents are dead. The kids are all over."

"What about Mason and Zane?"

He looks at me, frowning, thinking I didn't keep my half of the bargain. He's right.

"Last I heard they were both getting free room and board, courtesy of the state of Wisconsin. In different places. Zane's done minor shit, robbery, breaking and entering, stealing rings from women at a shopping mall. Mason's in for harder time."

"They're both out."

"Yeah?" He doesn't seem surprised.

"Were they ever suspects? In the murder case?"

"I told you, Harding. The case was closed so fast there were no other suspects. But it doesn't take a genius, seeing the way the Wilders turned out, to think them capable of it."

"But you haven't kept tabs on them."

He shakes his head.

"One thing I don't understand—"

"Only one?"

"Knowing all this—when you heard about Miner dying, didn't you want to talk to me?"

"Why?"

"I was there around six. I was probably the last one to see him alive."

"You were there at six-fifteen. The lady next door remembers seeing you right when the weather came on the local news. She's got a wonderful view from her kitchenette. And you weren't the last to see him. There were two others there a half hour later, talking to him in his front yard. Plus a woman. Those are the ones we'd like to talk to, if we thought it was a homicide."

"Which you don't."

"No," Reese says. "Which as of now we do not."

twenty

I PARK ON THE STREET near my place, pick up some beer, and head for Athena Gyros. I get as far as the front steps. Luther Toth's waiting for me. It's the first time I've seen him on his feet. He's Lurch-tall, maybe six-eight, wearing the same dark suit he wore yesterday for the funeral. I'm starting to think it's an everyday suit.

"Leonard wants a word," he says. "Down at the TrueValue. Aisle two, cleaning products." Once again he shows me his gun, a steel blue automatic. I wonder if he'd like to sell it.

I can't think of any hardware supplies I need. I'm wondering how far Luther is prepared to take this when Alison comes outside the restaurant. She sees the gun. She stares at Luther Toth. It's a stare I know well and have come to appreciate, but this isn't the time for a fight.

"I'm going with Luther to TrueValue," I say. She's looking at Luther's knees, a prime target. Just like in football—hit 'em low.

"You better get lost, little girl," Luther says. Alison barely moves. I think her eyebrows go up a little. There's a row of winos on the sidewalk, watching the action. Nobody's calling 911.

"It's okay," I tell her, giving her the beer. "Leonard probably just wants to reinforce some of the points he made earlier."

"I was on my way to Hyde Park," she says, giving me the stuff right back. "The vet's, on South Dorchester."

"I'll meet you there. This won't take long."

"I've got my phone with me—call me if you need help. Big dumb white guys are a specialty of mine." Luther climbs into the truck with me. "Skinny bitch," he says, loud enough for both Alison and the winos to hear. His head hits the ceiling, his knees bump the dash. He doesn't seem to mind. We drive down Sheridan to Grace.

"I hear you had a little party last night," Leonard says. He's pushing another shopping cart, carrying a plastic clicker to check the prices on cleansers, waxes, floor polish. His gun's in a white Burger King bag on the child seat. "Guess my invitation got lost in the mail."

He's wearing shorts today, with a fuzzy V-necked sweater and sandals and a gold chain that lies in the black hair creeping to his neck like a snake. It's his West Coast look, I guess. The sunglasses perched in his hair will need a serious cleaning. So will the gold chain.

"Your girlfriend's okay?"

"She's fine."

"That's the way these guys operate, Harding. No class, no consideration. They come in from out of town, send three goons to visit you after hours, even involve a civilian like Alison. They don't play by our rules."

I nod. "You came in from out of town yourself, Leonard."

"You know what I mean."

"And I don't remember saying there were three of them."

"Sure you did."

"I don't think so."

He waves this off. Details, details. "What the fuck does it matter?"

"So you know who did it."

"I don't know who they are, I can guess who they work for. Quanh. And I can guess what they wanted 'cause I know what Quanh wants and Quanh wants the same thing I want: Cassie."

"You should all go in together on some kind of bloodhound. She's an actress on a publicity tour—how hard can she be to find?"

"Where is she, Harding?"

"I don't know. It's not a line—I really don't."

"Let me show you something," he says, taking a piece of fax paper from his wallet, creased neatly in three places. "I know you don't believe me. Look. Read. Learn something."

The fax is so smeared it's hard to tell if it's legitimate. It's certainly impressive, real or not—an FBI status file from the Department of Immigration, with a picture of someone who might be Quanh and a long list of his sins.

> Though now a U.S. citizen, it is believed he entered this country illegally . . . formerly an NLA intelligence officer and suspected assassin . . . deported from the Republic of Vietnam in August 1992 after serving fifteen years in Tin How Prison outside Ho Chi Minh City.

"Even they didn't want him," Leonard says, retrieving the fax. "That's like being kicked out of the Klan."

"I didn't know the FBI was sharing information with you, Leonard."

"I've got friends," he says, "like you've got friends. What in hell do you think he's doing around here anyway?"

"He said he was a fan of Cassie's."

"And you believed him?"

"I'm keeping an open mind. Like I am right now, with you. He didn't really strike me as a killer, though."

"Why, because he's short and polite? He's VC, Harding. Christ, we were practically neighbors in an Iron Triangle firefight —and you know what kind of sick bastard he was, Harding? He was a tunneler. He lived underground. You know the mentality at work here?"

"Who does he work for?"

"Some Hong Kong guys I wouldn't want to cross. This goes back years—there's more than just money involved here, Harding. There's bad feeling. With the people I represent it's just money."

He stops his cart to check out the C-clamps. Old habits die hard. "They're willing to make a deal. She can work off what she owes. She can authenticate a few items, sign a few forms, maybe get back to work—the point is I'm under strict orders not to hurt her. Not in any ways that the camera could see anyway, and since she works naked I'd have to be more of a finesse guy than usual." He puts a very heavy C-clamp in his cart. He's also buying a ball-peen hammer and a very nasty looking power drill. All brand names, very expensive. He must be on an expense account. "Quanh doesn't work for the same guys. They don't work the same way. . . . We were both sitting on that house, waiting for Cassie to show. Neither one of us expected you to be with her. You surprised the shit out of me, Harding, if you want to know the truth. And I guess we both decided to hang back and go after her later that night. Except she split. My gut says she left town. I know where she's scheduled next, and if nothing turns up I guess I'll head out there. I've got time. Like I said, Quanh isn't as easygoing. He'll want to find her now, tonight, tomorrow morning."

"And you're telling me all this out of the goodness of your heart?"

"I'm telling you because I know what Quanh's capable of and what he intends to do and what he *will* do if he gets his grubby little gook hands on her—and then I won't get a fucking cent. Understand?"

"How much does she owe?"

"It's not what she owes—"

"Just a ballpark figure, Leonard."

"I dunno. It's more what these guys will *lose*. The number they threw at me was close to a million. Okay? That's why I need to talk to her, to Cassie, our little ballerina. *Before* she shows up at this convention of hers. That's important, Harding."

"Why?"

"That's my business."

"How do you know so much about her past?"

"I was on the force then, remember? Lots of people know who she is. Nobody much cares anymore. I think you're the only one who didn't know. That's why it was so smart hiring you, Harding. You're probably the only one who didn't know—and the only one who'd care."

"What does Quanh have to do with the murders and the shoe boxes?"

"Draw your own conclusions," he says. "Connect the dots.

He was in the country when the kid disappeared, again when the family got butchered. Now he's back, looking for Cassie. Do I have to draw you a fucking map?"

"Why should I believe any of this, Leonard?"

"You'd better believe it. Because he likes hurting people. He enjoys it. Your girlfriend's gonna need all those black belts and she's gonna have her hands full—you should see what he did to the last guy that crossed him. I'd say go talk to this guy but you'd have to know the language—he talks now with his eyebrows, this guy. Up, down. That's it. Courtesy of Mr. Quanh. Myself, I don't operate that way. I like to keep a low profile."

A husband and wife are waiting politely behind Leonard— the husband finally taps him on the shoulder, says, "Excuse us"— Leonard tips an imaginary cap to the guy's wife and moves his cart by lifting all four wheels off the floor. As they walk past, Leonard grabs her rear with a Charmin-like squeeze—startling the woman and distracting the husband, just what Leonard was counting on. When he hits him in the stomach—fast and close, like a fighter clenched in the ropes—the guy bends over like a folding chair and then falls backward, taking a Windex display with him. Blue liquid covers the tiles like a Jennifer Bartlett mural. The woman hurries off, looking for a manager. The husband is facedown, gagging, trying to catch his breath.

Leonard checks something off his list, motions to a stock boy at the end of the aisle. He winks at me.

"We got a cleanup here," Leonard tells him. "You might need a mop, some kind of bucket."

twenty-one

ALISON'S IN HYDE PARK at another zoo, slightly
more upscale: Critter Sitters. She's returning Harold Two, a loaner
cat. I brought Harold One, her store's watchcat, here because last
Friday he swallowed an antique thimble, part of a collection Alison inherited. I thought he had a fur ball. Who knew he was into
collectibles.

"You're going to make somebody a wonderful father," she
says. "I go away for three weeks, I come back to find my plants
are at death's door, my kitty's coughing up family heirlooms." I
bring her up to date on Richie's break-in and Leo's mysterious
phone calls, Dr. Lee and Reverend Miner.

The vet puts Harold One in his carrier. "Pay the clerk," he
says. "Nothing strenuous for about a week."

"Good," I say, "I could use a rest."

"He means the cat," Alison says. "You, I've got plans for."
We drive to her place on south Harper, water the plants I ignored
for three weeks, unpack the few things Alison took to Tucson—
black shorts, black jeans, great in the sun—and put her Louisville
Slugger in the closet. Then we drive to her photography store on
Fifty-fifth Street and return Harold One to his watchcat position
in the back, just behind a skid of incoming UPS. Alison berates
her staff for low turnover, and Harold heads for the litter box,
trying to do his part.

I look through the notes she made on her phone calls. Richie had already tried Cassie's agency in L.A., but I thought Alison might have more luck. But nobody in L.A. knew where Cassie might be, and though everyone knew at least one Nikki, none of them lived in the Midwest. The tour was pretty much put together by Cassie, a one-shot deal that sounds like someone needed some quick cash.

I put in a call for Tommy, but he's out of the station; probably getting something to eat. I try reaching Devlin again, get a different salesperson—a woman this time—who would also love to get me into a pool. She mentions thongs, Speedos, midnight swims. Her sales technique beats Devlin's by a mile. Devlin's out of town. "Downstate, I think," the woman says.

Alison's waiting for me in the 4Runner, playing dashboard drums to Led Zeppelin's "When the Levee Breaks." The sun's out a little now, just enough to cause a glare. It's still raining though. There must be a rainbow somewhere. Despite the heat she's dressed all in black; running shorts, hiking boots, a loose tank top. Another shirt—black—tied around her waist.

I open the driver's door but I don't get in.

"What's the matter?" she says.

"Nothing." I'm looking beyond the 4Runner, across the Fifty-fifth Street median to eastbound traffic. That's where the red Ford sits. I can't believe this. Leonard Toth—so much for keeping a low profile. I just got rid of the bastard.

"Come on," she says. "You're getting water on the uphol-stery." I don't see anyone behind the wheel. I don't see Toth, which makes me more nervous than if I did. He's being very obvious with the damn truck. I wonder if he's got his hardware with him.

"You drive," I say, tossing her the keys. The truck begins a slow U-turn across the median. There's a glare on the windshield.

"What's the matter?"

"Just drive, will you?" She scoots across, adjusts the seat and the mirrors. I jump in beside her. "We're going through the park," I say. She nods, impatient. We drive into the rain, heading west. He's staying a respectable distance behind us. "This is the long way," she says. "Why are we going the long way?"

"I like the park, it's very scenic. Turn left up there." I reach for her arm. "Don't use your signal."

"It says no left turn school days nine to four."

"I know."

"This is a school day, Harding. It's between nine and four."

"I know. Wait, slow down, Alison, it's still green. Wait for the yellow."

She looks in her mirror. "Who am I running from?"

"The red truck. Don't worry about him, just watch where you're going."

"No wonder you let me drive," she says, taking her foot off the gas. "You never let me drive."

We zoom through green lights at Michigan and Indiana. A State Street bus cuts him off but he pulls around it, staying two car lengths behind us. The next intersection's crowded with traffic.

"Wait, don't use your brakes—"

"I know, I know."

We coast toward the intersection. She's good, she's straddling both lanes like a tourist. A guy beeps his horn. Nobody knows where she's going. The truck's three cars behind us now.

"Not yet," I say. "Steady, not yet, wait for the red light. Wait until the other traffic starts—all right now hurry up, come on go go go—"

"Jesus, you'd think we were in bed—"

"Alison, hit the gas, the fucking light's changing."

"I know it's changing—this thing handles like a tank and I can't hit that bread truck—"

She comes as close as she can. We leave behind a trail of bread crumbs, startled pedestrians, and—far back at the intersection— the red truck.

"Good job," I say. She nods, frowning, watching her mirror. Neither one of us says anything for a minute or so.

"Mr. Toth again?" she finally says. Her hands are steady on the wheel.

"I think so. You're okay?"

"I'm fine. Did that accomplish something or was it just whose engine was bigger?"

"I don't like being followed."

My pager goes off; I recognize the number as Tommy's. Finally—the fingerprints. Maybe he'll have an address for Mason. I tell Alison to pull over at the next gas station.

"If he wants Cassie why is he tailing us?"

"I don't know."

"Here's a thought. Maybe you could just ask him—"

"I will, the next time I see him."

"Meaning the next time you see him alone."

"Something like that."

The gas station's west of the Ryan. Alison fills the tank while I go inside to an office crammed with Slim Jims, baseball cards, chewing gum, a freezer full of Heath Bars and Eskimo Pies encased in white fuzzy snow the thickness of *Ice Station Zebra*. I came inside for privacy, but the clerk's about a foot away. He's got nothing to do but listen. Tommy's voice comes through loud and clear. I have to hold the phone an inch or so away from my ear.

"You didn't tell me you were attacked by a gang of biker chicks," Tommy says. "Her name's Lori Mercer. She has a nice yellow sheet. Priors for solicitation, narcotics, half a dozen DUIs on a Harley 883. It takes guts to drive a souped-up Harley when you're drunk." The clerk nods in agreement. I'm very glad to have this confirmed.

"Do you have an address?"

"The one on her license is downstate, Eighteen Blackbird Road, Dry Ridge. She's got DUIs there from March. But her last two busts were right here, at the lovely Hotel Richter. She's a working girl, Harding. She's using the name Lola."

"No kidding. I use that name myself sometimes." I ask him to check Mason and Zane Wilder. He takes the names, but I don't get the feeling he's going to rush to the police computer.

"L-o-l-a, Lola," the clerk says, slashing an air Fender. "La la la la Lola."

Alison comes in and puts a ten-dollar bill on the counter and pulls two ice cream bars from the freezer. I'm impressed; it's like King Arthur pulling the sword from the stone. "I need ice cream," she says, still upset over the chase. "You're the only man I know who can make my stomach hurt."

twenty-two

THE HOTEL RICHTER sits on a stretch of Lincoln Avenue known informally as the "hot pillow" strip. The cops love setting up stings here to catch suburban johns but Monday afternoons you don't find much action—too much guilt and empty pockets from the weekend. It usually picks up again by Tuesday.

Alison waits in the truck, slouched in the front seat, waiting for her ice cream to melt. It looks like the prop food she uses on advertising shoots. The Richter's a five-story building on the corner. It's raining hard enough that the girls are inside the front stoop. A metal frame hangs over the sidewalk, the awning's canvas long gone. So is the doorman. I leave the truck a block away on Lincoln and then go inside, past the local color. A cute redhead asks me if I want a party.

"I wish I had the time. I'm looking for Lola."

"We don't know her," says another girl, sounding like Sylvia at the day care center. Her hair's red too but with streaks of purple. "You want a room? How about a room."

"I think I'll just talk to the front desk," I say looking around the lobby.

"Go ahead. Talk to the desk all you want. There's no one there."

"Maybe I'll just have a look upstairs—"

"Not without paying for a room."

"How much?"

"That depends on what you want."

"I just want the room. How much for the room for an hour?"

"Seventy-five."

"I just want a look, I don't want to buy it."

"Give him a break," the redhead says. "What'd she do this time?"

"You know her?"

"Maybe. You a cop? You don't look like a cop."

"Is she here now?"

"No. She's not here much."

"What about her boyfriend? He's the one I really want. I just want to talk."

"You don't look like that's all you want." She stares at me. It makes me nervous. Hookers are very good judges of character. I take a twenty-dollar bill from my pocket. "All right," she says. "She ain't here now. And like I said, she's not here often. But when she stays here she likes three seventeen."

"Rita—" the other says, annoyed.

"Hey, the bitch has an attitude."

"Like you don't?"

"She thinks she's an actress because of one crummy little part in some community theater downstate—and she stepped on my foot last time, coming in with those fucking biker boots—"

"Lola's into leather," the other one explains. "How about you, baby—you into leather?"

"Out of my price range. I'm into leatherette. Does Lola live here?"

"No one *lives* here. 'Cept the welfare renters on two. Lola's here once or twice a month. She don't live here."

The stairs smell worse than the lobby. Three's an L-shaped corridor with barely enough light to read the room numbers. One of the doors is slightly ajar, halfway down the hall—317. I walk quietly to the left side of the door.

Then the light goes off, the door opens quickly, and someone steps out. But it's not Mason or Lola—it's Quanh. He's not expecting me or anyone else. He reaches for his gun but I get there first, grab his .32, hit him once. It's not much of a fight. I push him back inside and let his neck feel his own gun. Then I switch on the light.

He's sitting on the bed, probably the last place I'd sit. He's bleeding a bit around the mouth. In the movies this is where I toss him a handkerchief, but I don't have a handkerchief. I do feel like hitting him again, but I let that pass.

"Mr. Quanh," I say. "How's the siding game?"

"We shouldn't stay," he says. He wipes his mouth on the bedcovers; again, not something I'd recommend.

"Why not? Your hour's up?"

"They may come back," he says.

"Don't worry, they're not coming back," the redhead, Rita, says from the hallway. I didn't hear her footsteps on the stairs. She has a definite future in law enforcement. "They left this morning. They took their bags. You boys getting acquainted?"

Quanh's annoyed. He pulls out a Kleenex for his lip. I think it's the same one I gave him yesterday, but I'm not getting close enough to check. "Why didn't you tell me that before?"

"You stepped on my foot coming in," she says. "I can't stand people stepping on my feet."

"How many were staying here exactly?" I ask her.

"Just Lola."

"You said 'they left.' "

"Some guy left with her. That's not exactly unusual."

"What's his name?"

"I don't do names," Rita says.

"You ever see the guy before?"

"I think he was here last year," Rita says. "But that's all I know. And if I knew more I'm not sure I'd tell you."

"Why?"

"Because he's a nasty fucker," she says.

"What did he do?" I say.

"He don't have to do nothing," she says. "You can see it around his eyes." She's watching Quanh, trying to figure out what's going on. If she comes up with something I hope she lets me in on it. I give her another twenty dollars and a card with my pager number. Then I close the door. Quanh hasn't moved. He's been following the conversation impatiently. I get the impression nothing she said is news to him.

"We've lost them," he says. "Thanks to you."

"This gives us a better chance to get acquainted. Let me just have a look around the room—"

"There's no need. I searched the room thoroughly."

"Good, then all I need to do is search you, right?"

"This is all I found," he says, producing a scrap of paper with three words in light pencil: Holiday Inn Libertyville. It gives me a slight chill.

He says nothing.

"Where did you find this?"

"On the floor. By the bed."

"Let's see the rest of your pockets. And your wallet."

"Very well." Other than a pack of the brown cigarettes his pockets are empty. His wallet has a ten-dollar bill and a bus transfer. His driver's license says his name is Nguyen Binh Quanh. The picture's reasonably close. The address is Cleveland, Ohio.

"You're a long ways from Cleveland, Mr. Quanh." I keep the license.

"Can we go now, please?" he says, polite as ever.

"Not yet. Take off your shoes and socks."

"Why?"

"Just do it."

He shakes his head, sits on the bed, slowly removing one shoe, then the other. "If you're looking for money I have none with me. The girl took my last ten dollars."

"Ten? I gave her twenty. The socks, too." He's right, there's no money but there is a piece of paper, folded to the size of a Triscuit. "This kind of thing could give you bunions," I say, unfolding another variant of the vacation offer from Lost Moon Developers.

plenty of children to play with—just like home

"Where'd you get this?"

"It was here, under the bed."

"You'd better tell me what you're doing here, Quanh."

He doesn't answer.

"This is very tiring," I say. When I turn him over on the bed and twist his arm, just enough to get his attention, he seems surprised, but he doesn't cry out. His tone is still calm and measured.

"I told you before," he says. "I'm looking for my nephew."

"No, you didn't tell me that. You should get your stories straight. And what happened to your nephew exactly?"

"He disappeared."

"I'll need a little bit more than that."

"My sister immigrated to your country six years ago. She works as a seamstress. She is divorced. Duc is her only son. When he disappeared six months ago, she of course went to the police. But nothing happened."

"Where does she live?"

"In Cleveland."

"How did he disappear?"

"He was on a bus, traveling south. He left the bus somewhere between Chicago and St. Louis. That seems to be the only thing anyone knows."

He's watching me, but I don't say anything.

"There are others," he says.

"What do you mean?"

He hesitates. "I have a list—not with me—a printout I've compiled. Missing boys. Boys who have disappeared."

"There'd be thousands."

"No, I've narrowed it down, over the years—Asian boys, on that particular interstate, between those two cities. Asian boys who were kidnapped from bus stations. Asian boys who disappeared from that company's buses. Haven't you ever heard of this?"

"No," I say. I ask him a number of questions very quickly— sister's name, address, husband's name, Cleveland sports teams— he answers them smoothly. If it's a story it's well rehearsed. My knowledge of Cleveland trivia ends with the Dr. Shepard trial and the Rock and Roll Hall of Fame. He's familiar with both, though he seems surprised to hear about the Bee Gees' admission to the Hall. He's not alone.

I give up with the arm. I could never do Toth's job.

"Tell me what you know about Mason Wilder."

"Where should I begin?" he says, rubbing his wrist.

"How about what you're doing in his girlfriend's room?"

He looks at me quickly. "Mason is a suspect," he says.

"You think he took your nephew?"

"He may be the one, yes. And if he took my nephew, he may have taken the others."

"One man took all these kids?"

"I think so," he says, still rubbing his wrist. "But I'm interested in several different ones . . . especially since Leo Minsk and Marty Devlin bought the movie—"

"Leo? Leo's got nothing to do with this."

"He's an old friend of Devlin's."

"I've known Leo for years, he's harmless, and he's not a great friend of Devlin's."

"Did you know Leo bought his home from Devlin?"

"You're nuts."

"Ask him sometime. Devlin lived there before Leo."

I don't know what this signifies, if anything, but it catches me off guard. Leo should have told me.

"What does this vacation flyer and the ad and the movie have to do with your nephew?"

"I don't know," he says. "They're just clues. I collect clues."

"How do you know this guy, this kidnapper, exists?"

"Just a feeling."

"What do you know about him?"

"Almost nothing."

"Where does he live?"

"I don't know that either."

"You don't know if he exists at all."

"I know the boys existed, and now they're gone. . . . I have lists of boys and bus routes and road maps—sightings—I'm tracking him the only way I can, through the others around him. The way scientists find a new planet. By watching for the effect it has on other things, long before they actually see it . . ."

I take a quick look around the room, holding the gun on Quanh.

"Where have you been staying?"

"In motels. Nowhere just now."

"Where are all your clothes? Your papers? Your passport?"

"In a locker. There isn't much."

"How are you getting around?"

"My sister's car. But I take the bus a lot. Your public transportation system is excellent."

"Is your car downstairs?"

He hesitates again, then says no.

"Why don't I believe you?" I say.

"You can check my papers. And the rest of it. Run them through your police. Whatever it is you've been told—"

"I've been told you're a very dangerous man. I'm afraid you're after Cassie for some reason."

"I have no interest in Cassandra."

"You were looking for her at the airport. You were waiting for her at the video store."

"Coincidence," he says.

"Why are the Wilder brothers breaking into my apartment? What do they want?"

"If I knew that do you think I'd be rummaging around in here?"

"Mr. Toth says you're an assassin."

"Do I look like an assassin?" he says. "I'm an old man, trying to help my sister. It's Mr. Toth who is the assassin. The question is, Mr. Harding—which side are you on? Who are you trying to help? Other than yourself?"

"Let's go," I say, pulling him to his feet. "We can talk on the way to the police station. I want to hear more about the Wilders and Cassie, not your conspiracy theory. And why you sold Richie that tape."

We leave the room and head down the dark hallway. I don't have the gun out, but I have one hand in my pocket near its handle. Either he's quicker than the normal human or I'm distracted by the sight of one of the hookers coming half-naked out of a room, still fastening her bra. Quanh trips my legs and both of us tumble down the stairs. When I wake up five minutes later—one minute later than Quanh—I find Rita splashing water on my face. Quanh is gone. So is his driver's license. So is his gun.

"You're going where?" Alison says. We're heading south on the Drive.

"Dry Ridge. It's a small town downstate."

"You've got an address?"

"Yeah, for Lola. But she's probably not there either. Still, it's all I've got."

"Sorry I fell asleep. I didn't see the guy come out."

"It doesn't matter."

"How did he get away from you again?"

"One of those Oriental judo things. Like you see Arnold use in the Karate Kid movies. He's small but dangerous."

"You don't look very banged up. What sort of move was it?"

"I was walking toward the stairs when a woman came out of a room half-naked. He forced me to look."

"Insidious," she says.

"Inscrutable," I agree.

"What should I get from my place?"

"You're going? You don't have to go."

"I don't want you falling down all over central Illinois."

"Rain gear. It's gonna be muddy. Cameras, the usual. Field glasses. A toothbrush. And a gun would be nice."

"You won't need a gun. I'll protect you."

"Right. If you're awake."

She comes out of her apartment dressed in black, carrying a large gym bag and her Louisville Slugger. "You never know," she says. The radio's in the middle of another hour of commercial-free classic rock.

When you dance I can really love

"Is this a case you're on now? For real?"

"It looks like. I took her money."

"But what are you looking for? *Who* are you looking for? The missing brother? Cassie?"

I shrug. I wonder what would happen if I could get them all in the same room—Kim, Cassie, Miner, the Toths, the Wilders, Quanh. What would they talk about? What would they have in common?

"How long do we have?" Alison says. "Until Cassie comes back?"

"Twenty-four hours."

twenty-three

IT'S NEARLY TEN P.M. by the time we reach Dry Ridge, a small town on the Illinois River. The main road's closed. We drive in circles looking for a way into town. The rain has a thickness to it; visibility's very bad. Once or twice we pull over and just sit, listening to the lightning pop and crack on AM radio. The thunder's all around us.

"This beats THX," Alison says. The humidity has both of us sweating. We've brought umbrellas we could never open in this wind, slickers, rain boots. Alison's wearing black jeans, a thin sleeveless T-shirt, dark prescription shades. Her shirt's tied around her waist again. Somehow her long black hair stays straight despite the humidity. Probably she just orders it to.

"What's the address again?" I say.

"Eighteen Blackbird."

A window I thought I'd fixed last winter develops a slow leak; a line of water runs down the inner glass to the door frame.

Two local cops ask us what the hell we're doing out in weather like this.

"My mother lives on Blackbird Road," I say. "Is that closed too?"

"It's open," he says. "For how much longer I don't know. You're sure she's still there? Most of them are up at the high school."

"She's one of the stubborn ones," I say. "We're taking her back to the asylum."

159

When we pull onto Blackbird, it's more like a swamp. Lola's place is in a trailer park. The Illinois River is cresting about fifty yards away. Alison waits in the truck. I run to Lola's trailer. No one answers. The door's locked. I could pick it, but a cop is already walking toward the truck.

"Park over there," he yells, pointing to what passes for higher ground; a tree orchard. There's mud everywhere, just different qualities of mud. This mud must be better for parking cars.

"Don't tell me," Alison says when I slosh back to the 4Runner. She's already retying the laces on her boots so they cover her jeans.

"What."

"This reminds you of Woodstock."

"I didn't say that."

"You parked in the field, there was mud everywhere—"

"Furthest thing from my mind," I say. "Do you know if the Airplane's playing tonight?"

"God, you're old, Harding. You're very old."

We cross a small lot to the river. The houses here are already evacuated. This isn't the Mississippi or the Ohio; they don't usually have much flooding here, not like this anyway. So this is new and it started out almost like a block party, everyone helping out, but now it's just work, people scared to death they'll lose everything they own. There are fifty or sixty people filling sandbags, passing them hand to hand. Alison buttons her slicker, joins the line. I walk closer to the river, where a couple of men stand smoking.

"I'm looking for Lola Mercer—"

"Who?"

"Lola—Lori Mercer." My words are blown away. "She lives over there in eighteen."

"Haven't seen her." I walk along the levee asking the same question. No one's seen her, not for weeks. A woman lets her baby-sit her kids sometimes, she remembers Lori pulling out in her Camaro, when was that, all we can think about is the rain and the river. . . .

"You want to help, mister?" someone says to me, and so I

join the crowd, passing sandbags. The river is like a brown snake coming nearer and nearer.

We're there a half hour or so when I hear someone talking excitedly behind me. Then I hear a shout and then—it's amazing how quickly it happens—the sandbags give way at one spot, then another. The water seeks its level, the residents keep piling sandbags, but it's too late, too little. The water grows in force.

And so we retreat, the water rising around our ankles, then our knees, children at first playing, then screaming; women pushed back on their seats, the water running toward the mobile homes, most already up on blocks, most apparently emptied of valuables —people running inside, grabbing what's left, the water climbing the short steps.

"You looking for Lori?" a man says to me, suddenly appearing on my left. He's wearing a heavy-duty poncho and fisherman's boots. I nod. "Thought I saw her over there, past the barn. She must be looking for her dog."

"Thanks."

"Watch your step," he says. "The footing's real slippery over there. We lost one man today already."

"Thanks again."

I don't see Alison. The barn's on slightly higher ground, protected by a natural levee. I roll the sliding door open, call for both Lori and Lola, walk across a wooden floor that sags with each step. Light slips between the cracks. There's a square hole with cement steps covered with straw. I'm on the first step when I feel two boots against my neck. Before I can move they kick me down the steps.

My head goes last. My ankles scream when they hit the concrete floor. My attacker lands flush on my back, a Red Cross poncho flying up like a parachute. It's Lola. Now I see why Rita hates her boots. They're heavy black leather with small silver spurs.

I follow her outside. The wind's much stronger now; so is the rain. To the north I can see the water rushing over the sandbags. The mobile homes are sitting in a lake. I can see her footprints in the quicksand, heading toward the river.

The water pushes over the levee, surges toward me. She's by the tree. A chunk of earth just tears off, falling into the river. She tries jumping to the first branch. You can see the weblike roots now in open air.

I make it to within an arm's reach of the tree.

"You'll have to jump," I yell. She doesn't move. "The tree won't hold, it's already sliding—"

"Get the fuck away from me," she says. And then the ground gives way and the tree bends farther and she loses her grip—and then she jumps, not toward me but straight down, to the brown rushing river.

The Red Cross has a shelter in a local high school. The gym's full of cots and sleeping bags. My clothes are so wet I'm afraid to go in, but they give me a new pair of jeans, torn but clean, and a DRY RIDGE HIGH T-shirt. Alison's dressed the same way. I find her with the emergency workers, setting up a makeshift kitchen that smells of coffee and sweating concrete. Alison sits with a glass of milk and a cheese danish she wouldn't eat if her life depended on it.

"God, where'd you go?" she says, hugging me.

"On a wild-goose chase. I lost Lola, she decided to go swimming. Any sign of Zane or Mason?"

She shakes her head.

"Well, we're not going anywhere tonight," I say. "Tell them we're married, maybe we can sleep together."

"The women sleep over there," she says. "Besides, if we can't fool around there's not much point sleeping with you. All I get is the snoring."

"Such a romantic."

The night passes slowly, full of unfamiliar noises, small outbursts of crying. It reminds me of boot camp. At six A.M. Alison and I get coffee from a huge metal urn and sit on the bleachers until the state police say we can go.

Outside, it's a new world. The high school's on a bluff overlooking the town. Most of the roads are gone. Grain silos show how high the muddy water went, like growth charts penciled on a door. "Everything's gone," someone says. "Everything I owned."

And then Alison pulls my sleeve, points to the strangest sight of all.

"It's the graveyard," she says. Coffins are floating in the water.

"We lost half the grave sites," a state cop says.

"I can't worry about that," another cop says, "not while we've got fourteen people missing."

"They're dead," the first one says. "As dead as the coffins." A single canoe floats through the town, looking for survivors.

Thirty miles downriver is the town of Twin Lakes, where Kim's Bible turned up, sent to Miner by a man named Simon Gates. The chapel Kim's group was rebuilding is here, too, but it's not where he disappeared, fifty miles and two bus stops away.

Alison and I hitch a ride back to our truck and then crawl through one-lane traffic until both the roads and the sky open up. There's a flash of lightning like one last electric shock and then the air begins to clear. The land rises from the river. The sun comes out.

Twin Lakes Methodist is on West Fork Road. It's a white clapboard church designed to look like it belongs in New England or Lake Forest. Except this building is just concrete and red brick behind the facade, and the ground it sits on is red clay beneath an inch of topsoil. A fake rustic sign points the way down a sloping side yard to two small ponds, optimistically labeled the Twin Lakes. Metal signs nailed into the ground like artificial flowers say the Rotary, the Elks, and the Lake County NRA share the church for meetings once a month.

I knock, but no one answers. I can hear singing. I hate to interrupt choir practice. Alison hears it too; she bails out, wanders toward the water with her camera. The door opens to a small nave, then a large, plain room full of folding chairs and the smell of sweating concrete. There's no air conditioning; no choir either, just a middle-aged man dressed in jeans and a plaid short-sleeve shirt. He's polishing the collection plates with Liquid Gold, listening to country swing on the radio.

"I do believe Bob Wills had the spirit of the Lord shining through him," he says to me, as though we're old friends. We're not. The music's "Mexicali Rose."

"My name's Harding—"

"Reverend Bob McKaskins," he says, stepping forward to shake my hand. "Everyone calls me Reverend Bobby."

"How about Bob?"

"That works too," he says cheerfully. "What can we do for you?"

"I'm looking for Simon Gates." He's trying to place my accent. I didn't know I had one but everybody does. It's like a scent that tags you.

"Reverend Gates? He's not here. He passed on two years ago . . . could I help you with something? I'm the pastor here now."

I tell him more than I probably should; he has a disarming nature—more Baptist than Methodist. Since I'm used to dealing with tough Chicago priests he seems more like somebody's grandfather; PastorLite.

"Hand me those collection plates, will you?" He sees me using both hands to lift them, and he smiles. "They move down the row a bit slower if they're not so light."

"If you could tell me anything about where the Bible might have been found—maybe there's some kind of record—"

"He disappeared off a bus?"

"That's right."

"If it was found by a cave it must have been out on Keller's Ridge. That's on the other side of the river. That's where the chapel is too. And that road's closed on account of the flood."

I give Bob the only picture I have of Kim; it's getting a little dog-eared. "He's from Chicago."

"Looks like he's from a little farther east than that."

"The police thought he was a runaway," I say, taking the picture back. "But the father—his name was Ellis—the father made a number of trips down here, meeting with Reverend Gates. I was wondering if perhaps Reverend Gates might have spoken about this to you, or someone else in the church."

"I don't really know."

"Does your church have any outreach programs for runaways?"

"We have youth ministry, sure. But not what you're talking about. That's more a city thing. Why look out here? He must have lost the Bible working on the chapel. That doesn't mean he disappeared from here. The bus sure don't come down West Fork Road."

"I'm just looking everywhere I can. No one in Chicago remembers these trips or the chapel. Anything you could tell me . . ."

He gives me a minister's thoughtful glance. "Let's go upstairs to my office," he says.

We climb a narrow set of stairs to an office overlooking two baseball diamonds and a parking lot. There are about a dozen kids in lederhosen dancing between parked cars. *"The Sound of Music,"* he explains. "We're doing it in the parking lot, so the audience can see the hills in the background, imagine them as Alps. Actually . . . it's a landfill. But beautifully maintained." He looks around the office as though there might be something to offer me, but finding nothing, he sits down, putting a copy of the Revised Standard version over this week's *Weekly World News.* "What's your interest in all this, Mr. Harding? Are you writing a story?"

"No. Like I said, I'm looking for Kim Moon, and I'm basically going in circles—"

"Let's see—as I recall, the trips were actually sponsored by IAFC—that's InterAgency Faith Council. It's an outreach program. The kids came from all over the Midwest. Stillwater Methodist must have sponsored Kim. Reverend Miner probably went along because he was youth minister. Like I was, at the time."

"Did you know Reverend Miner?"

He shakes his head

"Is this IAFC still running these trips?" I say.

"Oh no, there's no council anymore, I'm afraid. Like everything else, no money. Didn't they tell you that at Stillwater?"

"No one there wants to talk about Reverend Miner, or these trips."

"Oh?" He glances at the clock behind me on the wall. He's too polite to throw me out, but I get the feeling he's not saying much more; not about Miner anyway.

"What about this chapel you mentioned, the one Kim and his group worked on. Would there be any record of that?"

"There might be, in the basement, somewhere."

"Ellis Moon would have come down here during the week-end," I say. "I don't think he went to church in Stillwater but if he was with Reverend Gates he might have come to a Sunday service. Are there any attendance records or a visitor's book from that period?"

"There's a visitor's book."

"Could I see it?"

"From that time frame . . . it would be in the basement."

I get the feeling he doesn't much want to go to the basement.

"We don't keep the older records up to date too well. Mind you, we probably should, but there's only so much you can do." He smiles and checks the clock again. Maybe he's cooking a roast. "Just so many hours in the day." The *Sound of Music* kids are singing "So Long, Farewell," and I think McKaskins is just about to add auf Wiedersehen when Alison knocks on the door behind me. She's used to bailing me out, and she's an expert on small-town social rituals. Before I can say anything she introduces herself as my wife.

"Ah," Reverend Bob says, smiling, instantly seeing me in a better light. "How long have you been married?"

"Not long," I say.

"Three years next September tenth," she says. "He's always forgetting the date."

"Do that myself," Bob says. "You have any children?"

"Two," I say, as Alison says three. Bob looks back and forth between us, awaiting clarification until Alison takes my hand and explains that she's already counting the one that's on the way.

"Another little Harding," she says.

"Praise the Lord," Bob says.

"Reverend, if you don't mind . . . I feel a little sick to my stomach . . . if I could just sit for a minute. While you got that visitor's book?"

"Take my chair," Bob says. "There's a soda machine down the hall. I've always found carbonation helps the stomach." He pats Alison on the arm as he leaves. "You're a lucky man," he tells me.

"I didn't know how lucky."

When he's gone Alison leans over and whispers, "Jesus, don't lay it on so thick."

"Me? You're acting like one of the Stepford wives."

But it works. Bob takes a half hour and brings us back both a visitor's log and a collection of sermon notes from the year Ellis made his trips. "Reverend Gates liked to note anything special about the service in the margins of his sermons," Bob says. "Between that and the log we should find out when Ellis was here, if it meant anything at all to the reverend. You'll find some of the notations are a bit trivial." He also found a photo album from around the time of Kim's trip, the only thing he could find about the chapel.

We spend an hour looking. We hunt through the sermons, we slog through the visitor's log. Simon Gates took note of the temperature, the drop in barometric pressure, the hour the sun rose, the suit his lay minister wore, if Mrs. Heedy from Riverdale made it to church on time despite her "drunkard" husband. There's no mention of Ellis. Just handling the sermons is putting me to sleep.

The photo album is more interesting. Again, there's nothing here about Ellis. But there is a picture taken on the front yard of the chapel: fifteen kids and three adults dressed in shorts and T-shirts, holding brooms and mops and paint brushes. I recognize two faces—Reverend Miner stands behind the crowd, a tight smile on his thin lips. Kim's kneeling in front like a baseball player, holding a paint roller across one knee. He looks very happy. Beside him is a girl, several years older. There's no caption, no names. Finally we leave, empty-handed. Bob gives us a pamphlet on "Children as God's Blessing."

I give Bob my card and twenty dollars for the collection plate.

We take the truck back to Blackbird Street, or as close to it as we can get. No one's around. We have to hike through a muddy field, the back pasture of a small farm. "We're in a county historical district," Alison says, wiping her boots on a clump of weeds. "Watch out for cow pies." There's a row of tall skinny trees for a windbreak and some overgrown shrubs that love all this water. I

catch my sleeve on a branch and some thorns and then tumble
through the last row of shrubs onto the open ground leading to
the water. Alison follows me calmly. "The element of surprise has
been somewhat compromised," she says.

The trailer's sitting in the middle of the river now, twenty
yards from shore. I take off my boots and my shirt and give my
watch and wallet to Alison and then wade in. The water reaches
my upper chest, but I don't have to swim. There's no way to get
the door open, so I go to the other end and pull myself in through
the bedroom window, which is flapping on its hinge. It's dark
inside with the drapes pulled and the power off, and I don't feel
like advertising my presence any more than I already have. It's like
a small apartment. When I get to the living room the trailer shifts
a bit, as though the ground's giving way under the jacks and the
cement blocks. With the rain and the wind I feel like Huck Finn
finding his father, especially when I find Mason. At first I think
he's still alive, but that's an illusion created by the water rocking
the trailer. His body's rolled under a kitchen table that folds up to
the wall. He's dressed in a black leather jacket, and I have to push
one of the curtains open to see the head wound. Half his skull's
caved in.

Because of the water I can't tell how recently this happened; I
can't tell much of anything. Every instinct tells me to get as far
away from this mess as fast as possible, but I have to check something out first. I look through each room as best I can without
finding much evidence Mason even lived here. But lots of things
floated away last night.

Lola clearly lived here, though. All her clothes are here. There
are six or seven pairs of leather boots with her shoes. I can't find
any sort of office or desk and I don't see personal things like mail,
bills, the normal paper trail, but in the top drawer of a cheap
cardboard dresser, under her bras and bright red half-slip, I find
last year's datebook. Judging by this, she didn't have much of a
year. Some of the listings are just a man's first name and a phone
number. One of these is "Marty" with the number on Devlin's
business card.

In the bottom drawer there's an old purse, empty except for

some pennies and paper clips and Kleenex and two small pictures, one of three kids around the age of ten; two boys and a girl, with *Lori, Mason, and Zane: Michigan vacation* on the back. The other is the same picture I saw in the photo album at Twin Lakes, and here there are names because the picture was taken for the local paper. The girl beside Kim is Lori Wilder. That's when I notice the calendar that's been hanging in front of my face the whole time— a giveaway from Devlin Pool Co. The address sticker on the back says *Lori Wilder Mercer 16 Blackbird Road*

With our compliments and best wishes for the season
to our family of employees and friends

Pinned behind it are two vacation offers from Lost Moon, one for Lori, one for Mason, but both sent to this address. His looks like Devlin's—"swim in our Olympic-sized pool"—except there's a fairly creepy photo of two boys arm in arm—"big brothers teaching the spirit of giving." Lori's has a similar picture but the kids are a boy and a girl.

Within the tiny boxes on the calendar are a handful of reminders scribbled in pencil. I think it's her work schedule at the Hotel Richter. But for last weekend the note says "Chicago," with my address, and "rock 'n' roll." I don't think she means the Hall of Fame. There are a number of doctors' appointments. The following months are bare.

I check the small bathroom, not much bigger than a 737's, and find bottles of Zoloft, Wellbutrin, and lithium, all with recent dates, all from a local pharmacy, all for Lori Mercer. I'd be depressed too living here. I leave everything as I found it, including the pictures.

I wade back to Alison. The land around her looks like a Georgia swamp.

"You should have left your pants here too," she says. "You're wearing your cute shorts."

"I don't go into water like this without pants. I don't like snakes."

"What did you find?"

"Mason's body," I tell her. "It's pretty clear he works for Devlin."

"You think he might have killed Mason?"

"Maybe. His name's on a couple of things. Either he's sloppy or someone's framing him. But I can't tell if Mason was killed here, or just dumped here."

"Too bad Lola jumped. She might have killed Mason."

"I don't think so." I tell her about the calendar. "She's Mason's sister, not his girlfriend. And she still has a picture of Kim, the same one we just saw."

"So she was on the trip with Kim?"

"Yeah." I wish we could ask if anyone's found the body. But that might not be such a great idea.

"Why was she living here?"

"I don't know. Maybe her husband lived here. If there really is a Mercer."

"Do you want to report this?"

"No." I look around. The area's still closed. There are a million places to hide. Every time a small breeze shakes the trees it looks like someone's spying on us. "Did you see anyone?"

"Not that I noticed." She hands me my watch and wallet. "You weren't wearing gloves, Harding."

"I didn't expect to find a body. Or my address on a wall calendar."

When they do find the body someone will remember the strangers who asked for Lori Mercer. I can't think of what to do except leave. Small-town police make me exceedingly nervous. Finding an out-of-state ex-con with a manslaughter conviction near a body's like winning the lottery.

It's eight A.M. I have twelve hours until my meeting with Cassie.

twenty-four

"POLICE WERE HERE BEFORE," Minas says as he wipes the counter. The restaurant's half full for lunch, shades pulled to stop the summer sun. Alison's upstairs changing. I'm wearing clothes she bought me at a Wal-Mart outside Peoria, probably off the first rack she saw—cuffed polyester pants, a shirt that feels more like a plastic tablecloth. I bet it repels water.

"They have to eat, too," I say. "Even your food."

"Not to eat. For you."

"What kind of police? Uniforms? City cops?"

He shakes his head. I reach behind him for the house ouzo and pour myself about an inch in a paper cup. It doesn't go down very smoothly, so I pour another.

"Didn't they tell you where they were from?"

"I get them confused," he says.

"Did they show you a badge?"

"Who can trust a badge, after seeing all the phony ones in your sock drawer."

"You should stay out of my sock drawer. Were they wearing uniforms or plainclothes?"

"Uniforms."

"Hats or no hats?"

"Hats."

"What size hats?"

"Big hats."

"And what color were the uniforms? And the hats?"

"Brown." Meaning state, following me from Dry Ridge, or DuPage County, way out of their jurisdiction. Maybe it was a social call.

"Should I have told them about the break-in last night?"

"No, that's the last thing you should have told them."

"Harding, are you in trouble again?"

"No, of course not." I pause. "And what do you mean, Minas, by 'again'—"

"I'm just wondering if I should possibly get your rent in advance."

"You don't have last month's rent yet. But thanks for the vote of confidence."

I'm halfway to the staircase when he calls my name.

"What now."

"Your shoes," he says, getting a greasy carry-out bag from under the counter. "Don't forget your shoes."

"What?"

"Your shoes. She said you left them in her car." He hands me the bag, white paper curled tightly at the top. Then he leans close. "I thought I better not let Alison see them."

"What are you talking about?"

"Don't worry, I won't say a word."

"Tell me at least." Inside's one of the shoe boxes. It smells like old grass clippings, halfway to rot. "Cassie left this? Very sexy blonde, bright orange clothing?"

"Yellow, not orange. But blond and sexy, yes. Very sexy." He makes vague movements around his chest, the international symbol for boorish men. "You know."

"I know. When was this?"

"This morning. Before you got home."

"When exactly."

"I guess it was about nine-thirty."

"Didn't she say anything?"

"She was hungry. I gave her something to go. That's all. She said they're shoes, but they don't feel like shoes. I didn't look inside."

"Join the club. Are you sure she didn't say where she'd be today?"

He shakes his head. "Will she be coming back again, do you think?"

"Why?"

"I might take a bath."

"Then she's definitely coming. Soon."

Cassie's back in town. It sounds like a B movie. I use the restaurant's phone, get the number for the Holiday Inn Libertyville and try the front desk, but she hasn't checked in, not under that name anyway. The woman answering the phone sounds a little harried: "We're all booked up—the place is full of monsters!" This would make a good ad campaign.

Upstairs, I decide I need something stronger than beer but it's a little early to start drinking straight Wild Turkey. So I make a shaker of iced tea; not Long Island, since all I've got is vodka. Leningrad Iced Tea. Alison's sitting on the bed, hunched over the phone, speaking very sternly to someone she owes money to. She has world-class dominatrix phone skills. I turn on the stereo and hunt through a crate of records I bought for ten bucks at a garage sale. It's supposed to be country/folk but instead of Ramblin' Jack Elliott or Townes Van Zandt, I have my choice of Andy Williams, Al Hirt, or the Anita Kerr Singers. All are good in small doses. Finally—between Jack Jones and Gisele MacKenzie—I find a classic Van Morrison, his best record, *Veedon Fleece*.

I open the living room windows. Then I take the shoe box to the living room couch and sit down with Cassie's past.

The box is overflowing, tied with string—I wonder if she's combined both boxes in one. Some of it's ordinary family stuff, childhood memorabilia: kindergarten pictures, a tiny 4-H key chain, Girl Scout badges. A small pair of copper dog tags with Kalani's name and address. There's a picture of a stage, a dozen small girls in ballet white; another with the girls and their teacher, who's not much taller than the girls. A schedule of practices and performances: programs from *The Blue Bird, Swan Lake, Snow White,* and a touring company of *A Chorus Line* at the Arie Crown. On the back of that program there are trial signatures written over and over: *Cassandra Moon, Cassie Moon.* She was already changing her name.

Other clippings feature different members of the family. Older brother Ethan led a rock band that cut a demo. There's a review and a photo, both very serious. Sister Beth won fifty dollars writing an essay for Presidents' Day. The original copy is here, with smudged type and crooked letters from an old manual typewriter, and another picture. A faded clipping on an Antiques Club formed by the locals, meeting once a month at the Moons'. Letters from a girlfriend of Cassie's away for the summer, preteen boredom. She saved this stuff for an afternoon like this, I guess. Here's that rainy day.

One packet looks like a collection of Ellis's papers—army discharge, birth certificate, letters . . .

Dear Ellis:
    Your wife mentioned at the eleven o'clock service that you were thinking of making another trip to look for Kim. I wish very much that I could accompany you, but my duties at the church unfortunately preclude my leaving at this time. However, I've been thinking about your request for the name of anyone who might be able to help, and I think your best bet would be to contact the local church where we stayed . . .
    Godspeed you on your journey.
    Rev. Lawrence Miner

Dear Mr. Moon:
    I received your letter of April 10 regarding your trip to our area. Certainly we welcome you and will do whatever we can to assist you in looking for your son.
    Regarding your request for anyone else who may remember Kim and the three weeks he spent with us—I've compiled a list of people who were here at that time. Part of it is memory, and part is based on a list I made when I heard of the disappearance. I don't remember any policeman following up on these names, since they believed he left the bus in Carbondale. Most of these people are local, and I honestly don't believe them capable of harming your son. I can imagine that you have only the worst associations with our town, but there are good people here, Ellis.

Please contact me upon your arrival. If you indeed bring the rest of your family, there is a potluck dinner every Sunday evening at the parish. We would be honored to have you join us.
Reverend Simon Gates

There's a list of names, typed on onionskin paper. Miner's name is on the list; so is Wilder's. So is Dr. Arthur Lee. Each have small neat checkmarks next to them. The letterhead on the paper says

SUNNYSIDE DAYCARE/STILLWATER METHODIST
COSPONSORS OF CHRISTIAN YOUTH TRAVELERS

At the bottom of the box is a pair of toe shoes, white points, soles worn and shiny. They're as hard as a rock and folded slightly. Tucked underneath are two neat white envelopes, legal size. There's no postmark on either, and both are unsealed. Inside the first is a letter addressed to Cassie, signed by the minister of the Lake County Methodist Church:

If you're reading this, Kalani, you must have somehow survived your terrible ordeal and found the strength to return home. . . . I know you feel that God has deserted you but you must believe it is not so . . . I saved these things not to be morbid but because I thought one day you might wish to see them—they belong to you and I know you left them behind but since you have no one here anymore . . . if I've judged wrong, please just throw them away and excuse an old man his fumbling attempt one last time to reach out to you with God's grace. . . .

I have had trouble myself dealing with your family's passing, along with other things beyond my control . . . so much seems out of our control . . . we must have faith that God has a plan, but I expect to be taking a brief rest soon from my duties . . . another reason I write this now. . . .

My thoughts are confused today, forgive me . . . every now and then things become clear . . .

Do you remember the hymns you sang with us in the choir Sunday mornings—"Father, I Stretch My Hands to Thee," "Faith of Our Fathers" . . . I think of your family when I hear them and of course I think of your brother Kim. . . .

God bless you, Kalani.
Rev. Lawrence Miner

The clippings in the other envelope are creased so tightly I doubt anyone's looked at them until recently. Some are newspaper stories, some are advertisements and flyers.

Public notice of auction hereby given . . . antique furniture, cane-bottom chairs, walnut dresser, rose marble top . . . estate sale, all items, jewelry, lamps, children's toys

. . . outside help not needed, insists local sheriff in crowded press conference today on the courthouse steps . . . "We take care of our own thank you very much."

. . . crops harvested early . . . neighbors' fields plowed under looking for undisclosed . . .

. . . public notice of . . .

. . . bone china, refinished cabinets, assorted farm implements . . .

. . . Lake County family tragedy . . .

There's a piece of paper typed like the letters in Cassie's shoe box. It's covered with yellowed Scotch tape, as though it was the label for something.

left to right: Daddy, Reverend Miner, Dr. Lee, the pool man, Mason, Kim—practicing Giselle 8/20/65

"Mrs. Loomis wants her bathrobe back," Alison says, coming into the living room. She takes a sip of my iced tea, grimaces, adds more vodka. "What are you looking at?"

"One of Cassie's shoe boxes. She stopped here this morning."

I turn down the stereo. Van is in the middle of his epic "You Don't Pull No Punches, But You Don't Push the River."

"She didn't say where she'd be?"

"No. I thought there might be something in here—some kind of personal message, but all I see is family stuff."

"This looks like a personal message," she says, finding an envelope in the other toe shoe: *Dear Harding, Don't forget our date!*

Inside the envelope there's a check for five hundred dollars and a small charm bracelet with a silver heart. Alison holds up the jewelry first.

"She's sentimental," I say. "It's a girl thing."

"It's a woman thing," she says. "You don't know what this is, do you?"

"It's a tiny charm bracelet. Very delicate."

"It's a nipple ring, double pierced. Very deviant."

"Are you sure?"

"Either that or she's got very small wrists." She looks at the check and whistles. The phone rings—it's Marty Devlin. He sounds like he's calling from the bottom of an empty pool. He's working in southern Wisconsin, why don't we meet in an hour—there's a bar not far from him called Dreamland—do I know it? I tell him I do. It's more a nightclub than a bar, but in rural Wisconsin that's not saying much.

Alison is already closing up the apartment. Everyone seems to be able to hear my phone conversations. "Is there some sort of plan today?" she says.

"It's implied."

"Wonderful."

"The general idea is to get to Cassie first. Keep her safe. Hopefully she can tell us what's going on."

"This is a bar we're going to first?"

"More like a strip club. But not the kind you see in the movies."

"Are the girls cute or yucky?"

"This is Wisconsin, Alison."

"Then I'll wait in the car," she says. "Bring me out a sandwich." She's holding the check for me. She's very good at holding checks. "You know, Harding, I don't think I've ever been on a job with you where you actually had some money."

"Puts me in a whole new light, doesn't it?"

"No," she says. "The light's pretty much the same."

Outside, Alison puts on her sunglasses, looks around for the red pickup. She learns fast. I'm thinking about the clippings and photographs. They don't look like they were all put there at once. In fact, one of them's from a year after the murders—when Cassie was in Topeka with her grandparents. So when was that box really put there? And by whom?

"Don't forget the alarm system you promised me," she says.

"That is, if you expect me to ever sleep over without checking every single closet."

"First thing tomorrow."

"You know, Harding, with the kind of work you do I can't understand why you never installed one before."

"It's not hard to understand."

"No?"

"No. Until you, there was never anything here worth protecting."

She rewards me with a smile. "Nice try, Harding."

I drive around the block once or twice, but I don't see the red pickup. I'm glad Alison's with me, to watch my back. I feel like someone's following us, but it's just a feeling. I don't really see anyone.

twenty-five

THE HOLIDAY INN LIBERTYVILLE sits close enough to the expressway to ensure a steady stream of impulse sales and diesel exhaust. It looks like it was last remodeled about when Bing Crosby opened his own Holiday Inn. The woman behind the counter looks a bit like Danny Kaye. She smiles at me and frowns at Alison, who's taken off her outer shirt—she's wearing her black T-shirt with a skull and crossbones on the front, DAMNED TO LIVE on the back. The lobby's full of people getting ready for the convention. There's a large banner for GoreFest '98 on one wall —TONIGHT LIVE—THE RETURN OF CASSIE RAYN—surrounded by a collage of pictures from her movies.

"We're booked solid," the woman says. "I couldn't give you the sofa in the lobby."

"I don't see a sofa," I say, looking around. I barely see a lobby.

"Then somebody's already got it," she says, frowning, scratching it off her list. "What I could do is put two folding chairs together by the ice machine. It's broke anyway, so the noise wouldn't be a problem. Though people trying to get the ice machine to work, that's another matter. People love their ice."

"We don't need a room," Alison says. "We want to talk with Cassie Rayn."

"Who?" the woman says politely.

"The woman you've built a shrine to." I leave her alone to negotiate for a few minutes and follow the signs to the Empire

179

Room, filled now with folding tables, booths, posters. A lot of middle-aged men with too little sun and too little exercise are arranging their displays of figurines, comic books, pins. Everything is a one-of-a-kind item, specially reduced.

"We don't open till five," a guard tells me. He's dressed like a fem Freddy Krueger, with a rubber mask made up with lipstick and rouge, and long curving press-on nails painted metallic gray. "If you'd like to buy a ticket, see Dorothy at the coat check. She's got the tickets."

"I'm a performer," I tell him. "Where do I register?"

"That would be Dorothy again. At the coat check."

"Have you seen Cassie Rayn here yet?"

He shakes his head. The rubber mask wiggles. "She's not scheduled until the finale, at eight o'clock. Dorothy's got the schedules." Freddy gives me a long look. "Are you performing with her?"

"No, no. I do FX. What does Cassie do, sign autographs?"

"They'll have posters or glossies for her to sign. You can have your picture taken with her—there's different prices for a sheet of pocket size or portraits—"

"I'm guessing Dorothy has the price sheet." He nods. "Thanks, I'd better talk to Dorothy."

"What kind of FX? Makeup? Explosions?"

"No, I do body work. I'm the eyeball popper."

"What?"

"Dangling eyeballs, hanging by a thread, being squished on the floor . . . any time you see an eyeball pop out and hit the floor, that's me."

"Gross," he says. He's impressed.

"I'll be seeing you."

"In my dreams, honey," he says, waving. I think he loses a nail.

Alison's waiting near a potted palm. "You made a friend. How nice."

"Is she here?"

"Checked in two minutes ago. She's coming down."

And just like that, Cassie walks into the lobby, ignoring the stares of Cassie groupies, signing one or two autographs with a bloodred pen. She sees us, and smiles.

"Is there a problem?" she says.

A crowd gathers around her—we retreat to her room, furnished in early Naugahyde, to reconnoiter. Alison sits by the TV, shoes on the air conditioner. Cassie sits on the bed. There's an awkward minute when I try to introduce them—Alison sort of nods hello, then sniffs as though catching an animal's scent. I smell something too, but I attribute it to the Naugahyde. Cassie's wearing old jeans and a loose-fitting top but I don't think it matters what she wears.

"I've had a crummy day," she says. "Actually, since I saw you last, Harding, not much has gone right—the friend I was hoping to stay with split two months ago from troubles with her ex and so I've been staying with this other girl I know who just started cosmetology school—"

"That's it," Alison says, sniffing the air again.

"What?"

"That's what I smell. You've had a permanent."

"I've had three," Cassie says. "Beatrice had nobody to practice on and since I was staying there I couldn't say no."

Alison nods, turns the air conditioner up a notch.

"So what's new with you?" Cassie says. Alison looks at me, I look at Alison.

"Let's see," I begin. "Shall we go chronologically or in order of importance—"

"Oh, I'd love to see you try figuring that out," Alison says.

"Chronologically then. After I left you, Cassie, outside Richie's—remember Richie? The guy you stiffed? I talked to Reverend Miner, we had a nice little chat about Kim and an hour later he killed himself. There's a bottom-feeder named Leonard Toth and a VC cowboy named Quanh and the Pool King and the late Dr. Lee and Lola and Mason and Zane Wilder—my apartment was broken into, Richie's store was broken into, Leo Minsk's house was broken into."

"And I was locked in a closet," Alison says.

"That's right, Alison was locked in a closet."

"Mason Wilder?" Cassie says. "And Zane? He did what?"

"Broke into my place."

"Mason . . . I haven't thought about him in years—"

"He's been thinking of you."

"And Zane? They're both around?"

"Zane is. Mason's dead."

"I think I'll check out the exits," Alison says. "And get something to drink."

When she's gone I go through it all again with a plainly baffled Cassie.

"I had no idea all this would happen," she says. It's easy to believe her; she makes great eye contact. Sometimes I forget she's an actress.

"See, I think you're right about one thing," I say. "Somebody did send those vacation flyers for Lost Moon. I'm starting to wonder, Cassie, if it wasn't you."

"Me? Why would I send something like that, to myself yet—"

"Maybe they're designed to get the case opened again—not Kim's disappearance but the murder case. Everybody around the household is getting them, and they're shaking everybody up."

"They shook me up too."

"You didn't send them."

"No," she says. "Of course not. But I *told* you something was going on—"

"Let's go through these people, one by one. Marty Devlin. Do you know him?"

She says no.

"He was around your house about the time Kim vanished, doing construction for your dad and the Wilders. He built the Wilders' pool."

"I don't know who he is."

"How about the Wilders?"

"Of course I knew them, they were our neighbors, but I haven't heard from them since I left home."

"Mason and Zane both have police records. Did you ever think they might have had something to do with the murders?"

"Not really. They were kind of hoods, even then, but so were a lot of guys. Mason was the worst, he always had extra money, but he never worked and hardly went to school. What happened to Mason?"

"Someone killed him, in the last few days—I found him in his sister's trailer, in Dry Ridge, near the flood—"

"How did he die?"

"It looks like he was struck on the head. Why?"

"Nothing. He was always so afraid of water . . . I was hoping he didn't drown."

"You two were close?"

"We were friends," she says. "All of us, we were in and out of each other's houses during the summer. What happened to Lori?"

"I'm not sure. I was trying to talk to her when she jumped into the river. The current looked pretty strong. You didn't tell me she went along with Kim, on the trip—"

"I guess I forgot. I really didn't think the Wilders had anything to do with Kim or my family. We were all friends. It's so strange . . . all three of them."

"I know." I pause. "How close were you exactly?"

"You mean was I sleeping with all three? Not quite. Zane was closer to my age and we started going together, then Mason. I had a major crush on Mason. Lori was seeing Kim."

"She was a lot older—"

She nods. "It was unusual. Mason was a lot older than me, but you don't expect it with girls. It's status. But, Jesus, we're talking high school—junior high for me and Kim. This was all so long ago."

I nod, remembering the picture Lori still had of Kim in her trailer, even after twenty years of other men, marriage, divorce . . .

"Did your parents approve of all this?" I say.

"Oh no. My father hated Mason. And he thought Lori was practically molesting Kim. But you have to understand . . . we were way out in the country. There was no one else around to play with. You sort of bond with the other kids. And both my parents were working—"

My pager goes off. I forgot I even had it. I recognize the number—Leo. I call him at once and hear the panic in his voice.

"Harding? You have to help me tonight—"

"What's the matter, Leo?"

"I keep getting these phone calls, where nobody's there—"

"Don't answer your phone."

"Plus Marty Devlin's coming here—he called, he sounded very upset about the tape—"

"When did Devlin call?"

"Just now, two minutes ago."

"Leo, why didn't you tell me Devlin sold you the house?"

"I told you we did business together, real estate, residential—"

"You didn't tell me you're living in his fucking house."

"I bought it twenty years ago, what difference does it make? And I bought it through a broker, a third party, I never even met Devlin until much later—I'm worried about right now, tonight—"

"Maybe you should go to Richie's for the night, Leo."

"I've got people coming over for poker, I'm not sure I can reach them—besides, the Cheese King owes me two hundred bucks—"

"Another night, Leo."

"And let Devlin just come here?"

"Why not? I'm sure he knows his way around. . . . Look, Leo, I'm gonna see Devlin in a few minutes, I'll talk to him. And I'll stop by your place later to make sure everything's okay. Go to Richie's. Leave the alarm off."

"You don't have a key."

"I'll get in."

Alison comes in quickly. She smiles at Cassie, then turns to me. "It's getting crowded out there. Too crowded to watch for someone. I can't be sure we're clear."

"Okay," I say. "Cassie, we have to move you somewhere. Until we figure out what's going on."

"Do you think I'll get back here tonight?" she says, meaning the convention.

"Why? Is it that important?" Alison says.

She hesitates.

"If there's something you need to tell us, Cassie, now's the time," Alison says.

"I didn't think it had anything to do with anyone but me. But maybe it's why those other two men are following me—what were their names?"

"Toth and Quanh."

"See, I don't owe anyone money but . . ."

"Yes?"

Alison relocks the door and sits down.

"I know there are people still mad at me, people in the business who were shut down or arrested when my age thing came out. That was my fault, I guess."

"Why would they come after you now?"

"Because . . . I was planning to announce something, tonight, at the end of the convention. About my age."

"Toth said something the other night—at the time I didn't make much of it. That you shouldn't go to this convention."

Alison looks at me sharply. It's a look that says she doesn't like being kept in the dark.

"What were you going to announce?"

"That I wasn't really underage when I made those movies. The adoption agency screwed up my age. I was eighteen. Everything I did was legal."

"That's great," Alison says, looking first at Cassie, then at me. "Isn't it?"

"Not for everybody," I say. "If you've spent a hundred thousand dollars over twenty years collecting her memorabilia and watching it appreciate—"

"Meaning everything these people have collected is worthless?"

Cassie nods.

"There's enough money involved that someone would kill you?"

"Some of these people," Cassie says, "are a little obsessed."

"If it was someone she burned the first time, when she said she was underage, and now they're getting burned again—"

"Did you know you were eighteen?" Alison says.

"Oh, sure. I had to lie to get started . . . then I had to lie again to get out. I was under contract, I couldn't just quit."

"Who held your contract?" I say.

"The man who signed me is dead. But there were investors. I really don't know who owned the company. It went under."

"We should find out who the owners are," Alison says to me.

I nod. "But let's deal first with who's already here. Cassie, how would someone like Toth or Quanh have learned about your announcement?"

"I'm not sure," Cassie says. "I didn't tell anyone here. I *did* tell a couple people in L.A."

"Toth lives in L.A.," I say. "Quanh, I don't know." I'm trying to figure out if this means Toth and Quanh are separate from the others in this mess. Toth makes sense. He rode in like the Lone Ranger with his faithful sidekick, Luther. All he's interested in is Cassie. But Quanh's been involved with the Wilders.

The phone rings. Alison answers it, turns her back on us and whispers for a few minutes, then says, "Thanks, Dori, we owe you one. Yes, I've got your number."

"Who was that?"

"Dorothy," Alison says. "I asked her to let us know if a short Asian guy starts asking for Cassie."

"Quanh's here," I say.

Alison nods. "Luther Toth is here, too."

"Great."

"We can leave the back way," she says. "Dorothy says go down the corridor behind the restaurants. A cook will open the back door for us."

"Dorothy must be a big fan of Cassie's," I say, and Alison smiles. "A big fan of one of us, then. When we get outside we'd better split up. Cassie, you've got a car?" She nods.

"A Jeep, a Grand Cherokee."

"Did you rent it here?" I ask her.

"Yes."

"Under which name?"

"Cassie Rayn."

"Then I'd better take it. Alison will take you somewhere safe."

"Which would be . . ." Alison says.

"Try one of those cheap motels on Route 41. Watch out for tails."

"Where are you going?"

"To see Devlin, and then stop at Leo's."

"Who's Leo again?" Cassie says.

"I'll explain," Alison says.

"I don't have a clue about any of this," Cassie says.

"That's okay," Alison says. "That's standard operating procedure for Harding. Some people work best under pressure. Harding works best in total ignorance."

"I'll call you in about an hour," I tell her. "You're ready?" She nods, flips her baseball cap backward. Now she's ready.

The cook escorts us out the back door. We walk around a handful of people sunbathing on uncomfortable wooden chairs. There's no sun. Lightning flashes; the sky breaks open with a fast, furious rainstorm. The pool is full of children.

twenty-six

DREAMLAND SITS on a strip of rundown restaurants and bars that feed off an Indian casino, not far from the state line. Its specialty is renting harder porn than you can get in Illinois, selling toys to adults, cigarettes to minors, running skin flicks between live weekend shows—local girls mostly, just dancing; no pairs, no performance pieces. Nothing gonzo. It looks more like a fishing lodge than a nightclub. Once in a while a fading porn star easing into secular life draws a crowd to the runway. When that happens the room's full of people enjoying the house specialty—Strohs and salsa, both watered down; stale chips like Soylent Green. The parking lot's full of Illinois plates.

Devlin's waiting for me at the bar. He's not alone. A hood named Jimmy Keys is tending bar. I knew Jimmy in my bouncer days, both of us ex-cons and out of state, violating our paroles if anyone cared to check, putting in time at a dive outside Madison where I worked the door and Jimmy worked whatever scams he could get away with. Like Dreamland, it fed off a casino—all Wisconsin casinos are on reservations—and Jimmy apparently liked the Indian dancers, even followed a cross-dresser named Hiawatha home once or twice before discovering what she had tucked beneath her ceremonial costume. Whether he'd actually dipped his toe in the Big-Sea-Water of Gitche Gumee was a matter of some debate among the rest of the staff.

Jimmy gives me a bartender's smile, like I'm just another

customer. I don't think he remembers me. He's lost a few brain cells since then.

"What are you drinking," Devlin says to me. He's wearing standard business attire: nondescript pants, short-sleeved white shirt, a tie that could match any jacket. The jacket Devlin wore today is folded on the next bar stool.

"Bourbon, a little ice." I find the ice slows you down. It's like weighing down the collection plates.

"Make it two," Devlin says, and Jimmy automatically reaches for the good stuff. Devlin must be a regular. "One of my sales managers," he says, meaning me, as close as Devlin gets to an introduction. Why he feels he has to lie, I don't know. Jimmy nods.

"Long fucking day," Devlin says.

Jimmy pours two drinks. Devlin slides one in front of me, waits on his. I take a long sip. It tastes very good. If I could afford it, I'd probably be an alcoholic.

"Five estimates," he says, "four follow-ups, two jobs half a state away, everything a month behind because of the weather. I'm being sued in Chicago and Milwaukee for drownings in my pools, as though I was there holding their heads under water. Half my workers are on vacation in Mexico, the other half are home pumping water out of their basements. Then there's the filter problems." He shakes his head. "People think anything goes through a filter. The stuff I've seen in this business you would not believe. Hell, it's barely afternoon, the stuff I've seen this morning alone would gag you."

"Lots of water," Jimmy says. "*Way* too much water."

"It's bad all over," I say. "It's really bad downstate in Fulton County, a town called Dry Ridge on the Illinois River. . . . The whole place is flooded." Devlin says nothing, his eyes straight ahead, as though staring at a trophy case behind the bar filled with gold-plated bowlers, fishermen with bent rod and reel. "A lot of people lost their homes, their trailers. Even the cemeteries flooded. Coffins floated away, some of them thirty or forty years old. . . ."

Devlin reaches for the peanuts.

"I'm moving to Arizona," Jimmy says to no one in particular. "I play Lotto all three states and video poker and slots and as soon as I hit I'm out of here. Moving to Arizona, building an adobe house."

Devlin wants another drink. Jimmy refills his glass. I'm falling behind. I'm trying to picture Jimmy Keys building an adobe house.

"It's tough selling swimming pools in this weather," Devlin says. "People are sick of the water. Who wants to get into the water?"

"You know what they've got out there?" Jimmy says. "In Arizona? A cactus museum. This is how dry it is. A museum with nothing but cactuses."

"Cacti," I say.

"You have to *hunt* for water," Jimmy says. "You could walk for *days* and not see water."

"Sure," I say. "As long as Hoover Dam holds, you'll be fine."

It must be sixties night at Dreamland—the strippers have come down off the runway; the early shift dancers are climbing into their cages. One of them puts her hand on my shoulder as she gets in. She's wearing an Indian costume and white go-go boots. She smells like jasmine.

Devlin takes a look around the bar. "Look, about the other night, I have to apologize, bothering you that way."

"That's okay."

"Probably woke up the whole building, scared your girlfriend —what's her name?"

"Alison."

"Probably scared Alison half to death."

"She doesn't scare that easily."

"At any rate, I was out of line and I'm sorry."

I nod.

The music starts up from ancient JBLs; Paul Revere & the Raiders.

It's just like me. Music to frug by.

Devlin waits until Jimmy leaves to take care of a customer.

"What we talked about, just forget it. Forget I was even there."

"You weren't the only one to drop in unexpectedly that night."

"No kidding."

"While we were talking somebody snuck into my apartment, waited until we'd gone to sleep, and then opened the back door. There were three of them."

"No shit."

"You know two of them."

"Really?"

"A guy named Wilder. Mason Wilder. And his sister, Lori. Though you might know her as Lola."

Devlin sips his drink.

"You must be mistaken," he says.

"I don't think so. You're featured prominently in Lola's address book. And Mason Wilder worked for you. I saw your name on stuff in Lola's trailer—did you notice the time they came in Sunday, Marty? About an hour after we had our little chat. See, they didn't break in—the first guy snuck in while I was talking to you. And I remember how you pulled me away from the stairs, over by the restaurant—"

"You think I sent them? Why would I do that? You've got this all wrong."

"Educate me."

"I don't owe you any explanations," he says. The back of his neck's getting red. It might match the blazer he usually wears.

Jimmy asks if we need anything before he takes off. I shake my head but Devlin raises one finger from his glass; one for the road. One of the strippers sits down next to me and says I should buy her a drink, she loves Tom Collinses, and so I pay ten dollars for a glass of ginger ale. She says her name's Sari, she's from Katmandu, she was Miss Playboy—Far East. She has amazing blue eyes. It's hard to tell the Indians from the Indians around here.

"I think Mason's working for you again," I say. "I think you sent him inside my place last Sunday night—"

"Mason is the one I wanted you to take care of, asshole," Devlin says.

"What?"

"Mason's been on my back for a month now, from business dealings he feels went the wrong way—"

"He works for you."

"No, he *worked* for me. Not now, not for years—I haven't seen the fucker since God knows when and then he shows up on my door with his hand out—"

"And his brother, Zane?"

"I don't know him. I've heard the name."

"And his sister, Lola?"

"I know her, yeah, I met her twenty years ago when she was a kid, same time I met her brothers, doing work on their house, and I met her again in a bar and we've gone out a few times and I'm not surprised my name's in her fucking trailer. Turn me in to the vice squad, they'll be stunned, a guy seeing a hooker."

The lights dim, the music cranks up another notch; Los Bravos, "Black Is Black."

Devlin throws a twenty on the bar. "Somebody else talked to Mason, I guess. Somebody else gets the two grand." He walks toward the door, slowly, looking at the crowd as though expecting recognition applause. I'm about to follow when my pager goes off.

Jimmy points to a black phone on the counter. I don't recognize the number but the voice on the other end is familiar enough —Leonard Toth. He sounds like he's at a frat party.

"Do you have her?" he says.

"No." Devlin's talking to somebody just inside the door. Then a third person joins them. Jimmy Keys.

"Look, Harding," Leonard says, "let me level with you, okay? All I want from her is that she doesn't show at this convention."

"What are you talking about?" I say, distracted. Devlin's paying them both off. I can't tell how much. It could be a nice tip. It could be two grand.

"If I tell you the truth will you help me?" Toth says. Even though I say nothing he goes on. "She's gonna announce at this convention that she's two years older than everyone thinks—she was legal, Harding. It was all a scam and first my people got burned when they pulled all the product and now they're gonna get burned again—really burned—they've got a million or so invested in her, selling her shit all over the world. It's all worthless now. They want me to stop her, they don't want me to hurt her. Just convince her not to make the announcement. That's all I want."

The stripper, Sari, puts a five on the bar. She wants change for the slots. The bill's redolent with sweat, stripper's perfume, left over from the last place it was deposited. She's wearing less now than when she was stripping.

There's a new bartender. I need another drink. I tell Leonard I'm in the middle of something. That's the best way I can describe it. Sari's taken off her G-string. She's sitting on a corner of the runway in a half-lotus, eyes closed. She's getting more tips meditating than most of the dancers in their cages.

"This is just business," Leonard says. It must have looked like an easy payoff, just the sort of thing to attract someone like Leonard. "I just want to earn my money so I can go back to L.A."

I give Sari another ten. "Transcendental," Sari says. The bartender is looking at me as though I know something. I don't.

twenty-seven

THE JEEP'S PULLING to the left, like that Mazda I had a few years ago. I should have checked the tire pressure. The first gas station I come to is a King Kwik on high ground with old-fashioned rounded pumps and an air hose snaking down an ivy-covered wall. The sign's turned off, but the light's on inside. I fill the tire and then go inside to prepay the gas and borrow the key to the john. The owner's getting ready to close. I buy a map and some coffee. The map's five years old; the coffee might be older than that. I fill the gas tank, then move the car around back.

The parking lot's covered with storm victims—flowers, twigs, someone's mailbox. The sidewalks are wet with sand and more earthworms. Two minivans pull in and unload waterlogged Cub Scouts. Luckily they're headed for the store, not the bathroom. The owner's trying to close, but the Scouts prevail.

I'm washing up when someone tries the doorknob. My hands are so slippery—all the towels are on the floor—it takes me a minute to open the door. When I do there's no one there.

NO MORE THAN FOUR KIDS AT A TIME says a sign on the convenience store window, forcing the Scouts to mill around outside, replaying gruesome movie deaths from their field trip to the multiplex. The rain's dropped down a notch in intensity but the Scouts don't seem to care one way or another. A couple of them are sitting on the Grand Cherokee; I have to shoo them like pigeons. It's only then I see the red Ford sitting at the far end of the lot.

I walk over and take a quick look inside the window, see a thermos and notebook and a map like the one I just bought. The truck's tires and splash guards are covered with mud. The doors are locked. The coffins on the back are locked too. I look inside the store, but I don't see Toth. There are kids everywhere, yelling, screaming. A clerk's distracted, muttering, trying to fix the Frostee Freeze machine. His world stops there. I need a job like that.

I go back to the bathroom door. It's locked now. I knock and someone yells "Occupied" in a muffled voice.

I go inside the store and go quickly through the aisles, looking for a knife or a screwdriver but there's nothing here. So I buy a glass bottle of Bosco and a ball of string and then borrow a red CLOSED sign from the front door. Then I hang the sign on the door of the men's john and try the handle again and bang on the door.

It takes him a minute to open it—you need a key on either side. I guess it reminds you to bring it back. By then I've found an oily rag to wrap the Bosco bottle in—I want to slow him down, not kill him. I'm tired of him following me. The sun's at my back. When the door opens I kick him inside the bathroom but it's not Toth, it's the shooter from the other night, Zane Wilder. I recognize his face. I recognize his smell. *Put her down, Zane.* The key lands in the sink. I hit him across the face before he can say anything. It takes a bit of self-restraint not to hit him again. I kick the door closed and lock it, break the bottle on the edge of the sink and put it to the fleshy folds of his throat.

"What are you doing here?" I say.

"Fuck you," he says.

This gives me an excuse to hit him again, this time with my right hand. I don't have a bad right hand but I suspect it's the way his head bounces off the toilet bowl that knocks him out. There's some cleaning supplies on the floor behind the toilet—rags, sponges, a lovely bottle of Little Bo Peep ammonia. I go through his pockets and don't find anything but lint. I tie his hands behind him, and look outside the door. There's no one waiting. It's getting darker.

Little Bo Peep wakes him up when I wave an ammonia-soaked rag under his nose.

"Jesus, man," he says, coughing and spitting into the rag. "I can't breathe."

"That's the general idea," I say, squatting down so my face is right before his. His breath could clean windows. "I don't have a lot of time here, Zane. So I'm going to stop your breathing permanently in about two minutes. Unless you tell me what the fuck's going on."

"I don't know anything."

"Nighty-night, Zane," I say, prying his lips apart with the rag and raising the bottle. The ammonia slops against his mouth.

"Oh, Christ," Zane says, looking down at his pants, which just got a little wetter.

"Why are you following me?"

"I'm not."

"You just stopped for gas?"

He's not looking at me. His head moves slowly up and down to some internal rhythm. "You murdered my brother."

"Mason? I didn't kill Mason, Zane."

"I saw you there, coming out of the trailer—"

"He was already dead, Zane. It wasn't me."

"Somebody said a couple from Chicago were looking for Lola. Now she's disappeared. And Mason's dead, and I saw you coming out of the fucking trailer—"

"What were you doing in my place Sunday night?"

"Looking around."

"Zane, you're going to have to be a little more forthcoming. I'm really losing patience here."

"Mason was worried," he says, coughing. "He thinks someone's trying to frame him—we were looking for some stuff—"

"What stuff?"

"A tape."

"Of what?"

"Just a movie—a tape, we thought you had it."

"A tape with Cassie Rayn on it?"

He starts to say something, then hesitates.

"I know who she is, Zane. I know your family lived next to the Moons, I know you were friends with both Kim and Kalani, I know you were living there when the Moons were murdered."

"It's not exactly a secret."

"I know your sister's a hooker—"

"That's not a secret either."

"I saw a picture of Kim in her trailer, Zane. An old picture like one Kalani's carrying around—I know she was with him on that trip that day—"

"So?"

"Did you have something to do with Kim's disappearance?"

"Me?"

"Any of you."

He shakes his head.

"What do you think happened to him?"

"I always thought his father maybe did it. But it's not something I lie awake thinking about, you know?"

"What brought you both back to Chicago?"

He hesitates until he sees me reaching for the bottle.

"You won't believe me," he says. "I'll tell you and you won't fucking believe me."

"Try me."

He tries to sit up a little. He tells me about getting Lost Moon flyers every day for a month at the rooming house in St. Louis where he's been living.

"Who are you working for, Zane? Devlin?"

"We can't stand that bastard. Mason thought he was the one sending us all this fucking Lost Moon shit, acting like he had some kind of tape to incriminate us—"

"You think Devlin's setting you up? For what?"

He pauses. The veins on his hands are like rivers on a relief map. "Mason wasn't sure."

"Come on, Zane, there must be something—the murders? Kim's disappearance?"

"Nothing like that," he says, coughing. "Geez, who do you think we are?"

"What then."

"Go on and kill me then, man," he says, something new in his voice. It might be the ammonia fumes. "You won't get nothing else from me." I think he's stupid enough to mean it.

"Where'd you do time, Zane?"

"Joliet."

"Who'd you hang with? You're not a skinhead. You've got too much hair. What did you do before Joliet?"

"I was a soldier."

"What, like a mercenary? Soldier of fortune?"

Zane nods.

I hear someone outside.

"Fought any wars lately?"

"Every day, man. Look around you."

I'd like to talk to him further, but there's no time. I tie his ankles, then put a rope completely around his belly and tie him to the cold water pipe. I put a rag that seems reasonably clean in his mouth. Then I lock the door from the outside and break off the key.

I don't think anyone saw any of this—the manager's still busy with the Cub Scouts. The ones who've had their Frostee Freeze are starting to form a line for the bathroom. "Sorry, it's out of order," I tell the adult shepherding them, who groans and heads them back toward the store. "It's pretty bad in there, too." One kid lingers a second, watching me. He gives me a little smile. He's got the merit badge for bullshit detection. There's one in every crowd.

twenty-eight

IT'S A SLOWER DRIVE the farther north I get. I pause at street corners, listening to the water rushing to the sewer drains, trying to picture the route ahead of me. After a certain point there isn't any choice; the detours lead me a different way than I'm used to. The roads are slick and winding and I have to follow hand-painted detour signs, like a road rally, past fallen trees and wires. The weather's making most of my decisions for me now.

There's a line of cars ahead, but one by one they desert me, frustrated by the detours, making U-turns, turning down back roads or driveways—they know the area better than I do. I stay on the highway, follow the signs.

We're going very slowly and eventually I see why, as the last of the cars in front of me disappears, and I find I'm following a logging truck, very slow, too long to pass. I crack my window to clear the fog from my windshield and hear the hiss of the logger's air brakes. He's been downshifting through his gears and now he's putting his left-turn signal on, slowing for the long turn onto Route 20. But he can't make the turn without a complete stop. His backup lights come on. There's a new pair of headlights in my rearview mirror, content to stay back there. They don't get any closer. I don't see a tan Chevy. I don't see a Ford pickup. I stop the Jeep.

The logging truck pulls onto the grass, trying to make the turn. He has to go right to go left. His wheels spin in the mud. I

199

take my cell phone out of the glove compartment and dial Alison's portable phone and get a busy signal.

What is this guy doing? The logger has room to make the turn, but he's not moving. I wind the window all the way down, letting the rain in. I dial Alison's number again, and as I get another busy signal I pull the Jeep around to the right, on the gravel shoulder. As soon as I do, the logger backs up, closing the road behind me. Now I see what's preventing the logging truck from completing his turn—a ROAD CLOSED sign blocking his path. I try backing up around the logging truck but there's no room, and in a minute my fancy 4x4 is turned sideways, spinning its wheels, stuck in the mud. I wish Cassie had rented a Land Rover.

I'm starting to wish I'd brought a gun.

"Hello?" Alison says, finally picking up.

"Remember the broom closet?" I say. The line's full of static. I hate cell phones.

"Harding? Are you all right?"

"Fine, never better. But I'm thinking you should go somewhere different. I'm in the middle of something here. I can't tell what."

I keep waiting for another car to appear, but the logging truck's done a nice job of blocking both my rear and Route 20.

"What is this bastard doing—"

"Talk to me, Harding."

I rub the steam from my window.

"Remember the broom closet, Alison? Just say yes or no. Don't say the building, don't say where you are now. Christ, I hate these fucking car phones. I feel like Walter Winchell broadcasting to all the ships at sea."

I see the logging driver swing down from his cab and walk to the far side of his rig. He's short, wearing a windbreaker and a baseball cap. I'd give anything for a pair of binoculars. Everything's in my apartment. I'm not supposed to be working. And actually, I'm not doing much.

"You mean where we—"

"Exactly. Twice. Meet me there in an hour. Okay?" The logger's walking toward me. It's raining harder.

"It's serious?" she says.

"I think so."

"I'm leaving now," she says, hanging up. The logger's slogging around his truck toward my car. But I see a blue Explorer like Marty Devlin's coming from Route 20. It stops by the logging truck's front and Devlin gets out, dressed as if he was expecting to be out in the storm—a long heavy green slicker.

There's a brief argument, then Devlin shoves the logger, who loses his balance, falling back against the truck bed. The logger falls on the ground; Devlin steps around him and moves toward me.

He's got a shotgun under his slicker. God knows what he thinks he's doing. "Now you want my business? What were you doing in my fucking business?" he yells, not getting too close. He must think I'm armed; only an idiot wouldn't be. "Harding? Why are you doing this shit? Why?"

I don't answer. There's so much fog on the windows it's like being in a tinted limo.

"Get out of the fucking car, Harding. Talk to me." He's holding the shotgun across his arm, like a hunter waiting for flushed game. His green slicker has his company's emblem on the front pocket. At this point my options are severely limited. Guys like Devlin become much bolder when they're holding a 12-gauge Remington. About all I can do is scratch him with my keys. . . . I get in the backseat with the cell phone. A roll of thunder shakes the ridge. Devlin starts toward me again. I start dialing 911.

I get to the second digit. Devlin gets maybe ten yards.

Someone's up on the hillside with a rifle. It sounds like a backfire. I flinch, thinking I'm about to be shot in the back. It's fucking loud. Shots strike the roadway and skip forward like stones on a pond.

"Are you fucking nuts?" Devlin yells. He thinks it's me shooting and he returns fire, emptying both barrels into the Grand Cherokee's front grille and tires. In the movies the hood would magically pop up, the radiator boil over, but the Jeep simply falls forward like a horse dropping to its knees.

"Are you getting out?"

I leave the car but not the way he wants. I use the phone to knock out the interior light and wait for the next crash of thunder before I crawl out the back door and drop to the tarmac. Once outside, I head for the far side of the road through rivers of coolant and oil; swirling rainbows on the wet road.

There are more shots from the hillside. Devlin must finally realize what's happening. From beneath the Jeep I can see his legs backpedaling.

I start crawling for the shoulder behind my car and when I leave the roadway and find solid earth, I keep going, sliding over the edge. It's dark as sin below. But I can see another truck now, presumably belonging to the shooter on the ridge—the red flatbed Ford, parked sideways a little ways down the ridge.

Gunshots mix with thunder. I can't see the ensuing battle but it doesn't last long. The man on the hill has the advantage of position and firepower. He doesn't have anything fancy, but sometimes the old guns are the best. It sounds like a deer rifle. Devlin's shotgun doesn't reach that far up the hill.

I see the logger get up off the road.

I'm discovering the earth isn't so solid. My hands are full of grass and weeds. The way the clumps of mud that my boots are kicking up fall below me and seem to drop straight down keeps me from letting go. The shoulder's washed out by the flood. My fingers claw, but there's nothing but mud. I hear an engine start. There are sounds of broken glass.

My hands slip on the ground.

I watch a pair of cowboy boots come toward me, then I see Quanh's face and an extended arm. His cowboy hat is pushed back on his head. Water drips from its brim. "Give me your hand," he says. I shift my weight. The ground's giving way beneath my feet. My legs are dangling, searching for ground. "Don't be a fool, give me your hand." He's holding the rifle in his left hand. Otherwise all I can see is the wet pavement and Devlin's Explorer backing up Route 20, minus a headlight now, courtesy of Quanh.

I take the cowboy's hand. I don't have any choice.

twenty-nine

WE'RE DRIVING NORTH in the red flatbed Ford. Now he says his name is Lo Binh Quanh, he lives on Hung Vuong Street in the city of Danang, where he is a tailor, a trade he took up after the war—before that he was a policeman—he tells me this in a growing rush, perhaps sensing the unease bordering on panic coming from my side of the truck. I keep reaching for the door handle, which seems to be missing.

"The Cleveland story, the missing nephew—"

"Just stories." His wire-rimmed glasses keep sliding down his nose. He can barely see over the steering wheel. "Did you buy them?"

"The Cleveland part was pretty convincing, yeah."

He seems pleased. He says he's been making trips to the United States—he calls them "hunting trips"—for the last five years. "This is what I've needed," he says. "You, Harding. A partner. *Ride the High Country.* Someone I could trust."

"You trust me now?" I say.

"Somewhat. Devlin coming after you with a shotgun was definitely in your favor."

"And if he hadn't come after me—you'd have shot at me too?"

"It's possible," he says. "Entirely possible." He's driving slowly, staying below the speed limit. His rifle's on the floor to the left of his seat; I assume he still has the derringer. He says his handgun was stolen last night. He asks if I perhaps might have it. I tell him no. He shows me the empty shoulder holster beneath his slicker.

The logger was back in his truck when we left, probably phoning in Quanh's plate. But Quanh's in no hurry. He says he'll take me wherever I want to go—after we stop at King Kwik to look for Zane, then stop at Devlin's, and then maybe go to Leo's. I'm anxious to see Alison, but I'd love to talk to Devlin myself.

"I'm looking for a store," he says, then abruptly changes lanes and heads for the parking lot of a garishly lit strip mall. "This won't take long." He jumps from the truck and walks briskly toward a gun shop. He might be taking an evening stroll. I think he's whistling. I could leave—he's left the rifle—but if that's what I'd wanted I'd have rolled down that hillside. I hate walking out of anything in the middle. And besides, when I do check the gun it's not loaded.

I look around for a phone—my cell phone's still on the back- seat of the Jeep—but nothing except the gun shop's open, and they're closing just as Quanh gets there. He's back in five minutes, rearmed with an air pistol sealed in a plastic bubble, like a squirt gun from Walgreens. We're all set for squirrel season. "It looks real enough," he says, tucking it into his holster.

I ask where he got the rifle, which is a Winchester, bolt action.

"Here," he says, meaning the gun shop. "I haven't had much chance to test it out."

"I'd say it worked fine. Did you follow me home from the airport Sunday night?"

"Umm-hmm."

"Then you must know they broke into my place. Mason, Zane, Lola."

"All I saw was your discussion with Mr. Toth. And your subsequent talk with Mr. Devlin. Which frankly did nothing for your reputation. You know now about Lola? That she's Mason's sister?"

"I discovered that, yeah. Were you in Dry Ridge yesterday?"

"Did I follow you? No."

"What about just now, at the convenience store? The fact I

left one of them half-dead in a bathroom didn't earn me any extra consideration?"

"I was inside, using the bathroom—"

"That's where we were. Outside, in the bathroom."

"I never use those. I always ask the owner to use the store's bathroom."

The store's closed now, the parking lot empty. Quanh circles the lot once to see if anyone's around, then backs the truck up to the bathroom door.

The passenger door doesn't open, so I have to wait for Quanh to jump from the truck. He walks to the store's front door, peering inside. I check the bathroom. The key's still broken off in the lock. There's a stream of water coming from beneath the door. I kick the door but nothing happens. The handle turns but the door won't budge. I hit it with my shoulder and it gives just a little, so I hit it again much harder.

There's a split-second when the scene's frozen and I can see Zane's body floating above me. Then the red water falls down on me even as the door gives way, and I fall inside the bathroom. Zane falls down on top of me. Debris from the bathroom floats by my face.

Quanh, leaning calmly against his truck, watches me stand up.

"Did you do this?" I say.

He frowns. "No, of course not." He walks carefully into the bathroom, barely glancing at Zane. "You tied him how? To the water pipe?" I nod. "He pulled it free, then was unable to stop the water. There's usually a valve—" he reaches around the toilet —"ah, rusted shut. He would have needed a wrench. I assume you had the door locked. He had nowhere to go."

I look at Zane's body. Did I cause this? Why is there so much blood?

"We should go," Quanh says.

He has a stereo—six speakers, CD, and cassette—worth more than the truck itself, with a wired remote running to one of the coffins in the rear of the truck. Whenever we take a hard turn something rattles, jarring the CD changer; the music skips. Quanh's taste runs to the standard repertory: Bach, Handel's *Water Music*. Richie could have put that on his tape for Cassie.

"You know that Leo Minsk bought his home from Marty Devlin?" he says.

"Yeah. I don't think it's real important."

"The summer Kim disappeared was the summer Leo bought this house—you don't think that's important?"

"Not particularly."

"It was very dry that summer, you know. And yet Leo sealed up the cistern, had the drains sealed up and covered with cement that was poured by—guess who?"

"Marty Devlin. Who told you this? There's no cistern at that house. It's two minutes from the lake."

"There are lots of cases like this," he says. "A cistern is a good place to hide someone . . . to keep someone prisoner. A man in Kentucky did that, kept a twelve-year-old boy down there and then said the boy hit his head accidentally, but they found the cistern clean and dry, like a small room—do you know what he said when he finally confessed?" I shake my head. "He said—'you can't understand the perfection.' He was going to bury him down there, fill it with cement like a mausoleum. So he'd stay the same."

"And you think Leo did something like this? With Kim? You don't know Leo very well."

"Maybe for Devlin. I don't know. They both wanted that tape, didn't they?"

"Why didn't you check out Leo's house before now?"

"I just found out about this," he says.

"From who?"

"The Wilders . . . the two boys helped Devlin that summer with his construction business . . . they may have been there at Leo's."

"Which Wilder told you? Zane?" He doesn't answer. "You did talk to him after me, didn't you—"

"No. I told you, I didn't do that." He glances at me. "I worked quite hard on the Cleveland story," he says, abruptly changing the subject. "You're the first one to quiz me on it. I've been looking for these kids for years and years. Whenever I could get a visa. At first my government supported me but now they wish to trade with your country and they'd prefer I not make any trouble. So I never get to stay very long."

"You do this for the sheer humanity of it?"

"I've been shot at, stabbed, spat on, cursed, nearly run over, dunked in water at a county fair. I've had swastikas painted on my truck."

"Have you ever gone to the police?"

"Once or twice. Some are more sympathetic than others."

"I'm not fond of the police either, but sometimes you have to make an exception."

"Two years ago I went to a sheriff in southern Ohio with my credentials and a number of leads. He was in the war, too. It was more a point of difference than a common denominator. I left town with ten stitches. This is why I need someone like you. A partner."

"Didn't one of them—Randolph Scott or Joel McCrea, in *Ride the High Country*—didn't one of them double-cross the other?"

"Oh that. It's just a movie, Harding," he says.

We stop next at the Devlin Pool Co. The main office sits behind a series of aboveground swimming pools. They're closed for the day, of course, but we drive around back, looking for the blue Explorer. The parking lot's empty. We get out and look through the office windows. The same calendar I saw in Lola's trailer is hanging next to a desk. The contents of the desk are on the floor. I try the door. It's unlocked. If there's an alarm it's silent.

The showroom smells of chlorine. I find Devlin's office—also unlocked—and nearly kill myself tripping over the junk on the floor. Someone went through here in a hurry. Devlin thought it was me. What did he think I was looking for?

None of the swimming pool stuff means anything to me. You'd need a forensic accountant to wade through the data. I'm trying to boot up one of the secretary's computers when Quanh motions for me to see what was in Devlin's office closet.

The door is marked MR. DEVLIN—PRIVATE and its lock has

been tampered with. It's the size of a pantry and contains all of Devlin's goodies—the porn he doesn't want to keep at his house. At least it did. Most of the tape shells are empty.

"Why would he keep these things here?" Quanh asks me.

"I don't know his home situation. Maybe he's here more than home. It's like keeping golfing trophies. It's his collection. He likes having it close. What was on that tape you sold Leo?"

"An old film of Cassandra's," he says.

"Pretty Ballerina?"

He shakes his head. "I don't think that exists. This one was called *Personal Breast*. I bought it in Manila for seven dollars. What are those?"

He means the folders hiding behind the tapes. They're full of NAMBLA literature, pictures of little boys—not X-rated, but not exactly normal either.

"This makes no sense," I say. I don't like the casual way they're sitting here.

"He likes kids. He's a pederast."

"They don't usually like *all* kids." I don't think I've ever heard of a bisexual pederast. Whoever broke in here might have planted this stuff. For us to find? Or for the police to find?

Quanh is going through the rest of the things in the closet. I think we should get out of here. I'm picking my way through the showroom, sidestepping the wet spots to avoid leaving footprints, when I see what's hanging on the wall. It's a crude drawing—an "artist's interpretation"—of a series of country-style townhomes surrounding a clubhouse and an Olympic-size pool. It's just as unsettling as the contents of the closet.

Family Living in the Country
Lost Moon Estates
Stillwater, Illinois
A Joint Project of Minsk/Devlin InvestCorp.

This sends me back to Devlin's desk, most of which is on the cheap shag carpeting. I don't see anything to do with Leo or Minsk/Devlin InvestCorp., which I've never heard of. I do find a green envelope with a couple of pictures of Cassie—studio head shots—and what looks like an old 8mm movie. The phone rings on four different desks, startling both of us, and when Devlin's voice comes on the answering machine saying how much he wants to get us in a pool and the caller leaves name and number with a complaint about a filter, Quanh and I get ready to leave. Somehow the disembodied voices have filled the room with ghosts.

Twenty minutes later Quanh is pulling the truck into Leo's long curving driveway.

The guardhouse at the front entrance is empty tonight. Jake's not here. The gate's half-open. Quanh pulls around the circular drive and parks where I always park, well past the house, nearly back to the street, an old habit—I like a little head start if I have to leave in a hurry. Quanh apparently does too.

He takes the Winchester and a handful of shells. I wonder what he's done with the derringer. I leave the 8mm movie I took from Devlin's desk under my seat. The broken passenger door's beginning to get on my nerves. We start walking back to the house. "I bought this truck for two hundred dollars," he says. "It's the first automobile I've ever owned."

"Don't tell me the Danang police ride bicycles."

"No, we had cars, of course. And motorbikes. But I could never afford one on my salary. They stayed in the district garage. And I've driven before—in Singapore, when I went to school, for example. But it's remarkably different owning the vehicle, isn't it?"

"Welcome to America."

The driveway's covered with mud. We walk up a stone sidewalk covered with wet sand, more earthworms. Quanh's wearing gloves, the kind you use to clean toilets. He's not hiding the Winchester.

There's a dull glare to the setting sun. Leo has the porch light on. There are no cars within sight but Leo has a garage around back. I know because of the used Eldorado he keeps trying to sell me.

"Let me go first," I say. Quanh doesn't argue. I ring the bell. No one answers. The door's unlocked, but I don't like going in front doors. I motion to Quanh and we walk around the right side of the house to a rear deck. Here the drapes are slightly open. The house is dark. The backyard has a swimming pool with more leaves and a gazebo that looks like a big wicker chair. A path leads to the dock and the lake. We go around the deck to a patio door that sticks but opens when I lean my shoulder against it.

All I know about the house is Leo's basement theater and the one glimpse I had of his bedroom yesterday. I've never been back here, in what must have been a den or family room when Leo still had a family. There's Ethan Allen–style furniture, a recliner, a wet bar. I turn on a small light with horses on the shade. Leo's den is full of hunting trophies—honorary degrees, awards from Wisconsin businesses; pictures of politicians, athletes, third-rate celebrities, all with one arm wrapped around Leo, the way his arm would be around mine right now were he here, asking me what's wrong, Harding, what's the problem. Come on in, sit down, let's talk this out. We walk into the dark interior of the house, wondering what might be wrong tonight.

There's an ornate curving staircase off the main foyer, the kind you see in Virginia plantations and Brian De Palma movies. A light's on somewhere upstairs. I wave Quanh ahead of me like a minesweeper—he's got the gun. It's always good to keep guns in front of you. "Check the third floor, okay?" I whisper.

"Where are you going?"

"To the bedroom. Don't forget the third floor." There's nothing up there but it gets him off my back for a while. I still don't know how much to trust him.

The house is closed up tight, but a few of the shades are open. There's enough light from the dimming of the day to see my way into the bedroom. It's warm and stuffy, like the other rooms. I have to turn on a small light over the dresser to see the numbers on the wall safe.

Inside I find a lot of cash, a large bulky envelope, some insurance papers, and a videotape. The tape's not marked. I'm coming up with quite a film library. I look through the papers; there's no mention of Devlin or any joint business. I leave the cash and take the envelope, put the tape in my pocket, wipe my prints off the dial, and close the safe. I turn on the hall light long enough to make sure I haven't tracked any mud from the driveway. I look out the bedroom window. It's silent and dark.

Quanh's on the third floor. I go downstairs to the foyer and then find the basement steps. At least I can turn on the lights down here. I don't have gloves; I don't have a handkerchief. I wipe the light switch with the tail of my shirt. The basement's cooler and familiar ground. I let myself into the projection room of the Mindy Minsk Theater. The projection room's like a bunker. It takes me a minute to figure out Leo's controls. There's a grainy western in the VCR, an old Republic serial that starts up in slow motion, six-guns blazing in Leo's AC-3 digital sound before I can eject the tape. Good thing Leo's had the place soundproofed. Why, I don't know. The nearest neighbor's a half mile away. *Pretty Ballerina* plays to an empty house. I watch through the small projection window in Leo's basement wall.

I think it is Cassie; the next sequence—after the one with the two guys I watched at Richie's—shows her without so much makeup, in a story where she's playing a teenager in jogging shorts and T-shirt, on a running track. There are other runners of both sexes and lots of lustful glances while the baton's being passed and then people stop running. Everyone's very sweaty. The action shifts to the infield grass. Cassie's on her knees.

I jump ahead a bit. The film's poorly dubbed, but there's nothing here worth getting killed over. I do find myself watching Cassie in a different way, now that I know she was eighteen and legal. It's as good as porn gets—Cassie was a good actress even then. She's very sexy. She makes good eye contact. But something's lost, all right. The taboo's gone.

The 8mm film we found at Devlin's is still in the truck, but there's no equipment here that would play it anyway. I eject the tape and turn everything off. When I get to the basement steps there are noises overhead, toward the front of the house. I go up the steps and through the foyer and then upstairs to the second floor. I don't see Quanh anywhere, but there's a light on in one of the rooms, an extra bedroom, the kind that's never used, filled with extra furniture, a bed, thick blue carpeting. A cedar chest is open beneath the light like buried treasure. Quanh's sitting on the bed with what look like scrapbooks.

"Find anything?" he says, not looking up.

"No. The house is empty. What's that?"

"Leo's collections."

"What?"

"His scrapbooks. I think maybe Leo helped," he says to me.

"What are you talking about—"

"Look at this. Like the one at Devlin's."

The scrapbook smells like cedar. He's holding it on his lap like a child with an oversized storybook. There's a feverish excitement in his eyes. I can see what he sees, but I'm not sure we're looking at the same thing.

The first few pages are reviews and show programs from different high schools, junior high schools—*Music Man, Bye Bye Birdie*. And *Snow White* is here too, the same program that was in Cassie's shoe box, but this time I notice something else. You have to hunt to find it. It's far below a picture of the band.

The producers wish to acknowledge the many generous donations made by the Leo Minsk Music Stores.

"So what?" I say.

Quanh tears a page from the scrapbook. "I didn't see a garage when we came in."

"It's around back. Why?"

"I might need some tools . . . did you call the police yet?"

"No, the phones are out."

"Then don't."

"Quanh, I don't know what's going through your mind but if you think Leo's connected to Kim's disappearance—"

"Just don't call anyone. Leave it. Okay?"

"I'm heading back, Quanh."

"Go." He waves me off. And he hurries ahead of me, down the steps and out the door.

I go out the back door. The rain's stopped. The moon's out, a bright contrast to the dark clouds streaming past it. Quanh is opening the coffins on the pickup. He takes out a shovel, a pick, something that looks like a posthole digger, drags them all to a corner of the house, then starts measuring the distance from the gutter spouts on the corners of the house.

"What are you looking for?"

"A cistern," he says. "That's where he buried him, I bet—"

"There's no cistern here, Quanh. The fucking lake's two minutes away."

The ground's like soft flesh. Quanh digs furiously, one spot, then another. It's raining again, but Quanh doesn't notice. This is the Quanh Devlin described, the one who burst into his office.

"They wouldn't have a cistern," I tell him again.

"Then I'll dig up the pool," he says. "You don't have to stay. Go."

I stop at the red pickup first, to get the 8mm tape. I take the long way around the house to the Eldorado. It runs rough but it starts. I sit for a minute trying to retrace my steps through the house, remembering what I might have touched.

I pull the Eldorado onto the back drive. My headlights catch Quanh near Leo's ancient pool, the cracked stone, the ivy and moss, his shovel raised, a spot of gleaming metal in the mud. He's standing in one of the holes like a gravedigger. When he looks my way his wire-rimmed glasses reflect the light, shining brighter than the moon. I put the car in reverse, spin the wheels in the rain. Then I drive slowly around the house and pull onto the street without lights or wipers, as though that would let me slip through the night.

thirty

THE GALLERY where I told Alison to take Cassie is south of Milwaukee. It's run by a friend of hers named Felicia and was the safest spot I could think of on a moment's notice. The neighborhood's full of bars and restaurants open late and though the local papers have begun to warn about gang activity, that's the least of my worries tonight. I could have used a posse of Disciple Kings back there on the ridge.

I park a block away and walk the wrong way to see who follows me. The rain's let up and the hot humid air has brought people out of their homes, filling the bars. It's just past ten o'clock.

The 4Runner's parked around back. Its left front tire looks flat. Another car with a slow leak. The gallery's closed, but Felicia responds to my knock on the back door.

"It's you," she says, peering through the chain. Felicia and I don't get along. Then Alison appears behind her—"Thank God," she says, pulling me in. Felicia bolts the door.

"Are you okay?" I say.

Alison nods. "Just a little worried. Everything's quiet here."

"And Cassie?"

"She's a lush," Felicia says on the way to her office. "And a fashion disaster."

"She's been drinking," Alison says.

"That's not unusual. What else?"

"She wants to talk."

• • •

But before I see Cassie I want to talk to Reese. I thought of calling Tommy, but this is Reese's territory. I use the phone in Felicia's office—she's standing as close to me as the gas station clerk. She's grumpier than him but smells a whole lot better.

I call the number Reese gave me, start to leave a message on his machine, but he picks up. "Where are you?" he says. I give him the gallery address. I tell him about Devlin and the logger and that he'll find Cassie's rental car on the ridge.

"But she's not involved," I say. "Not directly."

"Where is she?"

I hesitate. "At her hotel, I guess."

"She needs to come in."

"I know . . ."

"From what happened on that ridge . . . you're saying Devlin's trying to kill you?"

"I don't know."

"But he was coming after you . . . are you sure Quanh wasn't shooting at you too?"

"I didn't read it that way. I might be wrong." I'm debating whether to mention King Kwik when Reese asks if I know where Quanh is right now.

"No, why?"

"Zane Wilder's body was discovered about an hour ago. We've got witnesses who put him there. . . . You don't know where he is?"

"No."

"Do you have any idea where Devlin might have gone?"

"No. He's in a blue Explorer, he's armed with a shotgun."

"Well, we'll pick him up. There's been a warrant out for his arrest since six o'clock. The Dry Ridge police found his prints all over the late Mason Wilder. This was in his sister's trailer. And the sister's disappeared. . . ."

"How did Zane die?"

"Gunshot, just a .32, made to look like a drowning."

A .32, like Quanh's gun. Which he says he lost. So much for dumb suburban cops. They put this together fast.

"How soon can you get to the station? So we can sort this all out?"

"About an hour, I guess."

"Do you want a squad car to pick you up?"

"No, I can get there."

"And you're where again?"

I give him the gallery's address. He's not familiar with the area. I don't think Reese does much gallery hopping.

"I'm home, so let's say an hour and a half," he says. "Lake County Police. If you need help call me back."

"Do you think Devlin's working with Quanh?"

"Actually, Harding . . . I don't know. Somebody *was* seen with Quanh earlier tonight. But it wasn't Devlin. To tell you the truth, the description sounded like you. Two men, riding in a red pickup."

"Yeah?"

"Yeah."

There's a short pause.

"So if you've got anything to say . . . like maybe where Quanh is right now—"

"I didn't do anything. I sure as hell didn't kill anybody."

"Were you with him earlier tonight?"

There's another pause, this one much longer.

"Why don't we talk about it when I get there," I say finally.

"It would help if you could give me something," Reese says, "a good-faith gesture, something to take to my captain so he doesn't start running your prints along with Quanh's—"

The pause this time is very short.

"You'll find Quanh at Leo Minsk's house in Lake Geneva." I give up the address too. "He's armed with a rifle. And a shovel."

"Good. Thanks."

"Don't mention it. I didn't do anything, Reese."

"You're coming in though, right, Harding?"

"Yeah, Reese. I'm coming in."

The studio is a collection of shadows. Odd-shaped partitions with photos from an upcoming show divide the room like a maze. Cassie's sitting at the back, near a small broom closet where Alison and I spent a memorable evening a couple months ago, escaping a very dull fund-raiser. She's sitting on a folding chair, holding an ashtray and a glass.

I check the locks on the other doors and go into the front gallery. The current show, "Iconography & Place in Self-Expression," is a collection of amateur photos downloaded from the Net—mostly naked people showing off their butts, but the curator isn't interested in the bodies, just the rooms they're posing in, especially the backgrounds—ashtrays, couches, the artless way a book or glass sits by the bed. The catalog has a ten-page treatise on headboards. Alison finds me by the windows. She slips her hands around my waist and presses close.

"What happened to you tonight?" Alison says.

"A little car trouble." I tell her about Devlin and Quanh and Zane. "It turns out Quanh's the one who's been trailing us in the red truck, not Toth."

"You talked with him?"

"He saved my life."

"Really? He's one of the good guys?"

"Could be."

"You don't sound convinced."

"I'm not. He keeps changing his story. And he's a little obsessed." I describe the scene at the Lake Geneva house. I tell her what Reese just told me. And I describe the Devlin Pool Co. and what we found there. To be consistent the gallery should be showing van Dongen or Dufy. The wild beasts. Not headboards.

"Devlin sounds a little obsessed too," Alison says. "Does he know Cassie?"

"That's what we need to find out."

She barely looks up when we enter the room. She's dressed as she was at the motel—jeans and a shirt—but she's been drinking and her eyes are bloodshot, her mascara smeared. It's only been a couple of hours; the motel's only ten miles away. She's traveled a long way in a very short time.

"We've got a few minutes," I tell her. "The police would like to talk with us. A detective named Reese is going to meet us at the station."

Cassie frowns at this.

"He's okay, he knows what's going on. I spoke with him yesterday and again just now."

"What do the police want with me?" Cassie says.

"Remember the story you told me, about Asian boys disappearing all over the Midwest?" She nods. "And remember the Vietnamese, Quanh, I mentioned at the motel? Well, Quanh told me the same story. He believes it. And according to him, he's been looking for the kidnappers for years now."

"The police think he killed Zane Wilder," Alison tells her.

"Zane's dead?"

"Before tonight I wouldn't have believed it but after seeing Quanh with his posthole digger in the rain—"

"What?" Cassie says.

"Nothing. The other guy we talked about, Marty Devlin, is also a suspect, for killing Mason. At this point the best thing we can do is go to the police. They're going to pick up Quanh and Devlin. With everybody there maybe we can straighten it out." I don't mention that I'm a suspect too. When you've been in prison it's the last thing you feel like telling someone.

"Why would Devlin kill them?" Cassie says.

"I'm not sure he did. I'm not sure of anything except I don't trust either one, Devlin or Quanh, at this point."

"Since you asked me at the motel, I've been thinking," she says. "And I remember somebody we called the pool man. If it's the guy I'm thinking of, he came to a couple of our recitals. Our dance pageants."

"When?"

"That summer. And the next."

"You met how? With him coming around your house?"

"Mason introduced us," she says. "Along with the others . . ."

The others included a De Paul sophomore who seduced her in the high school cafeteria; Bob, a photographer on the Gold Coast; an airline pilot introduced by a stewardess friend; even, incredibly, the father of one of her best friends in high school, who would pick them up after school in his car, with Cassie sitting in the middle hoping her friend wouldn't notice.

"I don't understand," Alison says. "Mason introduced you to these men? He knew airline pilots and photographers?"

"No . . . other men at the church."

"Arthur Lee?"

She nods.

Arthur Lee was then forty-four; their affair had lasted six months and then after it ended he still called, still occasionally took her to lunch, gave her jewelry, once even a Nikon camera that she took back to school after lunch, clutched in a brown paper bag.

"He took me to lunch at Barney's Market Club, in downtown Chicago . . . I was fifteen, but they served me anyway. I drank Shirley Temples with real gin. I got drunk really fast."

"That's why he took you there?"

"No, it was the drive, he liked the fact it took so long—"

"Jesus," Alison says, seeing the picture before I do.

"That's why I understood about Lori and Kim. Nobody else got it. She was a couple years older and girls didn't do that, but I think he was just *nice* to her. Less threatening than the men she saw around her . . . the men I was going out with . . ."

I can hear Felicia moving around upstairs. I'm glad she's left us alone. Sitting in this gallery of exhibits and statues is like sitting in a graveyard. The music she's playing is some sort of New Age jazz, Oregon or Pat Metheny.

Wichi-tai-to

The gallery has several old Super-8 projectors they use for multimedia. I remember the movie I found in Devlin's closet. Alison sets it up while Cassie uses the bathroom. She comes back with coffee from Felicia's little kitchen. She stands, watching. I sit on a folding chair that might be part of some exhibit. It's uncomfortable enough. Alison sits on the floor against the wall.

The image dances with light, overexposure—it's an old home movie. A small girl is dressed like a ballerina, with a white skirt and shoes and a small tiara on her black hair. The only thing connecting her to the Cassie in this room is the candy-colored nail polish she's wearing. She's dancing in a small room; it takes me a minute to recognize the living room from the farmhouse, here crowded with furniture. The girl dances the entire time. Only once does the cameraman turn around and pan the room, in a shaky motion, with the light seeping in to show the five adults sitting in high-backed chairs pulled from the dining room, protesting, no, don't take our picture, laughing, their hands raised . . .

left to right: Daddy, Reverend Miner, Dr. Lee, the pool man, Mason, Kim

I recognize Lee from his photos. Miner looks younger, less gaunt. Kim looks bored. "The pool man"—Devlin—looks uncomfortable, out of place, his chair a little farther away from the others —or am I reading too much into a simple home movie? Ellis is smiling proudly, watching his daughter.

"My mother took this," Cassie says, her eyes moist. "Where did you find it?"

"Devlin had it. He's got a huge collection of your stuff."

"About to be worthless," Alison says. "Which might make him a little angry . . ."

"You could always tell when my mother took the movies," Cassie says. "By how the camera shakes . . ." She turns to Alison. "Do you still have your parents?" It's a funny way of putting it. But it keeps death out of the equation.

"My mom's gone," Alison says. "My dad's alive and kicking, chasing women around Florida."

"What did it feel like when your mother died?"

"I missed her," Alison says. "Why?"

"The first time Harding and I talked we were outside my house. I asked him what made him afraid—"

"What'd he say?" Alison says, curious.

"He didn't really answer."

"I thought so," says Alison.

"I said nothing made me afraid and I meant it, sort of— nothing *violent* makes me afraid, nothing like robbers or rapists or getting shot—certainly nothing like scary movies—because after that day it seemed impossible to be frightened by anything else. What could compare? And I've never blocked it out. If I even just see a farmhouse or smell something like my mother's cooking —it's like I'm there again, in the shelter, hiding, with all hell breaking loose over my head and someone in my family yelling for me to run and then the metal door closing . . ."

"Jesus," Alison says. She never read the news reports. This is all new, and firsthand. "But there's nothing wrong with being afraid. It's part of nature—fight or flight."

"Your problem is you forget the flight part," I tell Alison.

"What makes you afraid?" Cassie asks Alison.

"I guess the first thing that comes to mind is my father. If something happened to him. If I couldn't help him."

Cassie nods. "I have trouble remembering my father," she says. "I remember how he was when I was little and I remember the way he looked in the news photos after the murders and the way he was described in the articles and I can't make the two fit together. I lost him somehow."

"You lost two families," I say. "You've been orphaned twice."

"I know. And it sounds selfish but that was almost the worst thing that happened to me that day. Leaving me alone, not just physically . . . even my memories were stolen. I don't think I'd feel so alone if I could think back to those years with something—*one thing*—to hold on to. That's what frightens me now. Going on like this, without finding Kim, having nothing to remember that doesn't cause me pain."

It occurs to me that being truly fearless is having nothing to care about. It's been a while since I've felt that way . . . I remember traveling on a prison bus through southern Indiana after my trial, crossing the Ohio River west of Cincinnati on a high bridge that seemed to be swaying in the air, and thinking, crash or not, I don't much care. Prison was eighteen months. A year after I got out I met Alison.

"There's someone outside," Felicia says, appearing suddenly. "I think he said his name's Toad or Tooth—"

"Leonard Toth," I say. "I didn't hear the bell ring."

"After hours the bell only rings upstairs. He says he wants to talk to Harding, and Cassie . . . I told him you weren't here, but I don't think he believed me."

"I'll talk to him," I tell her.

"How did he find us?" Alison says, getting to her feet.

"One of us must have left a trail of crumbs." I tell Cassie why Toth is probably here—to get her to cancel her announcement about her age. She nods. It doesn't seem like a high-priority item.

"But I should stop at the convention, for a minute anyway, or I won't get paid," she says. "And I'm broke."

Toth is outside the front door, swinging his arms as though trying to warm up. It must be nearly eighty. Maybe he's doing calisthenics. He's wearing a navy blue windbreaker with some sort of union symbol on the back and pleated pants. Dockers maybe. I don't invite him in.

"Which one of us did you follow, Leonard?" I say, joining him on the sidewalk. He's got a calfskin briefcase that looks like it doesn't get much use. Maybe it's supposed to impress me.

"Your girlfriend," he says. "Tell her she telegraphs her left turns."

"And you waited for me?"

"I knew Alison wouldn't go anywhere without you. And to tell you the truth, she makes me a little nervous, all that jujitsu shit. Cassie's here, right?"

"What do you want, Leonard?" I say, ignoring the question.

"Just an hour of your time. Her time." The sky's very dark but Leonard reaches into his jacket pocket for aviator shades, light blue. "If she would just come up to the convention, show she's not gonna make that announcement—"

"I thought you wanted her *not* to show up?"

"I know, but I think it's better if she shows up and says something positive—it's to her advantage really, Harding. To wrap this up, once and for all. If I don't take something concrete back to my guys they'll just send somebody else around—"

"And you won't get paid."

He shuffles his feet. "Well, there's that to consider, yeah."

"This is really the last thing on her mind right now, Leonard."

"So she is here?"

"If you followed Alison you already know the answer to that."

"Just ask her, will ya? Listen, if she says no I'll be on my way. Okay? Fair enough?"

"We're on our way to the Lake County police, Leonard. They know we're coming."

"Fine, great. I'm not gonna kidnap her. Here, I wrote something she could say. Just as a for instance . . ."

. . . glad to be here tonight with so many of my fans, I'm happy to say I may be making more movies soon. . . . Anyone here with some of my earlier work, I'm afraid I can't sign those things, but I do want to say I'm sorry if anyone was hurt by my age problem. . . . When you're that young—sixteen—you make lots of bad decisions. . . .

"I'll show it to her," I tell him. "Give me a minute."

"Sure. I'm not going anywhere. Luther took my car."

"Let's say she's here, and she's agreeable—what's in it for her, Leonard?"

He sighs. "Now you're her manager? I could go maybe a grand. Maybe."

"It's pretty late. If she was here she'd be awfully tired—"

"All right. Two grand."

"They must be paying you a lot."

"Why else would I be here in fucking Milwaukee in the middle of the night?"

I leave Leonard outside, explain things to Cassie and Alison.

"But don't do it unless you want to."

"Like I said, I could use the money," she says. "But don't we have to go to the police?"

"The convention's on the way to the police station. You wouldn't have to stay long, would you?" She shakes her head.

"You decided not to make the announcement?" Alison says.

Cassie nods. "Maybe another time. In L.A."

"Don't tell Leonard that," I say. "He thinks this is closure."

Before we leave I call Tommy Mullaney at his house on the South Side. I ask him to meet me at the Lake County police station. "That's a ninety-minute drive from here, minimum," he says. "Two hours is more like it, since I'm sitting here in my underwear. You want to tell me why?"

I tell him about the shooting on the ridge, that I'm with Cassie, that I'd rather go into the police station with Tommy. "Oh yeah, I command a great deal of respect around there," he says. But I can tell he's a little flattered, and nobody likes playing Godfather more than Tommy. "I'll try for ninety minutes," he says.

thirty-one

THE 4RUNNER'S front tire is shot. We take Leo's silver blue Eldorado, the oil light blinking on the dash like DefCon Five at SAC headquarters—the damn car runs through a quart just backing down the drive—Leonard beside me in the front, Alison and Cassie in the back. The Eldorado's reconditioned automatic five-speed hesitates, grunts and groans. It's raining again and Leonard hates the lightning enough to let me drive. His hands grip the soft calfskin briefcase doing a lap dance on his Dockers. The air conditioner stinks of mildew, so we leave it off, but with the windows closed the inside air turns into a thick sweaty perfume. It's raining hard. And the closer we get to the sheriff's office, the more Leonard sweats; drops of salty rain filling the anxious furrows above his brow. Leo's genuine original AM radio keeps us company through the storm. Leo's dashboard Jesus blesses us from a superglued perch above the radar detector.

We're listening to the White Sox–Brewers game. Alison's doing the navigating, jumping out to ask directions, scaring the locals with her black poncho and heavy black linesmen's boots.

"You better turn left, Harding. That underpass looks flooded."

"I know, I know. The ducks are a good clue."

We hit I-94 going south just as the weatherman breaks into the game with a special storm bulletin.

"How much rain did he say?" Leonard says nervously. "I've got a flight to L.A. later, I hate to fly in a storm."

"He wouldn't commit to a precise figure," Alison says. "And he sounded very stern, never a good sign in weather forecasting."

"Oh, God," Leonard says. "This car isn't like your 4Runner, Harding. Be careful. I wouldn't push the envelope."

"I wouldn't *lick* the envelope," Alison says from the backseat. "I wouldn't *use* the goddamn envelope."

Cassie sits quietly behind me. Whenever I turn to see her she's staring out the window. The speech Leonard wrote for her is still in her right hand.

"Should I call her Cassandra? Or Kalani?" Leonard whispers to me.

"She likes Cassie."

"This is very nice of you, Cassie, doing this tonight," Leonard says to her, turning in his seat. "I understand it's been a very trying time for you."

Cassie nods.

"I just want you to know," Leonard says, "whatever your age was, you were one hell of a performer. The best, really. And I'm going back—I'm showing my age here—but I'm going back to the Kay Parker, Vanessa Del Rio days. Am I right, Harding?"

I nod. I can't tell if it's in bad taste to tell a porn star how great she is, or impolite not to.

We're just south of the Wisconsin border, near Zion, having a grand old time—the game's over, the radio's playing eighties hits —the Go-Go's "Vacation," Bowie's "China Girl"—when a Lake County squad car pulls into the lane behind us. Cops make me nervous. They make Leonard nervous too. "Keep it under forty, why doncha," he says to me. The squad car flashes its brights and I start to slow down and pull over, but he just wants to pass. When he's far ahead of us Leonard relaxes. He winds down his window. He takes several deep breaths. Then he leans over and whispers in my ear, "Take a right up there." His breath smells like onions.

"No, we keep going straight for another ten miles," I say, keeping my eyes on the road like a responsible driver. I don't see what's happening. Leonard has to jam his .38 into my ribs to get me to notice it.

"What in hell are you doing, Leonard?" I say, a little surprised. I'm more annoyed than alarmed. "I told you, the police know we're coming. They know you're with us." This of course isn't exactly true.

"Well, we'll be a little delayed then. You can call them in a few minutes and tell them you had car trouble. Another flat tire maybe."

Alison sees what's going on, but Leonard warns her off. Now I'm beginning to get alarmed. I'm a slow starter in the alarm department.

"Easy now, everybody," Leonard says.

"What's going on?" Cassie says.

"Prince Charming here turned out to be a toad after all," Alison says.

"Just shut up, everybody. Harding, just be the smart guy I know you can be, nobody's gonna get hurt. Just don't miss the fuckin' turn."

We leave the main highway, make two more turns, then stop at a shuttered fruit stand that sits at the far end of a rundown farm, facing an intersection of narrow roads more like rows in a cornfield. Devlin's blue Explorer is parked beneath a large elm. Its lights are off. Leonard asks me if there are any guns in the Eldorado. I tell him no, it's not my car. "That's what I thought," he says. He checks the glove compartment and underneath the seats and tells Alison to sit tight, don't try to run, nothing bad's gonna happen. I always hate it when someone tells me that. She doesn't answer.

Leonard and I get out of the car.

"This is basically a communications problem," Leonard says, as we walk to the front of the fruit stand. It's covered with peeling logos for soft drinks, chewing tobacco, banners for old county fairs. The ground is muddy. A rusting metal Coke sign in the shape of a bottlecap is nailed to the front door. I bet it's a collectible.

"We just need to talk," he says.

"We could have talked in the gallery, without ruining my shoes."

"I have to make sure the answers I get are right. Who have you talked to, about Quanh and the Lost Moon stuff?"

"You mean the mailings? Well, let's see. Devlin knows.

Friends of his. A county cop I talked to knows—by the way, he also knows we're together tonight—"

"What about Mullaney."

"Sure, Tommy knows. So do a dozen other guys. Maybe more." I'm not sure what they're supposed to know, but I figure the more people, the better. "It's not just the three of us, that's for sure."

"Has Quanh talked to the cops at all?"

I shrug. "He could have. He told me about other cities where he's gone to the cops and they'd helped him out."

"Why would they help a gook ex-con?"

"I don't know. Spirit of international brotherhood, maybe?"

It starts raining harder. The front awning's made of corrugated tin. It sounds like we're standing in a coffee can.

"Here he is." Leonard pokes me in the side with the .38. The red pickup is coming across the marshy cornfield, lights off. "We're gonna switch cars. You and me in the Eldorado. The others in the pickup." Leonard's voice changes just a tad. "Just a little drive," he says. Any doubts I had about why we'd been brought out here disappear. No one's leaving but Leonard. And whoever he's working with. . . .

Because it's not Quanh driving the pickup, it's Luther Toth.

Alison and Cassie are told to get out of the Eldorado. Leonard confers with his brother, who's holding what looks like Quanh's rifle. And wearing what looks like Devlin's green slicker. I have just a second to talk to Alison.

"What do we do?" she says. There's no fear in her eyes.

"If you get a chance, take it. This isn't going well. But wait for your spot. Be smart."

"Why start now?" she says.

There's a heavy black tarp covering the bed of the pickup, vague podlike shapes underneath. Cassie doesn't look frightened, just a little numb. They're made to climb into the cab of the pickup, Cassie in the middle, Alison next to the jammed passenger door. Leonard and I return to the car. The pickup waits for us to lead. We head west, rain beating down on the Eldorado's roof. It feels like it's been raining forever.

thirty-two

WE'RE GOING TO STILLWATER. The trip takes longer than it did Sunday morning; I don't have Cassie's bravado, her air bags, her blood-alcohol level. The pickup's headlights are in my rearview mirror. Leonard checks his directions every two minutes. He's taking us a different way than I'm used to.

He's quiet at first, then he opens up a little. The fact that he's willing to talk is a bad sign. It doesn't much matter now what I know or don't know. I'm sure he's planning to kill us.

"This is really all Quanh's fault," Leonard says. "And yours. I warned you not to get involved. I don't generally issue a warning like that. You shouldn't have ignored it."

"I didn't know how special it was." I'm remembering the squad car that passed us before. Maybe he called in our plates. Maybe Reese heard the call. It doesn't seem very likely. "Why is it Quanh's fault exactly?"

"If he hadn't come back and started sending all those Lost Moon vacation scams and running ads and selling movies—I mean, everything was forgotten, nobody cared anymore. But he wouldn't leave it alone . . ."

"Quanh sent the flyers—"

"Let me fill you in," he says. "Quanh's some kind of great-uncle of Kim Moon's. Miner traced him years ago through the Red Cross, sent him letters about Ellis and the family, sent him the shoe boxes. He's been in jail for years. Last spring he showed up in the U.S., started sending the flyers to anyone connected to the disappearance, hoping to stir up some trouble. Which he did."

I keep watching the road, hoping for a squad car, but there's almost no traffic. "How were you connected to Kim Moon?"

"I didn't grab him if that's what you think. I was still a cop then, in Lake County. I was the one that interviewed Ellis. Not the only one, but I was the guy who checked his alibi for that day. When I found it didn't wash I arranged for Ellis to start mailing me a check once a week."

"Bullshit. He didn't have that kind of money—"

"You know how it's done, Harding. You don't ask for more than they can pay—you just keep them paying. I was stringing along five or six guys like Ellis. It was tough making ends meet on a cop's salary."

I turned to Leonard. "You're saying Ellis killed Kim?"

"I'm saying Ellis drove down to see Kim, surprise him or something. To talk with him about what he was doing with Lori Wilder. I'm saying Ellis is the one he left the bus to see."

"And then what happened?"

"Lori was on the bus too . . . he wasn't real clear about this part, I think he saw them in bed together and then followed the bus—whatever happened, Lori never saw him, it was just Kim and Ellis. They had an argument, tempers flared, you know the story. Kim ran. He ended up at the bottom of a cave. Ellis wanted to cover it up. Even if it was an accident—which nobody really knows the answer to—he was sure they'd take his other kids away."

I can tell where this is headed. "Why would all this bother you, Leonard? Unless you were involved more than you say—I mean, you don't exactly have a cop's pension to worry about."

"Two years later I went to collect from Ellis. Only Ellis was having an attack of conscience. He was going to tell what happened. I didn't think that was such a good idea. I liked the fifty bucks he sent me every week. It was beer money."

"So you killed the Moon family? Over a fifty-dollar payment?"

"I've killed guys for less," he says. "I've killed guys for nothing. . . . Take a right up there," he says, grabbing my arm. "Put on your blinker."

I do. Luther follows me when I turn.

"And I didn't go there to kill anybody. I didn't even pull my gun out first." He sighs. "Things have a way of escalating."

"How'd you get away with it?" I say.

"I had friends."

"You knew about Kalani, where she was all this time, and never did anything about it?"

"She didn't know nothing, and doing something about her was riskier than just letting it sit, especially since once she hit the porn circuit she had a few run-ins with the law out in California. A friend of mine on the force had enough on her to get his own regular payment, probably worth a lot more than fifty bucks—she's an incredible fuck, you know, Harding? She's a screamer, Harding, she was screaming that day and I've heard her scream a couple of other times, courtesy of this friend of mine."

"Why didn't she recognize you or know your name?"

"I didn't do her. I watched."

"And your brother?"

"Luther doesn't know anything about this." He emphasizes the word *this* with a wave of his hand, as though he meant the Eldorado or the night air. "Luther thinks I work for corporate security."

"That's what I tell people I do, Leonard."

"Well, we're both crooks then. And killers."

"It's not quite the same thing, Leonard. Killing children?"

"You weren't in the war, Harding. You weren't in-country. The children would kill you just as fast as the soldiers. You don't leave children behind. No loose ends. Besides, I was higher than a fucking kite at the time, I can't remember half of it, which is probably why most of my shots hit the furniture, but I do remember fighting Ellis for his gun and then thinking, Jesus, now I'll have to finish this. There was no question about what I had to do after that first shot. I didn't think twice."

I can tell where we are now. The road looks familiar and

when we drive through a tiny main street, past dark feed stores and gas stations, I see a sign for Gaines Road, the same road Cassie's farmhouse is on.

"What did Ellis do with Kim."

"He says he hit him once and the kid fell and he panicked and dumped the body down a cave, but who knows? I think he'd been drinking."

"What cave?"

"What difference does it make?"

"I'm just curious—"

"By the church down there. On Dry Ridge. But you won't find nothing, the cave narrows down and drops—he went back there himself a dozen times, looking. He couldn't remember the exact spot. He was stoned a lot then too."

We pass the Moons' farmhouse, and then the fields turn to woods; we end up on a small road I assume is a driveway, leading back to a neighboring farmhouse. But it dead-ends at a broken-down fence. We're about a half-mile from Cassie's house. The pickup pulls in behind us. Luther, Alison, and Cassie get out of the truck. "Time to go," Leonard says.

We start walking.

Leonard's a city kid, like me, but he's a professional—he brought a good flashlight, wide enough to keep us in clear sight, and he keeps us bunched together, in single file. The top of the ridge is a graveyard. We come over the hillside with the sky crashing low overhead, enough noise to wake the dead, if any are sleeping. The Stillwater Cemetery dates from the Civil War—I know this from the bronze plate I trip over in the grass. Half the markers are pushed over.

The ground slopes away from the road, past a ragged fence to a barn and a rushing creek. The land's divided by barbed wire strung between locust poles. We cross a creek and slog through enough mud for five hundred facials. There's no moon, only Toth's flashlight and the flashes of lightning to guide us.

At the foot of the hill the woods become thicker.

The ground is covered with needles and pine cones and a wet mulch that sticks to my shoes. It smells like a jungle. There's another creek—this one's too wide to jump but there's a bridge made from old telephone poles. It leads to the cabin I saw Sunday.

Leonard runs his flashlight over the windows, which are covered with brown paper. There are footprints, some of them fairly fresh, leading to the cabin. Leonard's taken a very large circle; I'm not sure why.

"Inside," Leonard says. Cassie goes first. Luther waits outside. There's one large room, about the size of a two-car garage. It's much too clean for a deserted cabin. Someone's been living here. At first I think it must have been Mason, but when Toth lights a Coleman lantern I can see an ashtray filled with brown cigarettes. The wide-plank flooring has six new marks, spaced to the size of a one-man pup tent.

"Welcome to the home of Mr. Quanh," Toth says.

Leonard tells Alison and Cassie to sit down against the far wall. There's no other door, just the front window. He runs his flashlight once around the room. A mouse scurries into a corner hole. "This is very cozy," Alison says.

Just then Luther sticks his head inside the door.

"You'd better see this," he says to his brother. Leonard peers outside. I can see what's bothering them—a single pair of headlights on the long driveway leading to the farmhouse. I hear Leonard flip the safety off on his gun. "Whatever happens, don't be stupid, Harding," he says. I can't identify the car. It's rocking side to side a little from the bumps in the road.

"Stay with the girls," Leonard tells his brother, then pushes me outside and closes the door. "I want you where I can see you. My brother isn't used to this shit."

"So let me guess," I say, trying to distract him. "You're going to make sure everything stays pinned on Ellis by getting rid of Quanh? Why involve the rest of us?"

"I didn't know what you knew," he says, fumbling in his pocket for extra bullets. "I still don't. I guess it doesn't much matter now."

"You can still let Alison and Cassie go . . . they haven't heard any of this. They don't know anything."

"It's too late for that," he says.

The headlights creep closer.

Alison steps out onto the small front porch. Leonard sees her, but he's walking away, toward the driveway. Luther is standing next to her. He must be a foot taller. He looks like a funeral director. He says something to her and laughs. She bends over and carefully reties the laces on her leather boots.

I think the car creeping slowly down the gravel path is a police car.

"What I do with these girls depends entirely on you, Harding," Leonard says. "So you be on your best behavior."

The car stops about fifty yards away. It is a squad car. A moveable spot joins the brights lighting up the stage. Reese gets out and stands behind his opened door. He's holding a gun. I've never been so glad to see a cop.

The feeling lasts a good ten seconds.

"I don't like this, Leonard," Reese says to Toth. "This is getting too messy."

"It will work," Leonard says.

"Where's Cassie?"

"Inside," says Leonard, pointing with his pistol.

"And the others?"

"Quanh and Devlin are tied up in the truck."

"You've got Quanh's gun?"

"Three guns—a rifle, and a derringer too. We can be creative. Plus we found a gun at Devlin's."

"What about Harding?"

"He wasn't armed."

"All right," Reese says, still standing behind the door of his squad car. "There are warrants out already for Quanh and Devlin . . . we can add Harding's name to that. But I don't know. . . ."

"I tell you, this will work," Leonard says. "We can make Quanh and Harding good for the Wilders. We can say Harding's been helping Quanh, and they went after the Wilders for killing the Moons. And then Devlin killed Cassie and these two before killing himself."

"Like I said, it's too messy."

"It would be," Leonard says, "if we didn't have the law on our side. You're a cop, Reese. You can fix it."

I think at this point both Toth and Reese are trying to compute who needs the other more.

Looking back on it, I don't think Leonard started it. . . . He needed Reese alive, at least long enough to get him out of this. Next month he might've paid Reese a late-night visit. But right now Reese has his uses, and so I'm sure Leonard's upset when Reese adds things up differently and realizes it would be easier just to pin everything on both Toths. Maybe he was planning to do that all along.

He leans into the car and then steps out, holding a revolver with that confident air cops have even when they're outgunned. He fires once at Leonard, catching him in the shoulder. It's not a good shot; not a kill shot. Reese probably hasn't fired his weapon once in his career. He takes two steps forward. Leonard Toth doesn't let him take another.

Leonard fires twice. He's a good shot. His job demands it. Reese hits the gravel hard. There's a bewildered look on his face, as though he'd taken the wrong bus somehow. The gunshots bring Cassie to the door of the cabin.

The next part happens very fast.

I'm pretty far from Leonard but Alison's just a step from his brother, and I realize this may be our only chance. When Leonard gets to his feet, holding his shoulder with his gun hand, and starts toward Reese's body I do the same.

"What the fuck did you do?" I say, looking only at Reese, as though I were a good friend of his. I don't look at Leonard until I'm parallel to him, and even then I don't raise my head, just lunge sideways, knocking him against the squad car. I hear Luther behind me, saying his brother's name. I hear Leonard telling me to stay back, but by then we're both on the ground, scrambling in the dirt, reaching for the gun. I don't hear Alison. I hear the sound of bones snapping. I hear Luther Toth scream.

Leonard and I roll down a slight ravine. The gun has disappeared. We're both searching for it—there's no moon and everything is shiny from the rain. Leonard's on the hill just below me when he sees the gun—I see him looking behind me, up the hill. He grabs my legs before I can even turn around.

He's been shot, but he's bigger than me and his adrenaline must have kicked in. Still, before he can get into any sort of rhythm I manage to get one arm behind his back, pinning him to the ground. The ground's so wet little puddles keep forming wherever we step and Toth's face is in one now.

That's when I see what he was looking at, behind me—not the gun but Cassie, coming down to help.

"Harding," Alison cries from the top of the hill.

"I'm okay." Leonard's hit once in the upper chest; he's gasping when I lift him up from the water. He's not badly hurt. But he's still fighting.

I see Cassie's face in the moonlight. *Just leave me something.* And I see Alison as she starts down the hill and I hear Leonard say something and then, when he pushes up against me, I just push his head back down, into the muddy water. I lean against him with all my strength. I don't think twice about it.

"I broke Luther's knees," Alison says, climbing down. "Both of them. He's not going anywhere. What about Leonard?"

"He's dead," I tell her. And by the time she makes it down the hill, he is.

epilogue

McKASKINS IS WAITING outside Twin Lakes Methodist in a green station wagon. He's reading the *Weekly World News*. CaveBoy has eluded the authorities once again. I tell him I want to drive. He gets in the 4Runner wearing fishing boots and heavy denim pants and another plaid shirt and then shows me on a map where we're going.

"I can't follow that," I tell him. He has a picnic basket with cold fried chicken and Diet Snapple. I'm surprised he hasn't brought his rod and reel.

"Just drive," he says. "I know the way." The church windows are open. Choir practice is just getting started. A few voices join together, harmonies tumbling into place.

He shall come down
He shall come down
He shall come down like rain

"I heard a little bit of what happened," he says. "Reverend Daniels, the youth minister at Stillwater—I believe you spoke to him—sent me a letter. I'm glad everything worked out."

I nod. I got a letter myself a few days ago.

I heard from the police that they're reopening the case regarding the death of my family. . . . Maybe now I can deal with it better . . . it's easier, I think, when the demons have real faces and the cause of all that horror turns out to simply be Toth instead of what my imagination created over the years. . . .

They said Luther Toth confirmed what you told the police

. . . about them killing Mason and Zane and planting that stuff on Devlin and Leo, hoping you or Quanh would kill them. . . . Luther said the original plan didn't include killing anybody, just taking advantage of the paranoia and bad memories Quanh was stirring up . . . they thought we might just knock ourselves off— this is Luther talking, so I don't know. I hung around the police station longer than you, hoping to understand things better. I think I do now.

Quanh shared some things with me—letters from my father —there's no way to tell if he really was related to Kim, but clearly Reverend Miner thought he was. The letters gave him a starting place for his scheme but no clear idea who might have taken Kim. So anyone from that time was a suspect, even me. He thought the Lost Moon stuff and the ad for my movie would stir things up and I guess it did. . . . Like you suggested, Harding, I told the police I didn't know where he went or why he wouldn't stay . . .

Quanh wouldn't stick around for the police that night. After we found them under the tarp—Quanh and Devlin, tied with string like oriental carpets—we watched from the farmhouse as he threw his empty saddlebags onto the bed of the pickup. The rain had stopped; you could actually see the stars, hear the crickets and frogs, see the lightning bugs. Quanh's pants were still muddy from his dig at Lake Geneva. He'd lost his Stetson somewhere along the way but he saddled up the red Ford and spun it around in the gravel, then took the long driveway at full gallop. He didn't look back.

I decided not to make that announcement regarding my age, so if you'll keep it to yourself it will be our little secret . . . I'll let what's out there stand, real or not, let someone else decide . . .

Thanks again for helping me find out the truth about these things. And please thank your friend Tommy Mullaney. He was a big help with the police.

Give my love to Alison. Thanks for everything.

Cassie

p.s. I talked to Sookie. She says hello. Several times.

The cave is part of five chambers spread across the hills or maybe all five connect; McKaskins says no one's ever really explored them that well. "There's nothing of interest, you see," he says. "No gold or silver, no interesting rocks or crystals, no strange animal life. And the land's unincorporated. It's not a state park or anything."

"So why would anyone go near it?"

"They wouldn't," he says. "Especially the one you asked about. It gets too narrow too quick to even go very far inside." The drive takes only about fifteen minutes. We park on a half-moon of gravel that looks like someone started a driveway and then thought better of it. "On foot now," McKaskins says. He's been whistling Bob Wills again; I think it's "Time Changes Everything." "Not far."

We cross over one hill and then another, jumping rushing streams so wide we land ankle deep in mud, then pull ourselves free and continue on. I'm carrying a backpack with a flashlight and a small folding shovel. The rain stopped hours ago. It's nearly dawn. The air is amazingly clear and clean for such a humid day.

Halfway up the last hill, McKaskins stops me and points along the ridge to a small hole in the rocks, with tufts of grass and weeds around the opening like decorations.

"That's it?" I say, shielding my eyes from the sun. He nods. "What's that sound?"

"The birds, you mean? The rain's finally stopped."

"No, not the birds—"

"The river," he says. "Just over the hill. It's crested but it's still moving pretty fast through these smaller stretches."

How did they get up there, I'm thinking, and McKaskins must see my stare.

"What are you looking for?" he says.

"Loose ends," I say. "There's no other way?"

"Straight up," he says. "I'll wait down here."

As I climb I can see McKaskins below me, opening his picnic basket. He's spread a blanket on a large rock, opening a Diet Snapple. He's still whistling something from Bob Wills. I'm wearing rain boots, not climbing boots, but the incline looks worse from below and besides there are lots of cracks in the rocks, tiny stairs, and I'm at the mouth of the cave in about ten minutes. At first I'm not sure why I bothered—McKaskins is right, the thing's too narrow. No adult could get in there. But a kid? Like Kim?

I walk the rest of the way up the hill, which is covered with blackberry bushes. Most of the berries are on the ground, unripened, scattered by the wind and the rain. The river's on the other side and I see now why I heard it—there's a bend in the river just below where the newly risen waters are crashing against the hillside, making a new stream. I climb down the other side, which has more mud than rocks, slipping once or twice until I'm about thirty feet above the water. There's another hole in the hillside, its face fresh dirt where the river tore away the grassy covering, and when I get closer I see it must be part of the cave, the bottom of the cave that starts on the other side. It's not wide enough to climb inside, but I don't really need to. Whan I want, what I came for, is gleaming in the mud along with a small boy's bones, what's left after twenty years in a cool dark cave—just the bones and a pair of dog tags I dig from the ground with my fingers, all of it uncovered by the river.

I'm undecided what to do until the river makes my decision for me—as I climb back up, another part of the hill gives way and tumbles into the water; another small avalanche of mud reclaims the grave. The bones have disappeared. The ground with Kim's remains is buried in a new cave.

"What'd you find?" McKaskins asks me when I come back. He's looking at my dirty hands.

"Nothing," I say. He nods, gives me a piece of chicken and a moist towelette. Ellis had gotten close. He must have circled this hill a dozen times, while Kim lay dead at the bottom of the cave. Maybe he sensed how close he was.

McKaskins has a cold Snapple ready for me.

"What was that girl's name," McKaskins says. "The sister of the boy you were looking for—Cathy or Cazzie—"

"Kalani. Kalani Moon."

"Kalani," McKaskins says. "I'm sure Kalani was glad to find out her father wasn't a killer. After all this time."

I nod.

"I was telling Reverend Daniels how the chapel her brother

worked on was damaged some by the flood . . . he thought some
folks from Stillwater might come back down and paint it again. I
told him that would be wonderful. We might rededicate it, put a
memorial there to Kim. Maybe Kalani would like to come down
for that."

"I'm sure she would."

"They still don't know where this man Toth left the body?"

"Kim's body? No. With Leonard Toth dead I doubt anyone
will ever know."

"May he rest in peace," McKaskins says. "He's with the
Lord."

"With the Lord and Bob Wills," I say, and McKaskins says
"amen."

We walk back to the 4Runner. I drop McKaskins back at his
church and get some coffee and then head north toward home.
The dog tags are in my pocket. I might find a better grave for them
somewhere between here and Chicago. There's no point showing
them to anyone. They might be fake. I can't tell by looking at
them. I'm certainly no expert on collecting dog tags.